derelict for trade

A Great New *Solar Queen* **Adventure**

Andre Norton &
Sherwood Smith

A Tom Doherty Associates Book / New York

DERELICT FOR TRADE

This book is printed on acid-free paper.

Edited by James Frenkel

A Tor Book
Published by Tom Doherty Associates, Inc.
175 Fifth Avenue
New York, NY 10010

Tor Books on the World Wide Web:
http://www.tor.com

Tor® is a registered trademark of Tom Doherty Associates, Inc.

Library of Congress Cataloging-in-Publication Data

Norton, Andre.
    Derelict for trade   :   a great new Solar Queen adventure   /
Andre Norton & Sherwood Smith. — 1st ed.
        p.   cm.
    "A Tom Doherty Associates book."
    ISBN 0-312-85919-8 (hardcover : acid-free paper)
    I. Smith, Sherwood. II. Title.
PS3527.0632D47 1997
813' .52—dc20   96-33221
                                                            CIP

First Edition: February 1997

Printed in the United States of America

0 9 8 7 6 5 4 3 2

I discovered science fiction when I was twelve years old and a friend eagerly recommended Andre Norton. In straight order I read every title the library had. By the next year, I was sending out my own books to publishers (never mind the quality of the typing or the stories!), and, of course, they came promptly back. In my environment I couldn't find anyone to take me seriously as a writer, to tell me what I ought to be doing and learning so that I could sell my books—not until I wrote to Andre Norton, who was the first professional to ever take me seriously. Her advice I took. I still have those letters, and treasure them. When the opportunity came to work with her in the universes I'd loved so long, I was thrilled. My heartfelt thanks to Ms. Norton for thirty years of pleasure—and debt.

—S. S.

Gratitude and appreciation to Dave
Trowbridge, who gave unstintingly
of time and effort to provide technical
advice. The Spinboggan was his idea.

—S. S.

derelict for trade

1

★

Except for the bleep from the computer consoles and the occasional rapid tick of keys, the control deck of the *Solar Queen* was silent.

Dane Thorson watched the tall, panther-lean man in the command pod, and felt his guts tighten.

Captain Jellico's gaze stayed on the constantly changing displays and readouts on his console. His face was emotionless, as always, but the subtle signs of tension were there to be read in the whiteness of the blaster scar on his cheek, and the taut muscles of his back.

At the astrogation console Steen Wilcox leaned forward, his fingers working steadily as he coaxed displays and readouts from his navputer—numbers that flickered so fast across the displays they were incomprehensible to Dane.

But Dane didn't have to be able to interpret them. As assistant cargo master, he had no job right now. He had squeezed into the back of the cramped control deck only because he couldn't just sit in his cabin, like his senior, Jan Van Ryke, or in the mess with the steward, Frank Mura, and the medic Craig Tau. Dane was not able to play a game of cards like those two, apparently ignoring the tension gripping the ship—nor did he have Van Ryke's unflappable attitude toward life. Dane knew they were in danger, perhaps the worst they'd faced yet, and he had to face danger straight on.

"Damn, damn, damn," Wilcox muttered under his breath. The display lights underlit his face with a weird yellow glow. "I don't like coming out of hyper this close to a planet, Chief."

"We have to." Jellico's voice was clipped, precise. "My calcs so far are proving true right to the tenth decimal—we don't have enough fuel left for snapout in flat space. We've got to use a gravity well."

Dane Thorson glanced again at the fuel-level panel. He'd been watching it for the last hour—he knew they all had. The captain had computed it very close, but he was right; unless they exploited the dimensional weakness caused by a planetary mass, they wouldn't have enough fuel to emerge from hyperspace—or rather, snapout wouldn't leave them enough fuel to rendezvous with Exchange, the Trade city in orbit above Mykos. As it was, it would be close.

"One minute to snapout," the captain said, and the engines snarled as they wound up towards the surge of power that would catapult them back into normal space. Dane pressed himself into his seat, reaching to connect his restraining belt—

And a tremendous bang shook the ship.

Dane's head rocked, and he clutched at his pod arms. Trouble lights flickered on the captain's console, and from the com to the engine deck came fluent curses from the usually taciturn Johan Stotz.

The pseudo-gravity of hyperspace suddenly vanished as the familiar fleeting nausea of snapout seized Dane, and he almost flew out of his seat before he managed to get his magnetic boots back on the deck and cinch up his seat belt.

"Snapout!" Wilcox exclaimed, and then, in a sharp voice, "We hit a knot!"

"Coordinates," Jellico commanded. "Find out where we are—and what lies on our course."

Wilcox's fingers were already flying over his console.

Dane looked at Captain Jellico, whose face was unchanged as he scanned his instruments. This was the most dreaded of all events, save plague, for the gravitational distortion that had thrown them out meant the existence of a close or large mass, and where there was one, there were likely many. Had they somehow flown into an uncharted asteroid cluster? Dane wondered. No, Steen Wilcox was too good for that.

As he watched the ordered haste of his fellow crew members at the controls, Dane became aware of a presence near him, and a faint, pleasant smell of lavender. He glanced up. The new medic, Rael Cofort, stood in the bridge hatch just behind his seat, a watchful look in her changeable violet eyes. So she too had to be on hand to see what happened.

It was something they had in common—a thought that made Dane vaguely uncomfortable. He turned his head to dismiss the thought, and watched the farseeing sensors of the *Solar Queen* slowly paint a picture of their course, while Wilcox's navputer oriented them.

"We're in the Mykos system, about twenty-five light-minutes from the sun," the astrogator said presently. He worked his console a bit longer. "No masses detected on course—we're about fifteen degrees above the ecliptic." Then he paused, looked from his console readout to his keys and back again. A chill seized Dane; it was rare to see the astrogator hesitate like that.

After another longer pause, without any change in his tone, Wilcox pronounced a death sentence on their careers as Free Traders.

"Insufficient fuel to reach any port," he said.

No one spoke. The truth was there on the screen for everyone on the bridge to see: they were billions of miles from where they had intended to emerge, without enough fuel to brake their tremendous velocity in time to bring them safely to the nearest port.

Dane cleared his throat, about to suggest they radio for help, but he pressed his lips together. That was for the captain to say. *The Old Man knows as well as I do that the salvage fees would bankrupt us,* he thought.

But Jellico was not looking at the screen. He had turned slightly in his pod, and was regarding Wilcox, his hard eyes narrowed in question. "And?" he said.

Wilcox's shoulders hunched. "We're headed straight at the Mykos cylomes at about five percent cee. Unless a salvage tug reaches us in sixteen hours or less, the habitat defenses will blow us out of space."

For a moment nobody said anything, and Dane reflected bitterly on the irony of their position. Few human Free Traders liked docking at the artificial habitats called cylomes—the cylindrical habitats favored by many alien races outside the human sphere of influence. Unfortunately for the *Queen* their low fuel situation had made the choice for them.

There'd been a lot of grousing in the mess-cabin strategy session when they'd discussed this option, even though the hospitality of the Kanddoyd race towards humans was well known. But now, even that option had been snatched from them, and they might not even have to worry about bankruptcy; ravening plasmabolts of the Kanddoyd defenses would see to that. Habitats were so vulnerable to space debris that their defenders tended to shoot first and ask questions afterwards.

The silence was broken by the leisurely click of magboots on the deckplates. Dane looked up, saw the comfortable bulk of cargo master Van Ryke looming over him, the white-blond bushy brows raised in mild question.

The captain said, "Ya. Send out SOS and Salvage Call. Standard terms."

As the Martian-born comtech turned to obey, Dane felt

the reaction of his crewmates. His own heart seemed to have been knocked awry by whatever they had hit. He remembered how, just minutes before, he'd envisioned the various ways his crewmates each responded to danger. He'd come to know them well in his time aboard the *Queen*, and he knew how much they trusted one another, and the captain. And now they seemed to have reached the end of their shiptime together.

Salvage would break the *Queen* permanently—there was no way out of that.

He looked down at his hands, which seemed suddenly unfamiliar. They were the hands of a man—a big, rawboned man, callused and strong. He'd been scarcely out of his teens when he'd come to the *Queen*, straight from Pool and training. He'd finished his growing up with this crew. The *Queen* was his home. He flexed his hands, thinking: *I guess I should consider myself lucky to be alive, even for a short time.*

A broad hand clapped his shoulder and squeezed. He looked up into Van Ryke's good-humored eyes and his reassuring smile. A faint hope awoke. If Van Ryke didn't seem worried, maybe there was an angle no one else had seen as yet.

Tang Ya sat back and sighed. "It'll be at least an hour before we hear anything," he said.

The captain nodded curtly. "Then we have an hour to plan." He keyed the com so everyone on board could participate. "We hit something, probably space debris, since there was nothing in the charts. We knew when we voted on this option that this was the closest margin we'd ever run—we had to balance our fuel and hyperspace jump against the needs of landing. I don't have to calculate the odds against running into something in snapout. We all know they're in the billions against one, but it seems this time our luck ran out."

Dane flexed his hands again.

"Not to complain, my dear friends . . ." From the engine deck came the familiar humorous drawl of the engineer apprentice Ali Kamil. "We all voted yes when we left Canuche, but it seems our luck ran out that day."

For a long moment there was silence, and Dane sensed everyone considering the wearing weeks they'd just endured.

Their hearts had been high when they left Canuche. The *Queen* was in good shape, and they had the generous sum given them by the grateful Macgregory for their heroic work there. They'd chosen not to stay on Canuche, though the cargo work promised by the equally grateful merchants would have meant a steady income. Steady—and boring.

They had decided unanimously to turn down the contract, for they were not cargo haulers, but Free Traders.

This was the risk every Free Trader took. Life was a gamble, and sometimes one lost. At least Captain Jellico permitted his crew to vote on the big decisions, and again everyone had voted unanimously to put all their earnings into the Survey auction on Denlieth, which had sounded so promising for Traders looking for new opportunities. Unfortunately the big Companies had heard the same scuttlebutt. All the *Queen* had been able to afford to bid on had been a Class D planet, and they'd scarcely gotten that as Combine and Inter-Solar had not only snapped up the better choices, but the I-S agent—probably in revenge for past encounters—had deliberately driven up the prices on the rest.

The *Queen* had just managed to get the one claim, and it had proved to be a dead one. Worse, the refueling station promised on the tape with the planet's coordinates had closed down probably weeks before their arrival, for lack of business, and the *Queen* had been forced to make what fuel they had last for this jump. They'd had no choice but to head for the nearest system, which was farther out on the frontiers of the Terran Federation than they had ever been. The Company ships seldom came out this far; even Free Traders were rare.

Most of the crew had groused about Mykos—all except Jan Van Ryke.

Dane looked up at the cargo master, who was watching the screens, his lips pursed. Van Ryke had admitted that he thought the Kanddoyds, and Exchange, might turn out to be a successful venture.

"Don't like habitats," Johan Stotz had growled.

"Me either," Ali had drawled, lounging behind his chief, his handsome face derisive. "If human beings were meant to live in gas tubes in space, we would have been born in vacuum."

"That's the way most humans feel," Van Ryke had said, beaming at them in triumph. "Which is exactly why we have a greater chance at success. Just think how little Terran competition we'll find!"

Now Dane looked around, saw Rip Shannon, the astrogator apprentice, tapping his fingers on his knees. "We might be able to work a deal," he said. "We all have good skills—"

"Right," came Craig Tau's voice over the com. "We might be forced to hire ourselves out to different outfits for a time, but if we pledge to save half our earnings and come back to rescue the *Queen*—"

"If she's not rendered down into scrap in the meantime." Karl Kosti's rumbling voice came from the engine deck.

"Which is why we cut a deal," Kamil said. "We have several silver tongues on board—"

All through their discussion, Dane noted abstractedly that Wilcox had not ceased his scanning of surrounding space; having satisfied himself of a clear course ahead, the astrogator had turned his attention in other directions.

"Captain!" Wilcox's exclamation brought everyone's attention forward again. "We've got a tail! Matching velocity—"

"Tang!" Jellico snapped. "Raise them."

Dane saw Rael frown and Van Ryke grip a handhold in the hatchway. He suspected they had the same thought as he did: was this some new form of space piracy?

"Working, Captain—" Tang Ya muttered. The comtech crouched over his console, the muscles in his broad back ridged with his intense concentration. "No answer—"

"Try Shver and Kanddoyd frequencies," Jellico cut in.

Of course Terran frequencies might not work this far out—Dane didn't know much about their present location, except that the Mykos system was on the boundaries of two alien spheres of influence, Kanddoyd and Shver.

"Sent, Captain," Tang said. "No response." He paused. "And no engine emissions detectable, either."

"Rip, try to get visuals," Jellico ordered.

The astrogator apprentice worked at his console as Jellico went about setting up their defense system. Not that they had much in the way of weaponry—the *Solar Queen* was a Trade vessel, not a fighter.

For a protracted moment there was silence on the bridge again. Dane watched until the edges of his vision twinkled darkly, then realized he had been holding his breath too long.

Rip said suddenly, "There it is!"

He keyed his console and the screen overhead flickered. They all stared up at the sleek ship following them. A frisson of fear shuddered through Dane as he noted the unfamiliar lines of the ship—it was not of Terran manufacture, nor, he knew from his recent studies, Kanddoyd or Shver.

No lights shone from it. The ship looked dead.

"Plague ship?" Jasper Weeks's voice came over the ship's com. The jet tech's apprentice was obviously watching on Kosti's screen.

Wilcox looked over at the captain. "May be, and maybe abandoned." He tabbed a key and the ship jumped even closer to view, showing dark scoring down one side. "Looks like she's been fired on."

"She's Terran registry," Rip exclaimed as their angle on the gleaming hull changed. In silence they read the registry numbers, and next to it, in Terran script and another script Dane had never seen before, was the word *Starvenger*.

"If she's Terran registry, chances are the crew were human, or humanoid," Tau said.

Kosti's voice came over the com: "Question is, if we use fuel to match speeds and cable it in, we're going to be running on fumes. Unless it's got fuel on board . . ."

No one spoke as the captain studied the ship on screen. Jellico's thumb stroked absently at the blaster scar on his cheek, a sure sign he was thinking furiously. This was the Free Trader life: a risk versus a gamble. With no fuel at all, the salvage fees would be even higher, due to the tug's greater fuel expenditure to match velocity.

Dane looked up at that dead ship with its blasted hull, and felt the old cramping all over again. Even though the ship was alien, its fuel, if any, would probably be usable by the Queen—the basics of fuel technology were universal, for no race, save perhaps the long-dead Forerunners, had ever cracked the secret of antigravity.

"Even if there's fuel on board," Johan Stotz said, "do we want to risk being contaminated by whatever killed its crew?"

"If it doesn't kill us," Kosti said, "and we do find fuel, we've got to have time to adapt the Queen's catalyzers and engine feeds before the Kanddoyds vaporize us—"

"With, of course, infinite regret," came Ali's irrepressible voice.

The captain slammed his hand down flat on his console. "Let's find out," he said suddenly. "We're no worse off if it doesn't. Wilcox, bring us into cable distance. Kosti, make ready the johblocks."

It took less than thirty minutes to bring the Queen up within cable distance of the strange ship and lay hold of it with the johblocks, whose atomically smooth gripping surfaces literally melded with any substance, no matter how obdurate—and there were few things more obdurate than a ship's hull. As Dane expected, the other ship gave the johblocks no trouble, and it was soon drawn within half a kilometer of the Trader vessel.

When Wilcox finally announced zero relative velocity, Jellico said, "I want an investigation team, full biohaz suits. Maybe our luck has changed."

2

Dr. Rael Cofort pulled on the flexible gauntlets of the biohaz suit and made sure they were fastened securely. Last came the helmet, fitting snugly over her crown of braided hair. As the helmet locked into place the suit's air system was automatically initiated, and the soft hiss of antiseptic air cooled her cheek. A green light flickered holographically, letting her know the suit com was also alive.

A moment later Rip Shannon's voice came over the com: "Ready, team?"

"Aye." Four voices, including hers, echoed in her ears.

"Then let's go."

Rip Shannon had been appointed squad leader for the expedition. Rael could see his dark face inside his helmet, his black eyes characterized by good humor and the formidable intelligence which marked him out as a natural leader. Behind him loomed Dane Thorson, the tall cargo apprentice who looked like the ancient illustrations of his Viking ancestors. Next to Rael, the short, slight engine tech Jasper Weeks checked the tools at his belt one last time, then stepped into the lock, moving with the characteristic high-step shuffle of free fall.

They waited in silence as the air pressure slowly dropped.

"Half air," said Rip. "Suit check."

Rael slapped the diagnostic tab on her chest; after a moment the ready light flickered to green.

"No leaks," she reported, and was echoed by the others.

Rip tabbed the lock control and then, at zero, keyed the outer lock, which slid silently open onto the jewel-pierced blackness of space.

Their helmet lights came on as each member of the squad hooked onto the cable uniting the two ships. Rip pushed off and glided along the cable for a moment; then his suit thrusters flared and he dwindled rapidly towards the alien ship. Dane followed. Then Rael flexed her toes to demagnetize her boots and pushed off into space. At first her movement merely intensified the feeling of falling; then, as she reached a safe distance from Jasper, she ignited her thrusters and her stomach settled as acceleration gripped her. Now it felt like flying. She grinned, remembering Weeks's thin face, grim behind his faceplate. He hated free fall outside the safety of a ship. For her, it was a feeling of freedom that never failed to boost her spirits.

The hull of the mystery ship glowed in the light of Mykos's primary, showing up the heavy scoring that marred the smooth fairing. Rael was not a pilot, but she knew that this ship would not be easy to land on a planet.

It was time to decelerate. She pivoted around and triggered another blast from her thrusters, then pulled herself along to join Rip and Dane.

Against the hull Rip was already working quickly, mute evidence that this investigation was a race against time. Rael heard a soft click, knew that the open communicator had switched to a two-way link so that Rip and Dane could talk to each other without flooding everyone's head with chatter. The two men worked quickly at the ship's outer lock. Rael watched, aware of her adrenaline-pushed heart rate. Though she felt nothing, and saw nothing, she knew they were hurtling through space at tremendous speed. Any kind of space dust could rip through their suits and kill them and they wouldn't necessarily see it coming.

As they waited, Rael saw Jasper pat the weapon at his side, and wondered if he, like she, was also thinking of the hazards they were exposed to—only in Jasper's case, he seemed to be worried about the very real possibility of space pirates. Not that they carried blasters, but the weapons they nicknamed sleeprods were better than nothing: the blast of sonics they emitted could temporarily scramble the nervous system of any oxygen breather.

The lock opened; they went in.

The general communicator clicked on again.

"All right, let's do this just like we've drilled," Rip said.

He and Dane moved in first, scanning swiftly for anything amiss—from bodies to obvious traps. They gestured Jasper and Rael in. Rael was glad to be inside the relative safety of a hull once again. She clicked on the mags in her boots, and stepped to the decking.

The inner lock showed nothing wrong; it was clean and plain, and on the control console green lights peacefully glowed, except for the red light indicating the lock still open to space.

Rip worked quickly at the controls, which Rael saw were arranged differently than those on the Terran ships she was used to. But they were located at the same general height, indicating use by beings about the size of humans.

Rip gave a short exclamation of satisfaction and the outer lock shut behind them. She heard the hiss of air pressure, and after a minute or so the inner lock opened. The two checked it, stepped through, and Rael and Jasper followed.

Now it was Rael's turn. She activated the scanner clipped to her suit, and watched the ripple of the diagnostics in its display. Within a few seconds she had her readout, and looked up to report: "It's breathable, pressure lighter than we're used to—about the same as Terran high mountains."

The information was for the general report. They would still keep their suits intact.

"Humanoids, just as Tau predicted," Rip said, sounding interested. Then, "Let's get going."

Moving fast, they headed for the engine deck, finding no one dead or alive on their way. Life support was still running, which indicated the ship had some power left. When they reached the engine deck and found no signs of tampering or presence, Rip nodded at Jasper, who almost dove at the complicated engineering console.

"Let's head for the control deck," Rip suggested. They worked their way forward, still finding no sign of occupancy. When they reached the control hatch, Rip opened it and looked through. "No one here, either. Chances are there's no one on board, then." He turned to Dane. "You check the cargo hold and hydro. Doctor, check the galley and surgery."

Rael made her way back along the curved accessways toward the galley and surgery. Her sleeprod was again clipped to her belt. In one hand she held her diagnostic scanner, this time keyed to the heat sensors in the unlikely case there was someone hiding in one of the storage areas.

Nothing showed up, and she moved to the surgery console, and stopped to look around. It was almost familiar— the arrangement of cupboards and slide tables was accessible to humans, but the organization was unlike that which she was used to on most Terran Federation ships. She found a computer console, and looked it over, again surprised by the unfamiliar layout, the width of the keytabs.

She tried a series of tabs, and at last reached a combination that activated the console. Lights flickered. An unfamiliar script flowed across the screen, in a color combination she found odd. Even the prompt was slightly different than she expected.

"Weeks here," came Jasper's voice, quick and eager. "Fuel is about ninety-eight-percent max."

A moment later Rip's voice was heard: "Relayed it to the

Queen. Stotz is on his way with the fuel tap equipment. Dane? Rael?"

"Cargo hold is full," Dane's voice reported. "Can't read the script. Maybe we can open these boxes later. I just entered the hydro lab—" He stopped, then Rael heard a short intake of breath from the apprentice cargo master.

"Found something?" Rip's voice was urgent.

"Someone," Dane said gruffly. "Two someones—not human. Ship's cats. They're in pretty bad shape."

Rael winced. "I'll be right there," she promised.

She turned her attention back to the surgery computer. With great care she experimented with key combinations. At last one caused a flicker, and a menu of icons appeared—but next to each entry was a pair of symbols that looked like empty brackets.

She hit the keys that had gotten the results, came up with more empty brackets. "Surgery log seems to have been cleaned out," she reported.

"Ship's log and navcomp same," came Rip's voice. "Looks like an organized abandonment."

Rael shook her head as she closed the computer down and moved to the galley. Again she scanned for known biohazards, but nothing came up on her scanner. She found the galley console and activated it, using the keys that looked most like the active ones in the surgery. She was rewarded with a lit display, which not only included the galley console but also caused lights to flicker on various storage compartments around the little room. But nothing else was to be gleaned from this console.

She retraced her steps, and hurried down to the cargo area. The storage space was larger than the *Queen*'s, and it took a little time to find Dane Thorson.

The cargo apprentice turned away from the console area and fell in step beside her. "Over here," he said.

He led her down a corridor of stacked containers to another hatchway. Rael braced herself—and despite her determination to be detached and professional, when she first saw the two small bodies, her eyes stung. The cats were unmarked by any signs of violence; they lay curled together, quite close to the door. One lifted its head, then the other, and four eyes regarded her weakly.

"Just gave them a few drops of water," Dane said. "Seemed to help."

His tone was apologetic, as if he expected to have made the wrong decision. Rael said, "You did right. I'll give them a bit more now, and I think we'd best leave them. Craig and I can bring over a case to transport them back to the *Queen*'s lab."

She busied herself with her diagnostic tool, glad for the time to gain control of her emotions. Again the display indicating no known biohazards—of course, there was always the chance of some new, and lethal-to-humans, biotics. They could isolate the cats on board the *Queen*, and check more carefully as the animals recuperated.

"Looks like they were accidentally shut in," she said, glad her voice, at least, sounded detached.

"Nearly starved," Dane said, nodding.

She carefully dripped a few drops from her water cache onto each cat's muzzle, and watched the raspy tongues lick it off. When the cats showed no more interest in the water, she detached a thin, light shock blanket from the equipment in her backpack, snapped it open, then refolded it, gently making a nest for the animals. Even for the short time they had to wait for better care, she wanted them warm.

At last she moved back, and looked around the hydroponics setup. Dane indicated the rows of plants. "Luckily they left this lab on automatic. The cats must have gotten water by licking moisture off the leaves after they were misted."

Rael stooped to examine several unfamiliar plants. Some of them showed gnaw marks; the cats appeared to have experimented with eating the plants. "There might have been a few vermin in here. Otherwise, it looks like they tried to make do with vegetables." She pointed at a half-eaten, yellow gourdlike shape.

Dane nodded, moving slowly among the plants.

Rael turned in the other direction, and was arrested by the gleam of console lights through dark blue-green leaves. She moved quickly toward it. A tiny console, set into a little cubicle mostly hidden by tall plants and by a high stool, was lit. Directly below it rested a pile of books, holo cubes, and miscellaneous personal paraphernalia. She wondered if these items had sat on the ledge into which the computer console was built—and if the cats had knocked it down.

When she touched the now-familiar key combination, this time the menu offered a row of choices that of course she couldn't read. "There's a live log here in the hydro lab," she reported over the general linkup.

"Good," Rip's voice came over the com. "Nothing up here—everything's been nulled out."

Rael stared at the screen before her, wondering if this was the only clue to the identity of the ship's owners. Her first instinct was to download whatever was in this computer, but she didn't try to extract one of the tiny quantumtapes from the pack at her belt. Whatever kind of data-transfer system this computer had, it didn't use Terran standards—there was no little round slot to drop a tape cylinder into.

Dane appeared. He half-reached for the console, then pulled his hand back. "Don't want to risk cutting off the maintenance cycle."

Rael nodded. "Right. We'll leave this for Tang. If anyone can figure it out, it's he."

They left the lab, and moved back through the cargo bay. In silence Dane Thorson paced along beside her. She glanced about at stacks of wares in the big bay, and to her surprise she recognized some of the scripts. "Isn't that Zacathan? And there's Persian. This ship must have been in the Zatah colonies, or traded for Zatahi goods. But the rest—"

"Most of this is Kanddoyd, I think," Dane said diffidently.

A spurt of amusement made Rael fight against a grin. Of course he would recognize that script. Most of the crew had been studying the sparse data on the Kanddoyd sphere of influence as soon as the *Queen* had gone into hyper. While Rael had focused on biological information, Dane Thorson and Jan Van Ryke had kept to the cultural end—everything they would need to know to aid them in the prospect of making trade.

That in itself was not amusing. Any good crew crammed available data when heading for new territory. It was his manner, and the fact that—encased as she was in a biohaz suit which was just as sexless as his—he still wouldn't look at her.

As she stepped closer to a series of oddly shaped containers to get a better look, she worked to make certain her face was absolutely straight, just in case he did glance down into her helmet. Her mind had gone straight back to Canuche, to the outdoor market of Canuche Town, when she had taken a length of gorgeous blue Thornen silk and moved through a few basic steps of an Ubis dance.

She had intended to help her old crewmate Deke Tatarcoff make a good sale, and hadn't thought beyond how spectacularly well the silk would drape and flutter through the air. She had forgotten the effect the dance had on watchers, and happening to glance up at the tall, blond cargo apprentice, she had surprised a look of what she considered to be perfectly normal, healthy male appreciation on his face—an expression which was almost immediately followed by dismay and then embarrassment.

"Cats, some human trade items, interior design reasonably accessible—it all points to humanoids, doesn't it?" she said, keeping her voice cool and professional.

Dane seemed glad for the unexceptionable subject. "There are some handwritten additions to some of the container labels. The script is nothing I've ever seen."

Rael nodded as they moved back through the silent corridors of cargo. Her mind was not on alien script, but on Dane Thorson, who was one of the *Solar Queen*'s most surprising anomalies. Memory also produced an intense visual image: Dane working like a madman to throw burning barrels of ammonium nitrate into the sea despite not only the painful burns he was enduring but the possibility of being blown into atoms at any moment. And the others—never Dane—had told her of equally heroic action on Trewsworld and other places. Afterward, instead of talking about his experience or expecting praise, Dane seemed to want to pretend these things had never happened.

Rael was a physician, and though her main area of study had been epidemiology, she had also done thorough studies of human and xeno psychology. Dane was a knot of intriguing contradictions, and the prospect of unraveling him was one that appealed to the professional in her.

But life experience had taught her patience.

In the hatchway leading back toward the entry lock, she said, "We'll probably never be able to categorize all the varieties of human biology out in space."

Dane said, "In training they told us that evolution took millions of years on Terra. On other worlds, especially where humans don't fit, it can take just a few generations."

"We are remarkably adaptable," Rael said. "Though in some cases there is a tremendous loss of life in the meantime." She thought of some of the terrible human tragedies behind the dry, academic prose of her study tapes. "It was inevitable that humans would try to help the adaptation process, in some cases, with bioengineering."

Dane blinked over at her. "I thought that was illegal."

"It is—in the Federation," she said. "But the farther you get away from Federation jurisdiction, the more chances people are willing to take. Unfortunately, not for the good of colonies, either."

She stopped there, but saw the impact of her words in Dane's sober eyes. Another tough lesson had been reading about some of the horrors perpetrated by unscrupulous bioengineers in their experiments to try to produce superhumans, or other variations. Most of those quickly failed; the ones that haunted Rael and her empathic fellow students were the stories about bioengineering meant to help humans adapt the more quickly to this or that planet, with unexpected and tragic results.

Shaking off the thoughts, she found the others gathered in the lock. Stotz had just arrived.

Rip said, "Captain wants you here to help the fuel transfer, Dane. Rael, you're released to get back to the *Queen* and see about the transfer of the cats. Tau's got transfer equipment packed and waiting for you at the other end of the line."

"Excellent," she said. This was the kind of duty she liked most—saving lives.

3

The engine crew, with Dane among them, watched anxiously as Johan Stotz lifted the platinum-alloy pipette carefully away from the inspection gland on the engine feed. A single drop of fuel glistened at its tip, not tear-shaped as it would have been planetside, but globular in the microgravity of the alien ship.

Carefully, the chief engineer inserted the pipette into the fuel analyzer, a bulky cylinder with a simple readout on it above a small console.

It was interesting, Dane reflected, that although the personal appointments of the alien ship were very different from the human norm, the engines were almost identical in design. That had been one of the lessons at Pool training: that cultures changed, but physics didn't.

Stotz extracted the pipette and locked the breech of the tester. He tapped rapidly at the tester's console, which hummed and clicked. Symbols flashed rapidly across the readout.

Then there was a muffled *whoomp* and the tester tilted slightly.

"That's it!" Stotz exclaimed. He peered at the readout. "Two third and one fourth array superheavy," he said. "Ganeshium, Kalium, and Lokium. Not our mix, but a number-ten catalysis screen and an oh-six-hundred feed should do it."

The crew expressed their relief and satisfaction in a variety of ways, from Jasper Weeks's quiet smile to Ali Kamil's jokes.

Ali hit the intership com with an extravagant gesture. "We've got fuel, Captain."

Stotz looked up. "Ask him how much he wants transferred over. We'll need a minimum of thirty percent in order to decelerate and dock."

Ali nodded and relayed the question.

After a brief pause, Captain Jellico's voice came back: "Take half. How long?"

"No more than four hours," Stotz replied.

"Make it three," replied Jellico and the com clicked off.

"You heard him," said the engineer.

The crew sprang into action. Kamil disappeared outside to attach the fuel hose already snaking over from the *Queen*, brought by Rip Shannon, and for what seemed far longer than the time allotted, Dane did what he was told, functioning as an extra pair of hands for Stotz and Kamil, who talked back in forth in their own cryptic shorthand. Dane's inner clock kept yammering at him about the length of time it was taking to make the conversion—he had no idea if the Kanddoyds would warn them first before blasting them out of space.

He didn't let himself look at the time until Stotz said finally, "We're done."

All four of them looked: two hours, forty-five minutes.

"Nice work, my children." Ali managed a graceful bow despite the bulky suit.

Stotz snorted. "Get back over to the *Queen*. Captain

wants us. Rip, you're to stay here with Wilcox. You too, Jasper. I want you down here monitoring."

Jasper Weeks nodded silently, and began drifting around the engine room, looking closely at the alien scripts.

Dane followed the others back to the lock, and one by one they blasted along the cable to the *Queen*.

As the lock of the *Solar Queen* pressurized around them, Dane felt excitement flood though him, and he rotated his neck, trying to ease the kinks out. Immediate danger seemed averted, though they were not in the clear yet.

"Decontamination cycle commencing," came Kosti's voice, and Dane squeezed his eyes shut as the UV lights flared on. He felt the needle-sharp spray of biostop even through his suit, and he raised his arms and turned slowly around, letting the deadly solution hammer against every square millimeter of his suit. The actinic light died, and as Dane opened his eyes his almost giddy sense of relief provoked a snicker at the sight of his crewmates in an identical posture, for all of space like a troupe of Parnixian Devil Dancers.

"Stand by for acceleration," came the captain's voice. Jump seats swung down from the walls of the lock, and they sat down and strapped in. The engines roared, and weight returned, building swiftly towards what felt like about 1.25 gees.

"We cut it close!" Kamil exclaimed.

"Damn close," Stotz muttered, but Dane heard the relief in his voice. The Kanddoyd defense monitors would see their engine exhaust, and soon their change of course. They were safe.

As soon as Kosti released them from decontamination, Dane stripped off his suit and ducked out of the lock bay. Carefully, he swung onto the downdeck ladder and climbed down three levels, feeling the increased acceleration in his thighs.

He found the two doctors in the surgery, hovering solicitously over the cats from the *Starvenger*. The two animals were in an isolation box. Both were sleeping; to Dane they already looked better.

"Not safe to touch?" he asked.

Tau shrugged. "They exhibit no signs of anything we're familiar with, but we can't take any chances—they could be infected with some rare new bacteria."

Dane put his hand into the gloveport and reached down to stroke one of the black-and-white heads, when a flicker on the periphery of his vision made him pause. Tail high, Sinbad, the *Queen*'s cat, marched in, and leaped up onto the table next to the isolation box.

One of the cats seemed to sense another feline, and raised its head. Delicately, with proper detachment, the two cats touched noses to either side of the plastic, sniffed, and with a little chirrup of affront that sounded to Dane just like one of the matrons at the orphanage where he'd lived before Pool, Sinbad turned away. Clearly these animals, while trespassers, were not deemed a threat to his territory.

"We're calling them Alpha and Omega," Rael Cofort told Dane, her blue eyes glinting through long, silky lashes.

Dane turned away, hoping his neck wouldn't look as hot as it felt. "Which is which?" he asked, making a business of stroking one of the cats behind its ears with one gloved finger.

"That one's Alpha," Tau said. "And that one Omega."

"No, no," Rael Cofort said promptly. "*That* one is Alpha."

The two doctors looked from the nearly identical cats to each other, and laughed.

"Two females, probably from the same litter," Tau said. "It seems a poetic touch, somehow, if we never do figure it out."

"They're safe enough now," Frank Mura said from the doorway. "Captain's waiting above."

"Conference time," Tau said, nodding. "Let's go."

Dane followed the others back up to the galley level, to

the galley mess room, which was the largest gathering area on the *Queen*. It was cramped—the *Queen* had been built in the days when luxuries like extra space were deemed too expensive. There were a lot more comfortable ships flying around known space, particularly for a man who seemed about two inches taller than the architect had planned for, but the *Queen,* with all its quirks, was home. Dane felt another flood of relief and gratitude that once again they were safe—and ready to plan for their next move.

As they crowded into the mess, Dane started heading automatically to the farthest corner of the cabin, a somewhat secluded spot under a bulkhead from which one could see everyone. As his footsteps took him in that direction, he saw Rael Cofort settle into the seat, and he turned aside, caught Van Ryke's genial eye, and dropped down beside his superior.

Opposite Cofort, Captain Jellico stood. There was no sign in his hard countenance of their recent scrape with death and danger. As soon as everyone was in place, either sitting or ranged along the wall, he said, "Ya was able to cancel the SOS before anyone responded. Wilcox, Shannon, and Weeks are conning the other ship on a matching course." He gestured at the communication grill. "They're patched in with a laser link. Anyway, our velocity is too high for a direct approach, so we will have to loop around Mykos before we pull in, which gives us a week. During that time I want everything on the other ship catalogued, from the hydro to the galley."

He paused, and Van Ryke and Mura nodded silently. Dane felt a spurt of anticipation—he could hardly wait to get over there and poke around that cargo bay with lots of time to spare. From the pleased smile on Van Ryke's face, he could tell the cargo master was thinking the same thing.

"What we have now before us is a decision. Legally we should be able to lay claim to the *Starvenger,* for we rescued it. Though we are no longer in Federation space, my understanding is that in the Kanddoyd-Shver-Terran Concord of Harmony set up here when humans were first invited in, cer-

tain Federation laws were guaranteed. One of them is the right
to salvage."

Van Ryke nodded silently.

Jellico went on, "What we need to vote on is whether we
sell this ship and her cargo—or whether we keep her and expand our cargo capabilities."

"If her cargo turns out to be low value, we'll really have
to scramble to get something to trade with. Not to mention
fueling two ships," Johan Stotz pointed out.

"And dockage for two ships in the meantime," Ali put in,
from where he lounged against a bulkhead. "After all, this is
new territory for us, and there's no telling how long our dear
friends in the City of Harmonious Exchange will keep us
paying for their hospitality while we clear up the legalities."

Mura nodded soberly. "I vote we sell it."

"The dockage problem isn't necessarily as bad as you
think," Van Ryke said, looking around the room. "We won't
have to pay double fees if we leave the *Starvenger* outside,
which costs considerably less. We'll bring the *Queen* inside—
we do have Macgregory's letter of credit to cover the initial
docking fees. It's only the duration we'll need to pay for."

Mura rubbed his chin, frowning silently.

Craig Tau said, "I take it, Jan, you're in favor of keeping
this ship."

"Of course." The cargo master spread his hands. "We not
only double our cargo space, but our opportunities—if need
be, our little fleet can investigate two possibilities for trade
instead of one." He nodded at Rael. "Is this not how your es-
teemed brother started his successful career?"

Rael Cofort nodded. "We sank everything we had into our
ships, and he expanded as quickly as he could."

Tau said, "I'll admit, it's disheartening when we start to
build up some steam, then lose everything. Who knows how
many Denlieth disasters are waiting in our future? At least
we'd only lose half."

"That second ship would stand as security," Van Ryke
added. "If we had to we could always sell her later. No mat-

ter where we are, a good ship is expensive and will bring a good price."

Jellico looked across the room at Rael. "Any opinion, Dr. Cofort?"

"What do Steen and Rip think?" she countered.

"I'll go with the majority, Chief," Wilcox's voice came promptly over the com. "But let me add this: if we expand, there are three apprentices and one jet tech who will be promoted at last, and each of them has earned it several times over."

Ali grinned, bowing toward the com grill. Dane felt his neck go hot, and he fought against the urge to tug at his collar.

"Of course that means we have to hire on new crew," Stotz put in with a frown. "That's a tricky venture, particularly as we still have years to go on our embargo from Terraport. We can't rely on Psycho to synch us up with good crew."

"With all due respect for Terra's excellent psychological evaluative computers," Van Ryke said, "we have two equally excellent doctors aboard who ought to be able to screen possible employees."

Mura smiled wryly. "I'm less worried about finding good shipmates than I am about paying them."

Jellico looked up at Dane. "What do you say, Thorson?"

"If they're Traders like us, they'll go with staking their pay against getting better cargo. When we win, we all win."

"Well said, my boy." Van Ryke nodded genially. "If steady pay was our first priority, we'd all be cogs in one of the big Company drives. We don't have to move at once—we can split crew and pilot both, as we did with the *Space Wrack*, for a time. But when we find likely prospects, if we are straightforward about our situation, we'll get a straight answer."

Jellico gave a short nod. "And you, Karl?"

Kosti jerked his thumb in Van Ryke's direction. "Jan hasn't pushed us into a nova yet."

The captain looked from face to face. "I'm hearing a consensus," he said. "Anyone against keeping the *Starvenger*? Now's the time to speak up."

Mura lifted his hand. "I don't know . . . my own feelings are mixed, but like Karl said, we've trusted Jan's hunches before, and they've played out. I'm in."

Stotz laid his hands flat on the table. "I'll admit I'd like more time to poke around that engine. I suspect there are some nice improvements on our old drives I can learn from and improvise. Why not keep her for now? As Jan said, we can always sell her if need be. But getting out with some cargo now will be tricky."

"Leave that to us," Van Ryke said, thumping Dane's shoulder.

Jellico looked around again. "Then it's settled."

"What I want to know is," Mura said, "how in the Five Hells of Krantuvi we managed to hook up with her out in space?"

"Pure luck," came Steen Wilcox's voice over the com.

"And about time," said Kamil.

Wilcox continued as if Ali hadn't spoken. "We just happened to intersect her realspace position during engine windup, when the ship is most vulnerable to gravitational knots."

"The engines seem to be intact," Kosti said. "No signs of tampering or sabotage."

"No signs of violence anywhere," Rip's voice came over the com. "I checked all the cabins. Belongings were all gone, no signs of any scuffles or breaks."

Jellico's eyes narrowed. "But the comps were stripped, which contraindicates an emergency evacuation. That takes time."

"All the comps except that little auxiliary one in hydro," Ya spoke up for the first time. "I'll get to work on that right away."

"Everything gone," Tau said, "except the cats. That's puzzling—even if they had an emergency, it seems to me any crew would take the time to scoop the cats into their suits, if nothing else."

"We're not talking about Terrans here," Stotz said.

"But they had cats, which is a human and humanoid custom," Rael countered. "And despite the shape Alpha and Omega were found in, we think they were well cared for."

Tau nodded, tapping his fingers on the table. "They were overlooked. This, with the computer wipes, bothers me." He looked up at the captain. "From what I remember of salvage law, we are required to report any sentients on board a derelict, whether alive or dead."

"True," Van Ryke said. "There's always an investigation to make certain the salvagers didn't get their ship through foul play."

"We don't have to mention the cats, then," Tau said. He leaned back and folded his arms. "We'll need to keep them here in any case, for it'll be a while before they're strong enough to set free again. When we make our report, I really think we should sit on this particular item."

Jellico's brows lifted slightly. "Then you do suspect foul play."

Tau shook his head. "I just think we ought to keep the cats to ourselves."

Rael Cofort said quietly, "I have to admit I really dislike the idea of acquiring a ship that might have been abandoned under coercive or suspicious circumstances."

Jellico's chin lifted slightly in a dismissive gesture that his crew knew well: his mind was made up. "No sentients on board, we found and rescued her fair and square. Salvage Law says she's ours."

"We may as well benefit," Ali said with a rakish smile. "If we don't, someone else will eventually come along and get her—and I really think we're about due for some luck."

Several of the others nodded, and Dane watched Cofort concede the point. Her eyes stayed serious, though, her expression reflective. He felt the impulse to ask her what she was thinking—but he was too embarrassed to speak and have that jewel-bright blue gaze turn his way. She might think he was an idiot.

"Let's have a formal vote, then," the captain said. "All in favor of keeping the *Starvenger*?"

The crew members spoke their ayes, and Jellico said, "Then that's it. We'll fly her in, dock her outside, and rotate crews of two out to guard her until we've finished our business and found ourselves a cargo."

"Then, my boy, we have lots to do before we dock," Van Ryke said to Dane. "No time to dawdle. Let's suit up and find out what we've inherited."

4

*

"That's the last of them," Van Ryke said, three fingers tapping with practiced speed on his hand comp. "Twelve cases of stridulation unguent."

"Seems most of this was meant for Kanddoyd trade," Dane said.

The cargo master nodded. "Certainly the unguent."

Dane ran his gloved hand over the cases of small containers, trying to recall what he'd read about the insectoid race. "What's it for? Alterations in stridulation tones, isn't it?"

Van Ryke gave a nod. "Indeed: a sonic analogue of perfume. Kanddoyd fashions also run to these carapace jewels." He held up a large, faceted jewel mounted on a kind of small corkscrew whose sharp tip glittered coldly in the yellow light from overhead. Dane shuddered even though he knew the Kanddoyd carapace was largely nerveless.

"And these cosmetic rasps, as well." Van Ryke grinned at him. "It might help if you thought of them as oversize fingernail files—that's pretty much their function."

Dane returned his grin as he pointed at another row of containers. "What about those?"

"My guess is that the metallo-paints are used by the Shver for clan rituals. Those scented wood chips are somewhat of a mystery, but I doubt they are a high-pri item. The solvents and alloys and friction preventives are standard trade for habitats."

"So it all came from Exchange," Dane said.

"Logical," Van Ryke murmured as they crossed the bay a last time. Dane could feel the extra quarter-gee in his thighs. Free Traders rarely boosted over one gravity except in emergencies, which this was. But at least their trajectory was now aimed away from the Kanddoyd habitats, so they need not fear destruction by the habitat antimeteor defenses.

"After all, the fuel was full, so they had to be starting their journey, rather than ending it. And since there is nothing here of startling value, one must assume something went amiss with the crew. Sickness, or a parasite—"

"Unless it was an attack," Dane said. "That scar on the hull."

"Could be old," Van Ryke said. "They wouldn't necessarily need to fix the fairing if they transported between habitats. It would only be dangerous if they attempted to enter a planet's atmosphere."

"Then there's the empty bay." Dane indicated the deck below them.

"Something might have been removed from it," Van Ryke conceded, "or it might have been empty all along. Unless Ya can read the script, we won't have a clue, I'm afraid. But more to the point, with this minimally valuable cargo, we're going to have fewer options for dealing." He sighed and looked at his chrono. "My time is up. The captain will be cutting boost in a moment, and I'm for the *Queen*. I'll tally the numbers, and start researching these items more thoroughly." He smiled at Dane. "Disappointing as our cargo seems to be, our experiences on Sargol should serve as a reminder of the potential of the most unexpected items."

"Catnip," Dane said. Inwardly he winced. He knew that Van Ryke was thinking only of the advantage the *Queen* had gained over their rivals of Inter-Solar when the indigenous people of Sargol had discovered the *Queen*'s catnip—but Dane's memory went right back to the near disaster he'd avoided only by luck when he'd thoughtlessly given the native youngster the sprig of catnip without even thinking about its possible lethal potential to another species.

Van Ryke did not throw past mistakes into anyone's face. Dane appreciated this, and reluctantly gave himself some credit for not making the same mistakes twice.

As he looked around the silent ship, he felt the impact of Wilcox's earlier words. It seemed he was about to be promoted—and this ship would be his first assignment as full cargo master. He felt an intense amalgam of emotions, with pride and apprehension foremost.

He'd learned a lot since that first day he stepped aboard the *Queen* at Terraport, but he still had so much more to learn!

A shrill chime sounded, an alien sound very different from the gee-warning Klaxon of the *Queen*. Automatically Dane triggered his magboots and grabbed the wall grips near the lock, as did Van Ryke. Moments later the subdued whistle of the engines faded and Dane could hear the structure of the ship creak around them as acceleration ceased.

"Coming, my boy?" Van Ryke stepped into the lock.

"I'll wait for the next boost pause, so I can look around a little more," Dane said. "Might find something else we've overlooked so far."

"Good idea," Van Ryke said, and closed the hatch. Dane watched the lights flicker, indicating the drop in air pressure, then he turned away, demagnetized his boots, and pushed off down the corridor, not thinking, just—observing.

Already he liked the spaciousness of the ship. He didn't feel the ceiling crowding the top of his head. The hatchways were higher as well.

He tabbed open one of the cabin doors and pulled himself through, looking around. Rip had already reported all personal effects having been stripped away, but right now Dane was just interested in the layout.

The cabin had the same basic components that just about any ship had: storage, bed, console. A narrow door on the other side opened onto a fresher. Dane noted that the water nozzles were higher than those on the *Queen*—as if designed for tall people.

A glimpse of color caught his eye. He looked down and saw something blue lying in a corner. He bent, picked it up. It was just a mug, with no handle, its color a deep cobalt blue that instantly appealed to Dane. Miraculously unbroken despite the changes in acceleration, its weight was impossible to guess in the microgravity of the ship, but its mass was pleasing. It seemed to have some heft, and as he wrapped his gauntleted hand around it, he realized it fit nicely into his palm. No worrying about dropping or cracking something like this, as he'd worried about most Terran-made dishes since he was about fifteen.

As he looked down at the cup in his hands, he felt a jolt inside, as if acceleration had suddenly resumed. For a moment it wasn't his hands he saw holding that cup, but an unknown being's hands, holding something long familiar.

The chime shrilled again, and Dane braced himself. Acceleration returned smoothly. Rip and Wilcox hadn't taken long to master the alien engines. Perhaps they felt as he did: that the crew of this ship had not been so alien after all.

He found a cupboard and put the cup in it, then retreated to the cabin, scanning it slowly. He saw the high seat, and on a portion of bulkhead near the fold-down console, a well-scuffed spot, as if the unknown inhabitant had habitually rested his or her feet there. Dane lowered himself onto the seat, leaned back and placed one boot on the scuffed rest, looked up—and there was the tri-D screen, placed at the perfect angle for perusal.

Despite the lack of belongings, subtle evidence was all around, indicating that this cabin had been someone's home, probably for a long time.

He rose suddenly and backed out, a conviction forming in his mind.

As he made his way toward the bridge, his eyes kept noting little signs of accustomed use, hints of personality. This ship had fit her unknown crew of Traders just like the *Queen* fit Dane's crewmates, and he wondered what a stranger would think coming aboard the *Queen* and looking around as he was doing right now. Would its worn spots and narrow, quirky design make it just another old ship—or would the visitor recognize it as someone's home?

On the bridge Steen Wilcox and Rip Shannon were busy at the consoles, experimenting with tools and hand comps. Both glanced up when he entered, and in their eyes, framed by their helmet visors, he saw question.

"I think we should find out what happened," he said to Rip.

Both of them stopped their work, and faced him.

"Find something?" Rip asked.

Dane gave his head a shake; the cup wasn't important. What he had to do was fit his ideas into words that made sense. "No good crew would just jump ship. Not a crew that's been with one ship a long time. The crew on this one had been here long—the evidence is all around. If we're going to take over their ship, well, I think we owe it to them to find out what happened. If we can."

Wilcox leaned back against the captain's pod. "That's not going to be easy—or cheap. Why? They're gone. There's nothing we can do about that."

Rip looked from Wilcox to Dane. "Maybe I see. You're thinking of the *Queen,* aren't you?"

Dane nodded, and Rip gave them a grim smile. "I have to say, I'd like to think someone would find out what happened to us, if the *Queen* was found empty, orbiting some distant planet."

Wilcox shrugged, and turned back to the unfamiliar navcomp. His interests obviously lay with the intricacies of the mysterious computer, not with the equally mysterious people who had used it. "You clear it with the Old Man, I'll do what I can to help. But I think this plan of yours is like jumping into hyper with fog for coordinates."

Dane said, "Might be no one will thank us for finding out. If we can find out. Could be it would lead to trouble. But I have to know."

"It seems more honest," Rip said slowly. "I think Thorson's right."

"What it is, is more trouble," Steen Wilcox said with a wry smile. "If all you uncover is some planet-bound distant family members who decide they want to lay blood claim and collect the price of a ship. But, as I said, it's your game. If the captain backs you, I'll do what I can to help."

Dane nodded, relieved. He sensed a kind of approval in the atmosphere—though he knew that was just fanciful thinking. "I'll ask him as soon as I get back."

Míceál Jellico entered the last of his report into his log, then sat back in his chair and rubbed his burning eyes. How long had he been awake now? He'd lost count of the hours long ago.

The ship was quiet; everything was under control. It was time to rack up. But first . . .

"Eeeeeyaaaagh!"

Jellico looked up at the blue hoobat, who stared back in typical detachment. "Yergh," Queex squawked again, and spat.

"Forgotten you, have I?" Jellico asked, and swung his arm out, hitting the hoobat's cage, which rocked and swung on its specially made springs. Queex grumbled and squeaked in contentment, its back four legs nestling and the two upper claws gripping the worn post. The hoobat appeared to settle down to sleep.

Jellico looked longingly at his bunk, but the insistent growling in his stomach reminded him that his last meal had been before his last rest. He got to his feet, tabbed his door open—and the smell of real coffee drifted in. Real, fresh, hot coffee, not the syntho coffee substitute called jakek that the crew made do with when times were lean.

He smiled to himself at this unspoken reminder, sent to him by his steward, that he needed to eat. Frank Mura would never nag. He simply set up an irresistible lure like this coffee, and made certain the air currents somehow carried the aroma from the galley to the captain's cabin.

He found Mura seated in his familiar alcove just off the galley, to all intents and purposes totally absorbed in the delicate process of creating another of his plasglas-bound miniature landscapes.

"I thought we were out of coffee," Jellico said.

Frank glanced up with the seeming imperturbability of his Japanese ancestors. "I had a bit left. Since we're docking soon, thought I might as well brew it up before it goes stale."

Jellico took in a deep, appreciative breath as he drew a steaming mug.

"There's rice and vegetables as well, and some spiced kursta sauce to go over it," Mura added without turning around.

Jellico found the plate waiting, the food hot and fresh.

He carried it and his coffee into the mess, and sat down. Four crew members were already there, empty plates set aside, hot drinks before them. The three men had not heard Jellico, who habitually walked soundlessly, come in; of the group only Rael Cofort looked up. She sent him a considering blue glance that was impossible to interpret, then turned her attention back to the others.

Ali's back was to Jellico. He had a recorder at hand. As the captain watched, the engineer apprentice keyed it, saying, "All right, how about this one?"

A weird sound emanated from the recorder, a quick sound that reminded Jellico of someone tapping a bow on a viola.

"I know," Dane Thorson said. The big cargo apprentice knuckled one vast hand through his yellow hair, making it spike up, as he said, "Agreement, with Elements of Distrust."

Ali hooted. "Wrong, old boy. Agreement, with Elements of Question."

Dane shook his head. "The question noise drops down a note on each beat. *Whoop, whoop, whoop.* Distrust sounds more like that did—*ik, ik, ik.* Surprise is even faster, like *kee-keekeek.*"

"Bet," Ali said promptly.

Dane snorted. "Play the tape."

Ali slapped his hand on the recorder—and a dispassionate human voice said, "Kanddoyd emotional modification indicating Agreement, with Elements of Distrust."

Dane grinned, Ali groaned, and Jasper Weeks snorted a quiet laugh.

"Another," Ali demanded. "One more."

Dane sighed. "Go ahead, but you've been right three out of—"

"Who's counting?" Ali cut in.

"Three out of eighteen," Dane finished remorselessly. "If I'd taken any of your bets, you'd be doing my chores for the next five years."

Ali threw up his hands in mock despair as the other three laughed at him. "All right, all right, I concede. Piqued, repiqued, slammed, and capotted, as my grandfather used to say. I see I have a week of studying ahead of me."

Dane said, suddenly serious, "We'll need that smooth tongue of yours. We sure can't afford to buy any data. And remember, this is just Trade lingo. There's a whole 'nother set of overtones we can't even hear." He nudged Jasper. "Show him."

Jasper pulled back his sleeve and showed the others a brooch band.

"Hmm. Handsome," Ali said. "Didn't know you were a man for jewelry."

"Not," Jasper said. "It's an ultrasonic detector I put together."

"We broke open a small case of the carapace jewels," Dane said. "Put this together—Weeks is making one for Jan and another for me. The detectors will let us hear some of the Kanddoyds' ultrasonics, but about all we'll know is that something else is being said. We haven't any translators for High Kanddoyd, and won't be able to afford them."

Ali rose to his feet with a loud sigh. "And here I had my leave time all planned out . . ."

"Cheer up," Jasper said. "You couldn't afford it anyway."

Ali waved him off, turned, and all three noticed Jellico sitting behind them. The captain repressed the urge to smile at the variety of expressions on their faces, each characteristic of its owner. Dane, of course, looked abashed. Ali grinned, hiding his surprise behind a mask of amused indifference. Jasper Weeks nodded respectfully, his shy gaze dropping to his hands. Rael Cofort, of course, smiled with her customary maddeningly enigmatic control.

"I'm for the rack," Ali said. "Thanks to you, to dream of Kanddoyds rubbing their exoskeletons in tuneful harmony."

"Just make sure you interpret them right," Dane said, with a salute to the captain before he followed Ali out.

Jasper Weeks drank off his mug, put it in the recycler, then softly bid everyone a good sleep. A moment later he was gone.

Rael Cofort rose and made to follow, her graceful form showing no sign of the high acceleration, but when she paused to glance back, Jellico gave in to impulse and stayed her with a gesture.

Her brows rose slightly, and he opened his hand in open invitation.

She sat down across from him, both her small, capable hands closed on her mug. She said nothing, but looked at him in question.

He glanced up briefly, his gaze not missing any detail: the long, auburn hair worn in a braided crown round her head, the thick-lashed dark blue eyes, the slight build mostly hidden in a too-large brown Trader's tunic.

"How are the cats?" he asked.

"Recovering rapidly," she said. "If the tests for unknown

biota continue to prove negative, we ought to be able to let them roam after we dock."

He nodded, and as she seemed poised to get up again, he pointed with his chin toward the place where the four had been sitting. "Still studying the crew?"

She countered lightly, "Am I hearing Question with Elements of Distrust?" Her eyes narrowed. "I thought I proved my intentions were honest."

He realized he'd started all wrong. The woman had proved herself trustworthy several times over—more than any of his other crew had had to do. And by now she probably knew it, and with typical compassion did not resent it. He owed her honesty, at least. "You're a valued member of the *Queen*'s crew," he said. "They all trust you. As do I. I'll rephrase the question: do you think it's necessary to study the others?"

The corners of her well-shaped mouth deepened. "That makes it sound like I regard them as lab experiments."

"Don't you?"

"Of course not. What makes you think I did?" She looked surprised—and a little wary.

Jellico frowned, trying to sort through his reactions. Everything he said to Cofort came out sounding antagonistic. He knew why. It had nothing to do with her brother being a rival, and very successful, Trader. It was simply because he found her attractive, so attractive he tried to counterbalance his reaction with a dispassionate attitude. "The way you talk to them. Ask questions about their backgrounds."

Rael Cofort smiled wryly. "I know the old Trader etiquette: you don't ask a person's past. I just happen to think it's wrong. It sets up an artificial barrier between people, keeps an artificial distance between them. A ship is like a family, or should be."

Jellico frowned, thinking this over. "In my own training I was told repeatedly that we need those boundaries, for the physical boundaries of a ship moving for weeks through hyper are cramped enough."

"Have you found that to be true?" she asked.

He shrugged slightly, drinking a sip of coffee. "My first posting—I was younger than Thorson when he came to us—the captain took me aside and said, 'Keep your background and your opinions to yourself. The less the others know, the less they'll use against you if there's a squabble.' Found out later there'd been two deadly fights. I've followed that advice ever since, and never regretted it."

Her long eyelashes lowered over her eyes, effectively shuttering their expression. He looked at the sweep of those lashes on her cheek, then transferred his gaze to the reflections in his coffee.

"So you're warning me not to talk to the crew, is that it?"

He repressed an impatient exclamation. "No," he said. "I guess I'm telling you why they are the way they are. A crew picks up the captain's habits, sometimes. They're all quiet, not by orders, but by inclination. Custom. Habit. But we've gotten on well together."

She nodded soberly.

"Then there's the fact that you're the only female. It's bound to make a difference. The last female we had was Thorson's predecessor. She hated serving on a ship full of men."

Cofort smiled slightly. "I know. She came to my brother, remember? She's now happily berthed on a ship with mostly women. But I think I can fit in here, if I am permitted to go about it my own way. Can you trust me to do that?"

He swallowed off his coffee, wishing it would make his brain work faster. "I will, but . . . just use caution. Especially with the younger ones. Kamil will be all right—I think he was born sophisticated—but, well, Thorson is at the other end of the spectrum. He might take your friendly interest as . . . well, something else."

Her eyes widened, and her mouth curved in a delightful smile. Jellico looked at the reflection of the bulkhead lights sparking in the deep blue of her gaze, then picked up his fork and made himself busy with it.

"I don't think you need to worry," she said, a quiver of laughter in her voice. "Part of our training in psych was in what you might call professional presentation. I have been very careful to project the aura of a fond older sister, and I think Dane will eventually accept me as such." She gave way suddenly to a low chuckle, soft and attractive. "Anything else and I think the poor soul would jump off the *Queen* and fly along in vacuum. He's terrified of women!"

"He's never known any," Jellico said. "Not socially, anyway. Orphan, went straight to Pool, and then to us. Did nothing in between times but work and study."

She nodded, unsurprised, and he realized belatedly that of course she must have read everyone's medical files. A good ship's doctor would, and Tau had made it clear he accepted her as a colleague.

As his fork absently pushed Mura's excellent food around on his plate, he reflected how glad he was that his own file contained only the briefest details about his medical history, and nothing else.

"Good night," Rael Cofort said, rising to her feet. "Sleep well."

"You too, Doctor."

A moment later he was alone with his meal, and his thoughts.

5

"Passed the inner beacon," Rip Shannon's voice came over the com from the other ship.

"Acknowledged," Tang Ya said. Then he keyed his console and looked up at Captain Jellico. "New instructions coming in."

"Pass them to my comp," the captain said, his hands steady as he piloted the *Queen* towards the immense construct now filling space dead ahead.

A moment later, they received word from the *Starvenger* that they too had received the docking and debarkation instructions.

Rael Cofort, from her vantage in the passenger's seat, looked up at the screen showing the slowly approaching habitat. They were vectoring in along the cylinder's long axis, straight toward the immense lock yawning at its center, surrounded by a wilderness of metallic complexity thickly forested with antennae and projectors and less identifiable objects. For a moment, dizziness seized her: the lack of scale made the metallic disk seem to suddenly swell to planetary size.

Rael shook her head to dispel the illusion, and instead saw the complexities of the habitat framed by the clean, plain, almost austere lines of the *Queen*'s control deck. During her years of trading with her brother Teague, she had visited two habitats, one of them Exchange. Each time she'd experienced the same vertigo: somehow, the artificial nature of a habitat made its size more viscerally awesome than any planet. Too, the uncanny silence of their approach was far too suggestive of the most terrifying of all sounds to a spacer: jet failure, which during the usual planetary touchdown almost invariably meant death.

"Velocity point zero zero eight," said Tang Ya. They were now moving as slowly as a ground vehicle, thought Rael. No, almost at a walk. But the beacon warnings on the way in had been unequivocal: here the speed limit was enforced by death, for despite its size, a habitat was fragile—a ship under full power that went astray could puncture through places that would cause the entire cylome to vent to space.

Now the disk of the cylindrical habitat's end cap was a plain of complex metal shapes stretching out to either side, while ahead she could see the docking berths, bright blue-white lights strobing from the one they'd been assigned. Slowly the edges of the immense lock slid past as the habitat swallowed the *Solar Queen,* and the ship trembled as Captain Jellico triggered the maneuvering thrusters in quick bursts.

Rael looked around at the *Queen*'s control deck. The contrast between the bristling technology outside the viewscreen and the functional ordinariness of the *Queen* was symbolic. On Exchange, fabulous technology was the norm—almost a fad. The Kanddoyds had to have the latest, the most complicated, the fastest, whether ships or food preparators. In contrast was Jellico and his crew, who worked with every evidence of contentment using ship technology that in some areas would be seen as outdated, and who lived plainly—as if on a planet—no matter what kind of gravity or environment they found themselves in. It seemed a part of their innate honesty, the straightforward approach to problems, to life, that had attracted her to them in the first place.

But she wondered how they would endure living in a place like Exchange.

"This is weird," said Ali, his voice rough. "Being inside like this."

"No degrees of freedom," agreed Van Ryke.

And that, thought Rael, was anathema to spacers, and Free Traders in particular.

A flicker at the edge of her vision caught her attention, and she suddenly realized that the immense space around them was alive with motion: small vehicles of every description and even figures in space suits swarmed around other ships in the huge bay and up into the vast corridors which radiated outward towards heavier-gee areas. They'd been assigned a berth in microgravity.

Tang Ya suddenly looked up. "General com incoming," he said.

Jellico gave a single nod. "Put it on."

Ya tabbed a key, and this time the voice that filled the bridge was a peculiar one, reedy—the kind of voice, Rael thought, a violin would have were it to speak.

"Welcome, Terrans of vessel *Solar Queen,* to the cylome graced with the cognomen The Garden of Harmonious Exchange. You will find here representatives of many worlds, far systems and near, conducting their important trade in perfect amity, hosted by three races, the Kanddoyd, the Shver, and the Terrans. Our laws, agreed in the Concord of Harmony between our peoples, can be found on Terran Standard Channel Twenty-seven. We wish, in the friendliest spirit, to draw your attention to those designed for everyone's safety, foremost being those governing relations between the three species signatory to the Concord."

"Standard hoo-la," Stotz muttered over the intercom.

"If you are puzzled, dismayed, astounded, or confounded, we invite you to visit your representative of the Terran Stellar Patrol, Captain-Legate Ross, who resides on level five, domiciled in the Way of the Rain-dappled Lilies."

Ali gave a sudden laugh. "I think I'm going to like it here."

"Our representative, Exalted Locutor Taddatak, will indulge himself the inexpressible joy of a visit to your vessel to negotiate the nominal fees that, alas, we must ask of our visitors in order to maintain our splendid facility for your pleasures."

The voice cut out just as a flurry of booms and clanks announced that the berth had firmly grappled the ship; but so precise had the captain's piloting been that they came to rest with almost no sense of deceleration.

"All right, we're in," the captain said.

Tang Ya watched his console. "They're bringing up the dock access tube; Thorson is overseeing the mate—" He frowned as a query light blinked. "It appears that they insist on controlling life support from their end."

Jellico looked up in question. Rael said, "Standard procedure, as you'll see when you have time to read their contract. We didn't like it either, though it turned out to have a benefit we hadn't planned for: dangerous biota from all three races are automatically filtered out. Our filters weren't that prepared."

Jellico turned back to Ya and gave a short nod. The comtech touched the intercom and said, "Go ahead, Thorson."

A flurry of activity then began, as both the crew of the *Solar Queen* and the dockside workers made the *Queen* fast, hooking up each life-support system and checking it before the *Queen* relinquished control. Once that was completed would begin the age-old process of negotiation for services and fees. Rael Cofort stayed out of the way; this was not her job, though she could help in an emergency. Right now her best help would be not to clutter the paths of the others.

So she moved toward one of the ports near the outer lock and glanced out. Though the *Solar Queen* herself was still in vacuum, the berthing equipment included a long tube bent at right angles, connecting the *Queen* to a lock giving them access into the habitat. Long strips at intervals on the tube were clear, affording her a view of anyone coming or going.

For a short time suited workers signaled back and forth as each system was locked in, checked, and equalized; then at last the green-go lights flashed. Moments later there was movement in the tube, indicating arrivals. From her vantage she could see the locutor moving toward the *Queen* at a rapid pace, with two or three minor officials scurrying behind. She glanced up, saw Frank Mura also looking out—and was surprised to see a look of strain on his face.

Her lips parted, but she repressed the exclamation she'd been about to make. Almost immediately Mura turned away from the port and retreated to his cabin off the galley. She heard the door hiss closed.

Once again she glanced out, this time trying to see the Kanddoyds with the eyes of a newcomer. They were mammalian beings, bipeds, and they had two arms, two legs, and a head, but there the resemblance between Terrans and Kanddoyds ended. Every centimeter of what would be skin on a human was protected by intersecting layers of chitinous material; the effect was a kind of elaborate armor, augmented by the decorations the beings were so fond of. Their heads were small, well protected by conical, flared chitin rather like a helmet; their carapaces were segmented, and also looked like armor. Not just any armor, but . . .

She frowned, reaching back in memory. She'd studied Terran history, and knew she'd seen something rather like the Kanddoyds before.

She turned away from the port, and her gaze fell by chance on one of the tiny trees Mura nurtured, and suddenly she had it.

Samurai warriors, *ronin*—the Kanddoyds looked like armored warriors from the days of Bushido in Japan.

Rael winced. Frank Mura did not talk about the cataclysm that had destroyed the Japanese islands, homeland of his peo-

ple for countless generations, but she had studied the effects
of cataclysm on people. They were capable of grieving for generations.

Should she say anything? No. But she'd watch, and listen.

Dane wedged himself between the curve of a bulkhead and
a wall in the mess. Eleven of the *Queen*'s thirteen were there.
Looking around, Dane realized that Steen and Rip had remained on the *Starvenger*. And this time they weren't radio-
linked with the *Queen*.

As if following Dane's thoughts, Captain Jellico said, "The
two who go out to the salvage ship on the next rotation can
report to Wilcox and Shannon. I don't want the comlink used
unless there's an emergency either way. This place has communication technology that we've probably never heard of.
We don't know who might be listening in, and why, and
there's no use in finding out the hard way. For now we'll do
our reports in person."

He paused and looked around. The others all nodded or
made murmurs of agreement. Jellico's hard mouth lost some
of its tension as he turned his gaze to Frank Mura.

The compact, quiet-faced steward said, "I calculated what
we have against the latest posted exchange rates, minus the
value of Macgregory's letter, and what it amounts to is this:
we can buy ourselves a Terran week or maybe two to resolve
our business—if everyone sleeps on board the *Queen*."

A couple of people sighed, and Dane grimaced in sympathy. He hated living in microgravity, and made a mental note
to find the equivalent of a Kanddoyd public gym—if there was
such a thing—down at the one-grav section, so he could work
out and not lose his muscle tone. *And to eat, if I can,* he
thought, remembering unfondly how spectacularly messy
food spills were in microgravity.

"I'll visit the legate and see if there's a way to shorten this
registry process," the captain went on. "What will take all of

your ingenuity, Van, is your managing to turn this cargo around."

Van Ryke smiled broadly. Dane couldn't help grinning at the blatant anticipation in his superior's face—the man lived for just such a challenge.

Jasper Weeks said soberly, "We listened to the entire Concord." He indicated himself and Kosti, who nodded. "From the sound of their regulations and formalities, it's going to take longer than from here to Terra in hyperjump to get the salvage claim going."

Jellico nodded. "I know. I heard it out as well. It seems to be the Kanddoyd way—a dozen extra visits for every piece of business, so that no one ever has to say no, and thus everyone saves face. This is why I'm going first to the legate. Ross is here to look out for the interests of Terrans. He ought to be able to tell me how to make this as quick and painless as possible."

Again there were murmurs of agreement. They'd had some run-ins with the Patrol in the past, but for strange reasons that had eventually been proven not their fault. Even if the Patrol were somewhat rough and ready in their approach to problems, Dane thought, no one had ever accused them of corruption or unfairness.

"We're now on dirtside shift schedule," Jellico said. "I've posted the rotations to the *Starvenger*; you'll each serve, in pairs, forty-eight Standard hours. Off limits are the domiciles of the Shver and Kanddoyds—stay in the Exchange areas. Also, stay away from the warehousing areas of the Spin Axis. Dr. Cofort?" He turned suddenly to the woman. "Explain?"

Rael Cofort said, "You won't find any mention of this in the official tapes, but there's a lawless element living up there. Apparently even the Monitors of Harmony, which is what they call their peace enforcers, don't go up there—at least the Kanddoyd ones don't go. The Shver arm of the Monitors do, but that's to keep an eye out for the Deathguard, which is a very dangerous gang of Shver outcasts who make their living through hiring out as assassins. There are other kinds of outcasts there as well, and my brother told me once that high-caste Shver sometimes go hunting the denizens there, for sport, and no one does anything about it. The Kanddoyds just pretend the area doesn't exist."

"So this supposed Harmony is a sham?" Mura asked, frowning.

Cofort shook her head. "Oh, it's stable enough—at least when we came here before, there had apparently never been any major trouble since the Concord was first hammered out. And the Kanddoyds are very friendly beings. The Shver are rather different."

"The Shver are all right if you respect their customs and stay out of their personal space," Van Ryke said. "But you've got to remember that at the other end of their sphere of influence they are still conquering worlds as a solution to their population problems."

Jellico's glance came back to rest, as if by chance, on Ali. "Get in their way—say something they don't like—and you've got a duel on your hands. They've channeled their aggressions into hunting for outlaws at the Spin Axis, and into formalized duels, but those aggressions are still there." He paused, then said, "Any other questions?"

No one spoke.

Jellico nodded. "Those scheduled for leave time can depart now. I'll see if the Terran legate can get us moving on the paperwork faster. Doctor, if you'd go with me and show me how to get around?"

"Gladly, Captain," Cofort said.

They left.

Dane looked across at Ali, who gave a little sigh. Dane wasn't fooled. Ali seemed incapable of permitting anyone to see that he had normal emotions, but just the same he knew that Kamil felt the same way that he and Rip did: what had happened to the crew of the *Starvenger* was their mystery to be solved, and if they couldn't solve it before leaving the Exchange, it wouldn't be for lack of trying.

✳　✳　✳

Rael Cofort was considerably amused to find that the evocative name of the captain-legate's corridor—The Way of the Rain-dappled Lilies—seemed to have originated entirely in someone's imagination. There were certainly no lilies in sight, rain-dappled or otherwise.

In fact, she thought as she paused outside the entranceway to the legate's quarters, hadn't the Kanddoyd world lacked rain? She recalled reading about the race's long battle against growing radiation from a swelling sun, and the fierce, hot, scouring winds that had driven them underground before they had finally abandoned their home and taken up life in space—one of the few races that did not live on planets. At any rate, these domiciles were all exactly alike to the human eye—plain steelplast doors set in blank walls. Only the nameplates varied; each was inscribed in three scripts, Kanddoyd, Shver, and Terran.

The corridor was situated in what inhabitants considered a prime area, Rael knew; the front of the domicile looked out over the breathtaking curve of the habitat. Odd, she thought, the dichotomy between enclosure and exposure: it was, she knew, a constant of Kanddoyd architecture.

"Coming, Dr. Cofort?"

Captain Jellico's voice interrupted her perusal of the corridor. She looked up, saw that the legate's door was open and a diminutive Kanddoyd waited just beyond for them to enter.

She glanced up into Jellico's face as she walked inside, expecting impatience with her lagging behind. His mouth was pressed in its familiar noncommittal line, but there was a hint of humor in his narrowed gray eyes.

"The honored legate welcomes sentients from his home planet with ineffable joy," the Kanddoyd said in its odd, grainy voice, while portions of its complicated carapace rubbed against other portions, making cricketlike chirrups. "If the imposing visitors from far Terra would ambulate this way?"

The being gestured down a narrow tiled hallway, then turned and led the way, its chitinous feet clicking rhymically. As Jellico stepped behind Rael, he murmured, "I sense it's been a while since the last Terran visited Ross."

Rael nodded, trying not to smile. A moment later the Kanddoyd and its odd Terran vocabulary were forgotten when she stepped through into a spectacular garden straight from Terra. A flower-scented breeze wafted in her face, and she heard the sounds of birds and insects, and the hush of leaves tossing—and realized, with difficulty, that this was a masterfully done holograph.

"Do you like it?" A quiet voice spoke from under one of the trees.

Rael realized she had gasped. Stepping forward, she peered into the shadows just as a tall, thin, spectral-featured man emerged into the light.

"I have eight projectors," Ross said. He lifted an arm and waved it—and the movement cast no shadow. "Keeps the proportions correct as well. The aromas are recent additions to my air system."

"Roses," Rael said. "Roses, jasmine, carnations. Grass."

Ross smiled. His features reminded Rael of a sad hound dog. "I hoped I had the proportions right. Six years it has taken me to program all the details. But I really think I have the proportions right. Do you?"

Rael looked up at Jellico, who said only, "I haven't been dirtside on Terra for a long time."

"I have been there more recently," Rael said, "and I really think you've captured the best of the gardens I've ever visited."

"It's a combination," Ross said eagerly. "I've seven specimens of the genus Rosa of the Rosaceae family, and that there is *Epilabium angustifolium* . . . and of course these varieties of Liliaceae . . ." He stopped suddenly, seemed to recall himself, and said, "Forgive me. I get enthusiastic over this hobby of mine. You are here on business. Shall we step into the office?"

He tabbed a control hidden in the holographic shadows, and a door seemed to open in one of the trees, making the whole scene seem still more unreal.

Once Rael stepped through, she felt that the universe had righted itself again. She found herself in a plain office, furnished simply in what was probably regulation for Patrol officers of Ross's rank. The lighting was efficient, and there were several ordinary chairs opposite the desk. Strangely, though, Ross's windows and view ways were completely blocked: there was no sign of the sweeping view that made outside domiciles so desirable to habitat dwellers.

Ross sat down behind the desk, and folded his hands. "Now, how may I help you? I take it you are not here on ordinary Trade business?"

Captain Jellico said, "Correct. We discovered an abandoned vessel on our way into the system."

Ross said, "There are standards set for the registry and claim of salvage under the Concord of Harmony."

Jellico gave a brief nod. "We've studied those."

Rael, acutely aware of the shades of Jellico's voice, sensed impatience. She said smoothly, "The explications that were sent along with the text of the Concord were admirable in their completeness, but it seems if we follow the directions contained there, we'll be spending weeks going from office to office performing polite rituals as we get passed from official to official." She opened her hands. "Unfortunately, we are facing a time limit to our visit here."

Jellico added, "I hoped you could assist in telling us precisely whom to see and what papers to file so we can keep this process as short as possible."

The Patrol officer said, "I have no jurisdiction in this area, of course, but I can see if there's a chance that the trade administrator will be able to aid you. Can you give me your ship ID and that of the one you found?"

Jellico quoted them, and Ross typed them into the computer, then sent his message. "As you probably surmised, business with Kanddoyds is a pleasant but leisurely affair. Ordinarily it takes time just to get an appointment. As it happens, you are in luck. The Administrator of Trade Executed in Perfect Amity is human—or at least, he was born human."

Ross paused, looking slightly pained; Rael wondered if whatever changes the administrator had gone through repelled Ross.

"Flindyk, isn't that his name?" Jellico said.

Ross smiled. "You have done your reading."

"Isn't that a Kanddoyd name?" Rael asked.

Ross turned to her. "It is indeed a Kanddoyd version of his name, which I understand was Flynn von Dieck. He doesn't use the Terran name at all anymore—hasn't for a couple hundred years."

"A couple hundred *years?*" Rael repeated.

Ross nodded. "He's a nuller now—lives in null grav up near the Spin Axis. He can go down into the low grav of the Kanddoyds for a certain amount of time a day, to work. If you can adjust to that kind of life, you can extend your years almost indefinitely, I understand." He glanced at the communications status light, and then looked up, his dark eyes expressionless. "It probably isn't going to work, trying to supercede the system, but it was worth a try—"

A blinking light suddenly went green, and a message flashed across his console.

Ross looked slightly surprised. "You are in luck. The administrator will see you right now, himself, if you care to go along to his office in the Trade Administration building."

Rael and Jellico got to their feet. "Thank you," the captain said.

"Do make certain that all your data is correct, though," Ross cautioned. "Flindyk is known to all three races as being scrupulously careful, a by-the-book administrator, favoring no one or no race over strict adherence to the Concord."

"Which probably explains why he has been successful for so long," Rael said with a smile. "Thank you, sir."

Rael led the way out, and they found the maglev that led to the Trade Administration building.

This building made the most of its lack of weather; it was open to the habitat, with spectacularly elaborate gardens on complicated terracing. The offices were mostly hidden behind flowering shrubs with exotic, delicate fronds that had never known lashing wind or punishing temperature changes.

Rael had been here before, had been happy to wander about as Teague executed his business. Now they were met by a Kanddoyd functionary who spoke Trade perfectly, and who complimented them each several times before finally asking their business.

Rael answered as best she could, inwardly hiding her growing amusement at Jellico's impatience. Not that he showed it, but she was sensitive to his moods, and felt him watching the time as the Kanddoyd led them along this garden path and that one—only to be introduced not to Flindyk but to yet another functionary, this one even more elaborate in carapace decoration (and wordage) than the last.

Finally, though, they were taken to a larger building at the back which had mosaic-lined corridors and offices at intervals along them. Flindyk's suite was an exceptionally large one, as would be expected for an executive.

The official took them directly to a door cleverly hidden in a fabulous mosaic. Inside was a room that looked more like a garden than an office. Many of the appurtenances were gold, and everything was screened by delicate ferns that had been nurtured in null grav and grew in fabulous patterns.

Rael gained a hasty impression of all this artistic beauty, but what drew her attention and kept it was the large holofract of Terra spinning slowly in the middle of the room. All the plants and furnishings were planned around the vast fractal image, evolving slowly to a logic of its own in mimicry of a distant planet that Flindyk would never see again.

Rael moved closer, admiring the loving detail that highlighted each familiar mountain range and body of water. There were even white spirals moving gently across each hemisphere, realistic weather patterns that made Rael feel a sudden, intense longing to go home.

"Beautiful, is it not?" a mellow voice said.

Rael turned, feeling heat burn up her neck.

Behind a truly splendid console-desk was the biggest Kanddoyd she had ever seen in her life. For a moment she stared at the elaborately beautiful carapace of fine amber-colored wood, gilded and jeweled, covering a body of gigantic proportions. Her gaze traveled up to a round, smiling face and she felt unsettled for a moment, as if her eyes couldn't decide if this was a Kanddoyd wearing a disturbingly real human face mask, or a human encased in a Kanddoyd carapace. This, then, was Flindyk, the human who was several hundred years old.

"We appreciate your seeing us right away," Captain Jellico was saying. "He probably told you we are on a tight schedule and want to expedite this business as fast as we can."

"Ah yes," Flindyk said, his hands touching the fine console inset into his desk. The keytabs were extremely costly porcelain, gold-painted. From the faceting on the status lights, Rael strongly suspected that these latter were jewels.

"You are captain of the *Solar Queen,* and you seem to have attached a derelict? The . . . *Starvenger?*"

"Snapped out of hyper and sucked her into our wake," Jellico said.

"Well, if you provide proper data, including your visual records and copies of your log, we will compare this with the records from Trade Central, and see if we can get your business moving along briskly," Flindyk said. His hands tapped lightly at his keys, then he sat back and waited. A moment later a spool extruded from a slot. "Here you go," he said, smiling. "Just have your communications officer append the data requested on here, bring it back to the prime facilitator, Koytatik, whose function this comes under, and you'll soon be on your way."

"Thanks," Jellico said. "We really appreciate the help."

"For my fellow humans it is a pleasure to extend the extra effort," Flindyk said genially. One hand waved gracefully at the holo of Terra spinning in the center of the office. "Though I have been happy enough here, I do miss the old world, and I envy you who can go back."

Rael felt a pang of sympathy for the man; she realized that at his age, and size, he could never risk being in normal gravity again. A visit to Terra would kill him.

"If there's anything else I can do for you, anything at all, you know the way to my office," Flindyk said cheerily.

They both thanked him and departed, Jellico tucking the spool into his tunic pocket.

"I think our luck has finally turned," he said, smiling.

6

Dane Thorson drew a deep breath, and fought the urge to grip the table with both hands. Most of the time he was fine—kept his visual orientation balanced with his inner ear—but if he turned too quickly, or got absorbed in watching the gyrations of the Kanddoyds, without warning he'd lose his sense of down and up, and see himself floating upside down in a revolving canister.

One breath, two. He looked up, saw an expression of sympathy on his chief's face. "Drink," Van Ryke said.

Obediently Thorson sipped at the straw that had extruded from the bubble of nilak, the Kanddoyd version of coffee. He tightened his stomach muscles, determined to conquer what he derided as physical weakness. A Free Trader—particularly a cargo master—ought to be able to adjust to any environment, he told himself.

As if reading his mind, Van Ryke said, "I have lost count of the number of planets I've visited, but of them very few rate as repellent to natural human instinct as one of these cy-lomes."

"It's inside out," Dane muttered. "I tell myself this is the best design for a habitat, but my guts know that down is out, with vacuum underfoot, and the horizon doesn't curve out of sight, as it decently should—instead it curves up and over. Then . . ." He glanced at a quartet of Kanddoyds passing nearby, and clamped his jaw shut.

He would not speak a criticism of the indigenous popu-lation, even in Terran, which apparently few of the other races understood. It wasn't the way of a Trader. But still, it made a person dizzy to watch the way the beings zigzagged back and forth across each other's path, constantly buzzing and humming and chirping and clicking. The tapes hadn't even remotely made him ready for that; he'd stupidly gotten the idea that they would speak Trade, and augment what they said with one discrete noise of emotional amplification at a time. The reality was, they never stopped making noises, so many it was difficult to distinguish what kind of noise, much less the patterns. He thought grumpily, *And this is only what they do in my sonic range.*

Van Ryke was watching the four Kanddoyds make their way down the concourse. To human eyes they walked in a continual braiding motion, veering only when they encoun-tered others of their kind. Then the pattern evolved into a mesmerizing series of intersecting angles, broken only if they were approached by other beings, especially the bulky, heavy-treading Shver. Then they flowed out of the way in deference, wide berth for high clan rank and just skirting those of low rank. The Shver, Dane noted, did not turn aside from their path for anyone save others of their own kind, and then only for those of higher degree; but they paused and exchanged gestures of formal recognition and obligation first.

Dane, watching the tall, massively muscled beings ges-turing as their low voices rumbled like distant thunder, won-dered who would be idiot enough to deliberately cross a Shver's path.

The Shver were even bigger up close than seen from afar. Their thick, coarse gray hides and massive bodies called to mind humanoid elephants. Even their ears were almost elephantine, so large and wrinkly were they, though the faces were more or less humanoid—a forbidding sort of humanoid. The sheer size of the Shver, plus their bulk and broody mien, and the savage-looking serrated honor knives worn at their sides, guaranteed that no beings, even the raffish and overdecorated Ylp, or the militant Rigelians, got in their way.

They seemed all-powerful, yet Dane recalled reading that they were phobic about flying insects—and were terrified of spiders. It made sense that their heavy gravity would not support most insect life as known to Terra and other worlds; fragile exoskeletons would be crushed by the creatures' own weight. Small fauna on the Shver's homeworld was apparently all vermiform.

But in addition, for some reason buried deep within the Shver's prehistory, anything with more legs than five—their sacred number—was considered daemonic. They apparently reacted at the sight of spiders the way most spacers would react to meeting a ghost.

Van Ryke's sudden chuckle brought Dane's attention back to the Shver walking by. As the two men watched, the smallest of three Shver stared at them intently, until one of the taller ones noticed and with a sharp gesture ordered the youngster to turn around again. Dane smothered the urge to grin. He remembered that the Shver considered it indelicate to eat in public, and the gawking youngster reminded him strongly of human children and their infinite capacity for entertainment at the prospect of impolite spectacles.

"A few minutes more." The cargo master's voice broke into Dane's thoughts, and Van Ryke turned to study Dane. "Do you wish me to accompany you, my boy?"

Thorson shook his head. "No. Thanks. I'll manage. With the start Flindyk gave us on the process, as the captain said, this is cut-and-dried work. You'll need all the time we have to secure a good cargo. That's top priority."

"Good enough, then," Van Ryke said. "Speaking of which, I ought to be about my business. The sooner I get started on those hours of flowery talk the better. I just hope it comes with suitable refreshments." He gave Dane a smile that the apprentice cargo master knew was meant to be reassuring, rose, and moved at a sedate pace down the concourse.

Dane sighed. He knew he had the easier job—which would be the more embarrassing if he failed. He fingered the recorder at his belt, with its variety of tones and tinkles that had been established as acceptable emotional modifiers for Trade Speech, then turned his eyes to another group of Kanddoyds who were busy settling at one of the tables nearby. Covertly Dane studied them, trying to muster all he'd learned in order to identify them. Three had huge, gold-faceted eyes, which meant they were females; of these one had light eyes, indicating youth, and the eyes of the other two were a darker honey color, indicating greater age. The four males were also a variety of ages, their green eyes reflecting varied shades.

All of them had complicated jewel insets and enameling on their exoskeletal components, indicating wealth; Dane did not bother to scrutinize the decorations any more closely, since they were supposedly indicative only of individual tastes—and might change from day to day, if the owner had enough time and money to constantly augment his or her carapace. Kanddoyd, unlike the clannish, hierarchical Shver, did not wear any insignia indicating rank—they were far too individualistic for that.

Sucking absently at his drink, he realized it was empty when the fragile bubble collapsed in his hands. He slid the crushed bubble into a recycle bin and shuffled out onto the concourse, careful to move slowly. A forgetful step and he'd bound in the air, legs and arms pumping for balance, making him look like the rawest newbie.

A glance up the concourse toward a place where bright lights and loud music emanated forth caused him to grin. There, right in the middle of a group of flashily dressed

Traders from half a dozen widely scattered civilizations, was Ali. To all appearances he was just partying, but Dane knew better. *Sometimes the quickest way to find out what you need to know is to go where the spacers hang out, and listen to gossip,* Ali had said when he and Rip held their planning session.

Better you than I, Dane thought, turning toward the maglev. His chrono showed it was time for Prime Facilitator Koytatik's duty to start at the registry office, something he'd taken care to ascertain earlier. He slid into a pod, moving around a pair of Shver. A cluster of other beings, all from different worlds but wearing the brown indicative of Trade, pushed in from behind.

"So they swapped them, cargo for cargo, and sold for double . . ."

". . . got a week of leave before we blast out for the Thstoths-Buool Run . . ."

". . . so they think the Deathguard must have done it. No evidence anywhere—"

Dane sneaked a peek when he heard that one, but the speaker's voice lowered, and he could not tell which being had said the words.

". . . the grace and beauty of your excellent ship, but we poor Traders cannot possibly hope"—Regret, with Elements of Doubt—"to compete with the great and powerful Traders from the Deneb . . ."

The pod drew to a halt, and the talk blended into general noise as the travelers pushed out, everyone bounding lightly into the microgravity and ricocheting off in various directions.

Dane looked up at the vast, terraced edifice with the holographic poles declaring in the three main languages that this was the Trade Administrative Center.

He finally made his way straight for the widest pathway in the middle. Just under an archway he saw a Kanddoyd spot him and come scurrying forward. The Kanddoyd escorted him to a pleasant waiting room while assuring him that the locutor would promptly interrupt her activities to serve him, using about four times as many words as were necessary.

While he was waiting, Dane forced himself to walk forward to the huge window overlooking the interior of the cylome and gaze out. The reluctance he felt triggered a sudden realization: that the Kanddoyd had doubtless put him here to exploit the well-known Terran aversion to habitats.

"The Kanddoyd are indeed the friendliest of all alien races," he remembered Van Ryke saying. *"That does not mean they do not desire their own advantage."*

Despite himself, Dane found himself fascinated by the view. The locutor's office was in the middle of the Kanddoyd levels: a compromise for the comfort of the many races who might visit here. It faced down the length of the habitat, and there were no obstructions to his gaze.

And the view was utterly strange. Dane found that if he looked straight ahead, it was much like being in an aircar above a planetary surface, flying through an immense canyon—*like the Slash on Immensa,* he thought—with distance softening the juts of buildings among greenery into analogues of distant mountains. But then the curve of the cylindrical walls drew his eyes up and over and vertigo seized him anew as he saw towering structures skewering out into the air far above him, apparently in defiance of all gravity and engineering. Fortunately, he thought, the radiants that lit the interior of the vast habitat blocked any view of the opposite surface—he didn't know if he could have tolerated seeing an entire half a world hanging upside down overhead.

"The hindbrain knows nothing of spin gravity," he remembered Craig Tau saying dryly.

It was clever, though, Dane thought, how the design of the habitat fit the nature of the two races who inhabited it. The inner surface was at 1.6 gee, giving the Shver not only the acceleration they'd evolved in but also the lion's share of the living space—just as that expansive race preferred. The Kanddoyds, on the other hand, lived high up in the immense tube-shaped towers that transfixed the cylinder from side to side, giving them the lower gravity and combination of en-

closure and exposure that they preferred. They did not mind
the imbalance in territory, for their long, losing battle on a
dying planet had bred them to enjoy close quarters.

In fact, the more he looked, the more he was impressed
by Kanddoyd engineering, despite his discomfort. The huge
cylindrical towers would have rendered many acres dark and
undesirable on a planet, but here, since they passed through
the Spin Axis, they cast no shadows. And elevators in them
gave rapid transit from one side of the habitat to another—
as long as you didn't mind the change in gees, and the flip-
over at the center, where gravity was zero.

His musings were interrupted by the cheery clackings and
whirrings of welcome from a Kanddoyd who bustled forward out of a cleverly concealed door. She was painted all
over in curlicues of pleasing shades of purple. Jewels winked
on her carapace as she made the complicated gesture that was
the equivalent of a human bow. She said in a thin, reedy
voice, "Welcome to the Bright Arrangement of Herbaceous
Delights, O Gentle Trader. Locutor Danakak wishes no
greater pleasure this day than to have the honor of assisting
you in your important affairs."

Dane said, "I have come to register a salvage find."

"Ah!" the locutor said. "May I congratulate you upon
your advantageous discovery—but at the same time we
salute the misfortune of the unknowns whose craft has
fallen, through the exigencies of fate, to your benefit." She
clacked her mandibles rapidly, and rubbed together the complicated ankle armor that reminded Dane a little of ancient
pictures of spurs. A deep droning sound rose, fell away. He
identified both sounds—Grief for the Honorably Fallen and
Acknowledgment of the Ephemeral Nature of Material
Ownership—and hastened to produce from his belt recorder
the corroborative sounds.

"Thank you," he said, and pressed another code on his
recorder as he said, "If you would honor me with the directions to the registry office of Prime Facilitator Koytatik, we

can both carry on our tasks." Underscoring his words were the musical chirps of Friendly and Honest Intent.

"Well, then," said the locutor. She made a series of rapid noises, the only one he recognized being Curiosity Appropriate to the Circumstances. "Your respected employer must rejoice in a worker so ready to execute her will in a timely manner! Permit me to introduce to your notice the humble Augmentor Laktic, whose greatest pleasure in life is the assistance of our Terran visitors in the expeditious discharge of their important affairs!"

Danakak led Thorson along a roundabout route past terraced layers of fragrant herbs. He curbed his impatience, knowing that this was intended as a compliment. To conduct someone the shortest way was not only to hint that the person had no taste for beauty, but to indicate that one wished to spend as little time as possible in his company. People came and went along the winding paths, past offices whose exteriors were painted with geometric designs or decorated with ceramic mosaics. Busy Kanddoyds scurried in between all the other sentients, moving with the startling swiftness Dane had hitherto associated only with Rigelians.

Under a flowering vine-covered archway they encountered a waiting Kanddoyd, and after a mutual exchange of compliments accompanied by rhythmic noises indicating good intentions, Dane found himself handed off to Augmentor Laktic. He was a young male, painted over with geometric shapes in metallic colors.

He offered, at great length, to assist Dane in finding the appropriate office for the initiation of his business, at which time Dane pulled out the spool that Flindyk had given Captain Jellico and a printout version of the data, and said, "I've already gotten the proper forms. What I need to do is find the office where I can register this information. If you can take me there, I'd appreciate it, Augmentor Laktic."

The Kanddoyd looked at the spool, glanced at the printout, and clacked in Surprise Tempered with Respect. "I contemplate with admiration the rapidity of Terrans in their business enterprise," he said, making a series of clicks and tweets that Dane sensed were interrogative.

Dane's time as cargo master apprentice had provided enough experience for him to instinctively endeavor not to give any hint of the time and money constraints forcing the *Queen*'s crew to act quickly. Though the business he had here was only a matter of form, he didn't know how much talk passed between the registry workers and those who dealt with Traders. It would be more difficult for Van Ryke if whoever he was working with found out about their desperate need.

So he said, "Terrans usually act quickly to execute business so they can get to their pleasures the more quickly. Our crew wants to have plenty of time to explore all the delights Exchange has to offer." And he pressed his belt in the code that produced the sounds indicating Fervent Anticipation.

The Kanddoyd laughed, a sound like a violin cadenza. "Ah! Of course! Then clearly it behooves me to bustle us along, the quicker to enable the Gentle Terrans to consort in the pleasure decks with other convivial beings. Since you appear to have all the correct forms, and filled out—as far as this humble augmentor is able to infer—correctly as well, I suggest we proceed directly to the august precincts of Registry and Claims."

Thorson tried to keep his face impassive, but inside he felt a spurt of joy. So he was going to be successful!

They proceeded up through levels and layers, all flower-bordered, with occasional views out into the habitat, to a door inlaid with a fabulous mosaic pattern indicating the birth of a star. Through the door, and into pleasant scents of fresh flowers. Kanddoyd music played softly from somewhere; not melodic, but the complicated rhythms were pleasing to the Terran ear.

They had to go through two or three levels of functionaries, each of whose jobs apparently existed to prevent the applicant the disappointment of discovering that his forms were incorrect. After the customary exchanges of compliments, Laktic proffered the spool, with its unmistakable sigil of Trade Administration, and the helpers all bowed them on their way.

Laktic seemed as pleased as Dane was, if it was possible to ascribe human emotions to a nonhuman. As they approached what appeared to be the last stop, Dane wondered if augmentors got paid for each successful piece of business they helped to resolve. If so, he had to admire all the more the indefatigable good manners that had detained them along the way; on Terra, though no one liked standing in line, Dane suspected twenty people could have gotten their papers filed in the time it was taking him just to find the correct person to submit his to.

But at last Laktic brought him to a low table where an older Kanddoyd waited, her carapace jeweled in shades of gold to match her eyes. This was Prime Facilitator Koytatik, Dane discovered, after a truly memorable exchange of flowery politeness.

At last, though, she dismissed Laktic, who thanked Dane—and on being thanked for his help, thanked him for his thanks—and after exchanging mutual wishes for each other's long and pleasurable lives, Laktic departed.

"Now, Gentle Trader," Koytatik said, making the clicks of Universal Goodwill. "Will you permit me the honor of requesting the data the augmentor has indicated you hold, so that we may persevere in your efforts to complete your business?"

"Here is the spool," Dane said, tapping his belt to play the code for Happy Compliance. "And the printouts, in case you need those."

Koytatik extended a grasping member to take the spool, which she dropped into a slot cleverly hidden among the mosaic patterns on the table. A thin screen extruded at an angle; Dane, from his height, could just see over the top, and watched Kanddoyd script flash up on the screen in ordered ranks of data.

There was a pause, and for a moment Thorson felt a flash of something—almost pain—through his temples. But then it was gone, and he realized Koytatik was making sounds that he needed to decode. He recognized Universal Goodwill again, among other more rapid patterns. "The *Solar Queen*," Koytatik said. "And the ship you found is the *Starvenger*, registered through the Terran Free Traders."

"That's correct," Dane said.

Again he felt that strange tightness in his head, and was reminded suddenly of Frank Mura's feedle pipe and its ten ultrasonic notes. He surreptitiously activated the jeweled ultrasonic recorder that Jasper had made—noting at the same time that the facilitator was rapidly making sounds that he recognized. All were positive ones, even the low droning of Important Business Proceeds Best with Care and Caution.

"We must check your data against the claims registry of your own Traders, as well as our registry," Koytatik said. "If, of course, the owners of the *Starvenger* or the heirs of the owners have made an insurance claim against the ship—thus indicating they in fact duly abandoned her—then she is yours. If not, we shall proceed to the next step in our process, which is to post the claim."

Dane nodded. "We understand all that. How long does it take to get transmissions to and from Terran Trade? A couple of days?"

Koytatik made a series of sounds so rapid that Dane was not able to follow them, and he felt for the third time that odd sense of pressure in his head, and he glanced down at his ultrasonic device, and saw that it was flashing blue. But she said, "About that long, yes, indeed, Gentle Trader. If you will honor us with your presence again in two Standard Days, which is three Cycles in Exchange time measure, I shall avail myself of the pleasure of furthering your business once again."

Dane nodded, mentally going over the questions he was

to ask about the next step, so the captain could plan for them, but to his surprise the prime facilitator made a bow, clacking away with complimentary sounds and chirps, and then withdrew behind a screen with all the rapidity of her race. Dane felt an impulse to follow, except the screen was closed—and with a shrug he decided that, taken all in all, things had gone well enough. He could always get to the questions next visit, and report with the answers straight back to the captain.

He got to his feet, and made his way back through the maze of flowered pathways, pausing only to exchange complimentary farewells with all the functionaries whom he encountered on the way.

7

✳

Rip Shannon was glad to get back to the *Queen,* and said so as soon as he and Jasper Weeks stepped off the shuttle, magged their boots, and joined the other apprentices in the mess cabin.

"Things quiet on the *Starvenger?*" Ali asked, lounging back.

Rip glanced around at the cramped mess cabin, and lowered himself into one of the battered old chairs. The *Queen* was both restfully familiar and a little bit strange; it had been a long time since he'd really noticed just how small her cabins were. Small, but comfortable. Everything fit—like his favorite pair of boots. And yet . . . and yet . . .

"Quiet as vacuum," Rip said, forcing a grin. He wouldn't talk about how he'd had to fight against envisioning himself piloting that ship. He looked across at Jasper Weeks, who was staring down at his tube of fresh jakek, and felt with a sudden, visceral certainty that Weeks's moods of abstraction after he'd returned from checking the engine rooms during their two-day stretch probably owed much to the same kind of day-dreams.

He saw a kind of sober assessment in Dane Thorson's blue eyes, and knew, with the same kind of inner conviction, that both of the other two apprentices felt the same. But he also knew that no one was going to say anything out loud.

Relieved, he stretched out his arms. "So, what'd I miss? Isn't it today you go back to registry, Thorson?"

Dane nodded. "Been three days Exchange time, so I'm going as soon as we're done here." He waved a big hand at his half-eaten breakfast.

"Other than that," Ali said in his mild voice, "we've all been taking in the sights—and the sounds. Lots of sounds."

"Lots and lots," Thorson added with a twisted grin.

"Any clues on our mystery?" Rip asked.

All three shook their heads.

"Ah, well, I guess it was too much to hope for that one of you characters would happen to walk into some dim bar and sit down in the next booth to some mysterious spacers, just in time to hear them discussing the strange happenings to their old friends, the crew of the *Starvenger.*"

"Only happens on the vids," Thorson growled.

Ali tapped his long fingers idly on the arm of his chair as he leaned back against the bulkhead. "Maybe it's my wicked nature, but I wouldn't believe it if I did hear it."

Jasper nodded. "Think we were being fed a load of horse-radish."

"For someone else's arcane and nefarious purposes," Ali drawled. "Exactly."

"Speaking of horseradish," Rip said, "how's the master progressing with swapping that cargo for something we can use?"

Dane sighed. "Looks good. He's found an eager Trader who likes Terrans. Name of Tapadakk. Some kind of complicated three-way deal is shaping up nicely, despite all the flowery apologies and excuses for their goods not being fine enough for the exalted Terrans."

"Van says dealing with these Kanddoyds is a fine lesson in patience," Ali put in. "As if he really needed the reminder."

"How are we holding out?" Rip said.

"It's tight, but Captain says if we can get everything wrapped in a few days, we won't tip into the red," Ali reported. "One option we have is to move the *Queen* up to the heavy-grav section. It's cheaper."

"I'd like it better," Jasper admitted. "I want to drink out of a mug, and not worry when I stand up too fast from a chair, if I forget to mag my boots, that I'll bounce my brains out on the ceiling."

Dane said, "Except we're a lot closer to the action here. May's well not lose what time we have in traveling the maglevs if we don't have to." He rose—slowly, Rip noted. "Speaking of which, it's time to find out whether we own two ships or not."

Rip said suddenly, "Mind company? Captain says I'm off-duty for another six hours."

Thorson gave a nod. "Glad to have you along."

As they started out of the mess, Frank Mura appeared from the galley, frowning slightly. "Anyone here have a mysterious appetite for carrots?"

The men all shook their heads, and Ali laughed. "If we've got rabbits aboard, the one you should ask is Sinbad."

Mura sighed. "I don't mind if someone got a sudden craving, but I just want to be told if they're going into my hydrogarden. I like to know what I have at hand and what I need to grow." As he spoke, he hefted something in his hand.

Rip watched the object, some kind of tool, it looked like, spin slowly through the air in a lazy parabola, then arc down. "What's that?" he asked, when Mura had finished talking.

Frank shrugged. "Found it on the deckplates outside the galley when I came on duty today. Kosti or Stotz probably dropped it. Looks like the kind of thing they'd pick up—it certainly isn't anything I use."

"Can always ask Stotz when he gets back from his stretch at the *Starvenger*," Ali said, yawning. "Well, it's been a long shift for me—I'm for some shut-eye. Night, gentlemen."

Rip demagged his boots and pushed off, following Dane through the outer lock into the tube leading to the access lock to Exchange. They emerged onto a concourse, and Rip looked around with interest as Dane pointed out a few of the sights. He listened with part of his attention; the rest of his mind was involved with imagining what it might be like to design and build one of these habitats.

They found an empty bench on a maglev, and the transport zapped them down into the Spin Axis towards the vertical shaft—the hollow core of one of the habitat-spanning towers—that would take them directly to their destination.

"Hey—what's that?"

Rip's eye was caught by the sight of what looked like a lush island moving slowly along a beautifully lit tube way up at the North Pole.

"That's the Movable Feast," Dane said, leaning toward the port. "We're seeing it change level."

"The Movable Feast? What is it?"

"Just what it sounds like. It's a kind of restaurant. Well, it *is* one, but it's also the center of Exchange. I guess Dr. Cofort knows some weird stories about it."

Dane's shoulders hunched a little, and Rip tried not to smile. Eventually the big Viking—who had to be about the shyest man Rip had ever met—was going to get used to being within two meters of a beautiful woman without feeling like she was going to have him killed for looking.

Rip said, "So what's the lure?"

"I don't know—food's supposed to be great, but then it's great in a lot of the eateries. Expensive, that I heard. But then you can just go in and get a bulb of drink. It stops at all the grav levels, which means everyone on Exchange finds it eventually at the grav they like best, and I guess over the centuries it became a kind of safe haven for talk. Nobody causes any trouble there."

"Let's take a look when we get done, if we have the time," Rip suggested.

Dane gave a nod.

They exchanged a few more comments about the sights Exchange had to offer as the pod sped along. Rip had a lot of questions on his mind, but the captain had expressly forbidden the *Queen*'s crew to discuss anything having to do with the *Starvenger* where they might be overheard, so he saved them. Besides, he thought as the maglev slowed and he followed Thorson to the exit, it made sense to first see what the officials said. Some of his questions might be answered.

They entered the splendid main garden of the trilateral Trade headquarters, and Rip looked around appreciatively. Soon he was feeling different emotions—a combination of amusement, bemusement, and impatience. He'd thought the others were kidding—or at least exaggerating—about the elaborate manners of the Kanddoyds, until they spent twenty solid minutes (he kept surreptitiously checking his chrono) walking around decorative herbaceous pathways and pausing to exchange smiling compliments with bowing, clicking, humming Kanddoyd functionaries.

"If I understand all this right, all we have to do is find this Prime Facilitator Koytatik and get her word on *Starvenger*'s status," Rip muttered out of the side of his mouth just after the third functionary bade them follow her.

Thorson gave a quick nod. "Right. My guess is she's busy with someone else, and the Kanddoyds consider it impolite to keep anyone waiting."

Rip fought against a grin. So, lines like those he'd grown up with back on Terra were impolite? He looked around at all the beings walking the pathways, pausing beside fountains, exchanging polite compliments. Maybe the Kanddoyds had a good idea after all. Walking around pleasant gardens seemed a lot more conducive to good moods than inching forward in a long line next to other long lines in a featureless gray building.

But the fifth time Dane had explained that they were expected by Prime Facilitator Koytatik, the latest Kanddoyd functionary, a Kanddoyd male sporting fabulous carapace designs in patterns of red, obsidian, and yellow stones, said, "It would please me the remainder of my days if the honored Terrans would permit me to escort them to the prime facilitator they seek, there to embrace quickly the important business that awaits."

While he talked, he was making all kinds of rhythmic noises. Dane tabbed his belt recorder and made similar noises as he said, "The greatest pleasure of our day would be provided in following your excellent self to this meeting, O Locutor Telkdidd."

"Then," the locutor said, humming and clacking away, "may I humbly request the Terrans to fall in step with me?"

"We shall do so at once, with pleasure and alacrity," Dane said.

Again Rip felt the impulse to grin. This sounded so unlike the laconic Viking he was used to! But Dane had changed a lot since he first joined the *Queen*, he thought as once again they started wending their way under vine-decorated archways and past tiled doors. Only Dane's change had been so gradual, no one had really noticed—any more than one notices oneself changing.

Finally they reached a fine set of doors with a beautiful mosaic depicting a nova. Inside, a splendidly decorated female Kanddoyd greeted them—adding, Rip suspected, five full minutes of compliments to honor Rip's being along.

Dane responded patiently, his fingers working his belt to make noises that matched those of the facilitator.

Finally she said, "And now I bring myself with glorious emotions to the enabling of your completion of your exalted business. Your estimable colleagues at the Terran Free Trade headquarters have obligingly furnished us with a copy of the quitclaim that the heirs of the *Starvenger* made upon their ship, duly abandoned after serious illness rapidly overtook their crew. I salute with sympathetic gesture this ill luck." She paused, and the noises she made reminded Rip of the keening praifu-dogs of Ypsilon IV. "But so is life in the remorseless universe, as all beings must agree: one's loss is another's benefit, and this time, the benefit goes to the honorable Captain Jellico and his distinguished crew."

Dane grinned, forgetting to make Kanddoyd noises with his belt recorder; he and Rip raised their fists and rapped their knuckles together in the old gesture of triumph.

The facilitator watched, making high chirping sounds and a pleasant series of notes almost like a guitar being plucked in cheery major chords. "Herewith I tender to you the official papers, and the chip whereon your ownership has been duly recorded. Your good captain is now free to acquire items for trade from our splendid markets, and to go forth into successful business ventures in Terran space!" She started to rise, her noises merry and rapid.

Dane took the chip and slid it into his tunic pocket. He bent over the paper, scanning it quickly, then looked up. "Might we beg a few more moments of your time, Prime Facilitator? I have a question."

Her mandibles clacked; Rip suspected the sound indicated surprise.

"Is not the paper in correct Terran ideographs? Is something amiss with the information? Our offices will be desolated if we have effected error—"

"No, no, it looks fine," Dane said hastily. "It's just that the paper here only lists the names of the former owners— Olben Kayusha and Nim Miscoigne. There's no communication code or even a world of origin. All it says is that the claim is relinquished, and the official notations to that effect."

"I do not understand." The prime facilitator's reedy voice dropped, now sounding like a violin slightly out of tune. "Here we have the correct forms, as agreed between our three estimable races in the venerable Concord of Harmony."

Rip saw Dane wince slightly and shake his head, and thumb the jeweled ring on his middle finger. Rip saw a blue light flash briefly. Then Dane looked up and said, "I just thought there'd be information about the former owners on these papers."

"Ah! You are careful, Gentle Trader, and this indicates an excellent being of business acumen. We congratulate you upon your perspicacity, for this is an attribute well loved among my people." She produced a flurry of sounds. "The papers are correct; if you had completed a sale, then indeed, gracing the forms would be all the information you refer to. But such is not traditional in relinquishment of title."

"Is there a way we can find out where the former owners are?" Dane asked.

Koytatik droned on a weird note. "Alas!" she keened. "To my sorrow I apprehend that our distinguished guests do not, in fact, trust the operatives of our registry precincts—"

"That's not it at all," Dane said. He took a quick swipe at his brow, and shot a pained look at Rip. "I, uh, we just had a question or two we were hoping you'd help us with. What we'd like to do is find out where those old owners are, or who their heirs are, and, well—"

Rip heard Dane falter. Captain Jellico had said they could try to find out who the old owners were—but they both knew he would not authorize risking an upset with local authorities just to satisfy their curiosity. Rip said quickly, "It's the custom where we come from to send our condolences to the relinquishing party. Just so there's no hard feelings."

Again the prime facilitator produced an array of sounds. None of them were unpleasant, but Rip felt a slight twinge behind his eyes, as if the air pressure in the room had dropped briefly. "I perceive!" she exclaimed. "Abject apologies do I owe to you, good Traders, for the length with which my poor faculties were unable to comprehend the laudable sentiments under which you labor. Alas, it is my profound regret to inform you that such is not customary through my registry. I must abase myself before you; it will take time for me to supplicate my superiors, to discover the proper forms with which to afford you this special request."

Dane glanced up. Rip knew he was hearing the same thing: *special request probably means special fees.*

Dane got to his feet. "Perhaps we can return to this question some other time, then. You are busy, and we have to give this data back to our captain."

The prime facilitator also rose, and again began the long litany of compliments, but this time the sounds seemed subtly different. Rip watched the blue light flicker on Dane's ring, and wondered what the ultrasonics meant.

As soon as they were out of earshot of the ubiquitous Kanddoyd guides, both men paused on the causeway. Rip said, "Dead end?"

Dane nodded. "Apparently so. I guess we could try to pursue it—if we had time, and money." He glanced down at the paper again. "The registry fees are stiff enough, but the captain said that they'd figured those into our budget. I hadn't counted on extra fees for this data. Thought it'd be included."

"I've got an idea," Rip said. "Why don't we try Trade's com center? If we get humans there, it might be easier to explain and initiate a search, at least."

"Good thinking." The tall cargo apprentice led the way back inside.

Rip realized that Dane had spent much of his free time exploring around; he knew exactly where to go.

Once again they encountered Kanddoyd functionaries, but this time, when they made it plain they wanted to go to the Terran Sphere's office in the communications center, they were passed on with what must have seemed to the Kanddoyds incredible speed.

It was a relief to both apprentices when they walked into the office and saw the usual fabulous holos of different planets with their relative times and dates ticking off the passing seconds, and the illuminated directions flashing in countless alphabets. Trade Service communications offices were much the same everywhere, then, right down to the preponderance of humanoid workers behind the counters.

There were even, Rip noted with an inward smile, lines; they joined the one below a holographic designation that indicated communications going to Solar system planets and moons.

The woman immediately before them wore the insignia of Inter-Stellar. She glanced back with disinterest, then turned around again.

Rip nodded politely when his eyes met hers, but he felt no compunction to chat. They'd had too many unpleasant encounters with I-S in the past, and instinct warned him against having to answer even the easiest questions now.

But the woman showed no disposition to talk to them while the man at the front of the line finished his business. At last it was her turn; she handed over a chip, apparently preregistered, received one in return, and she was gone a moment later.

The young man behind the counter scanned their Free Trader brown tunics with the apprentice insignia, then said in a bored voice, "Chip or flimsy?"

"Neither—" Dane started.

The worker cut in. "We don't write mail for you. Keyboards over there." He nodded to some little booths on the adjacent wall. "Translation charges flat fee."

Rip said, "We want to run an ID check first—Free Traders, just like us. We're off the *Solar Queen,* Terra registry six-five-seven-two-four-nine-one-zero-JK."

The bored clerk keyed in the number as quickly as Rip spoke it, and waited with unconcealed impatience for a few seconds. He plainly expected the ID to come up green so he could get on with the request; after a long pause, he gave an impatient sigh and tapped at his console.

"Must be a data jam," he muttered. "Just to make sure, let's have that number again."

This time Dane spoke it, slowly and clearly. The man typed it in equally slowly; then his boredom changed to perplexity as he stared at his blank screen. "My com must be down. Wait here." He shut down his console and disappeared through a narrow door directly behind him.

They stood at the counter as, on either side of them, several people came and went. Fewer people were left in the room now; none had come in for a time.

Presently Dane, who had been scanning the papers, said, "Interesting."

"What?" Rip asked, watching one of the techs close down her computer and blank the sign above her cubicle.

"Date the claim was registered is only in some local time or other. I thought everything was supposed to be in Terran Standard."

"Maybe not out this far," Rip said. "Look, that counter over there is empty—"

Just then the door behind the counter where they stood opened again, but instead of the bored young man, a tall Shver with arcane caste markings on his forehead and arms trod with heavy step to the counter, and looked down at the two *Queen*'s men. "Inquire you?" he said, his voice so deep Rip almost felt it through the floor.

"Thanks, we're just waiting for the other worker to return," Rip said.

"Is end of shift for his," the Shver said. "Am the Jheel of Clan Golm. Serve I now."

"We are trying to locate the IDs of some Free Traders, registered through Terran Trade Service, like ourselves," Dane said.

The Shver looked impassively at them, his thick fingers resting as if by chance on his shauv, the serrated honor knife all adult Shver wore. Rip wondered if the beings had any natural expressions besides a kind of detached glower. "Is your ID?"

"Dane Thorson, apprentice cargo master, *Solar Queen*, and Rip Shannon, apprentice astrogator, also of the *Solar Queen*," Dane said, and then for the third time quoted the registration number.

The Shver worked at the console, which was now tipped at an angle to accomodate his great height—and from which the others could not see his screen. "Is names of other Traders?" he asked presently.

"Olben Kayusha and Nim Miscoigne," Rip said, writing them hastily on a scrap of paper with his pocket stylus. He pushed the paper across to the Shver, who picked it up and laid it down again out of sight before he began to work at the console.

In silence the *Queen*'s men waited. Rip noticed that they were the last in the room.

At last the Shver looked up and said, "Data jam; take too much hours. Is close time. Return you tomorrow."

Rip opened his mouth, but it was too late. The Shver had closed down the console, and lumbered back through the door, closing it firmly.

A moment later plasglas shields came down, walling off the counters, and the holo lights all went off.

Rip and Dane looked at each other, shrugged, then turned and left.

"So we come back," Rip said. "Come on, let's go nose out the Movable Feast, see what's so special about their beer."

8

Captain Jellico looked up at his cargo master, determined not to show any of the exasperation he felt.

"So you're saying that I-S cargo master cut in and took your deal?"

Van Ryke's white brows formed a line of perplexity in his face. "I wish it were that simple," he said. "I don't think Mdango cut in on us—I think that Tapadakk offered her my deal, but did it in such a way as to make it look like I-S pulled the deal out from under us."

Jellico let his breath out slowly. "Any idea why?"

Van Ryke lifted his hands. "If I knew that, I could have done some fast talking and saved it. He's been most apologetic, but only over the com. I can't seem to get to him to agree to see me in person. But it's only been an hour; for Kanddoyds, that's an impossible rush. What I want to make certain of is if he's suddenly changed his mind and doesn't want to deal with us at all. If so, why?"

"Has Mdango or any of her crew been talking us down?"

Van Ryke rubbed his chin thoughtfully. It would be the most obvious explanation. The *Queen* had run afoul of Inter-Stellar ships in the past, and despite the fact that the *Queen* was only one ship, and I-S was a huge Company, big Companies were made up of human beings, most of whom were as loyal to their Companies as the *Queen*'s crew were to the *Solar Queen*. Jellico knew that there were plenty of people in I-S who might like to see a bit of revenge taken for the *Queen*'s wins over some of their colleagues.

"I don't get the impression they've heard anything about us at all," Van Ryke said slowly. "I think their ship, the *Corvallis,* has been making runs in totally different lanes than we've been used to. No one in our crew has reported any negative encounters, or even any comments, from their crew up in the recreation areas—and we humanoid Traders stand out up there, so it's not like they couldn't find us if they half tried."

"All right," Jellico said. "Then we'll rule out malice—at least on the part of I-S. Now, what about Tapadakk?"

Van Ryke sighed. "It is possible, except it wouldn't make any sense. We spent four solid days dancing around in their interminable negotiations, and I can't believe even a Kanddoyd would spend all that time for nothing. He seemed eager to deal; our cargo isn't all that tempting, but he's got a surplus of mosaic works of various sorts that we could move pretty well back in Terran space, where they are rarer, and he did have two or three buyers set up in a complicated ring. He just seemed to be waiting for us to get our papers on *Starvenger* and wind up our registry business."

"That was yesterday," Jellico said.

Van Ryke nodded. "Tapadakk and I finished our talk about the time Thorson and Shannon left registry yesterday, with our papers in hand, so we know it's nothing to do with that. Anyway, that's about the time we set up today's meeting. Then an hour ago, I get this com message—just before I'm to leave for our meeting to accomplish what I hoped was the last stage of negotiation—and he ups and tells me that he's not good enough, his goods aren't good enough, he's desolately and abjectly sorry but our exalted trade would grace another cargo better, et cetera et cetera. I thought I'd go over and try to get him in person again."

Jellico nodded. "Right. Do what you can. We're running out of time."

Van Ryke nodded and walked out.

Jellico leaned back in his chair and glared at the various calculations Wilcox had printed out for him. Then he tabbed the intercom. "Ya."

"Captain?" came the comtech's voice.

"Progress?"

"Still working—I have some algorithms roughed out that might be what we need."

"Keep at it."

"Right, Captain."

They both cut the connection. The hoobat let out a sudden metal-rending shriek, and Jellico grabbed his chair to anchor himself and reached to give the cage a swat.

"Fnerble," Queex squawked, settling down happily as the cage rocked and bounced.

"Just what I was thinking," Míceál Jellico said grimly.

Karl Kosti leaned back in the padded seat and stared out at the long tubes of the Kanddoyd buildings. He rather liked the crazy curves and angles, the strings of lights. He was in a good mood. His muscles ached from a good workout in heavy grav, and he had an excellent meal before him, and something interesting to look at. It entertained him to figure out how to power this habitat and the buildings inside it.

It would have been nicer if he could have eaten in decent grav, but the gym for Traders was down in Shver territory, a rare concession. Of course they wouldn't have food places there. The Shver didn't like outsiders, and they didn't like public eating. Plain, straightforward. Karl rather liked the Shver. He preferred them to the gyrating, buzzing, clacking Kanddoyds who talked in such convoluted sentences it was like their mouths were full of mush. The Shver said exactly what they thought, or they kept silent. He appreciated that—and he also liked them as sparring partners in the gym. For once he didn't have to worry about going easy on his partner, for they massed a lot more than he did. He liked that too. Few humans massed as much as he, and fewer of those were anywhere near as strong.

He tabbed the heat button on his bulb of spiced wine and sipped, enjoying the pleasant tang on his tongue, and the warmth down his throat. His eyes stayed on the buildings as, gradually, the chatter of the spacehounds around him resolved from white noise into individual words.

". . . hijackers," someone said.

Hijackers? Karl didn't want to look—ordinarily he despised gossip, but that subject would get anyone's attention.

"I wonder how much credit it takes to smooth that one over," a woman said. Her voice was sharp.

"Kind of makes you wonder what registry is worth, don't it?" a man's voice grated. "Knowin' you can get a quitclaim, free and clear, on someone else's ship?"

"Eventually," the woman said, "the New Hope catches up with 'em. You gotta believe that."

Another man laughed. It was an ugly laugh. "Yeah, I like that," he said. "Sanford Jones holds out his hand in welcome—you ship with him for eternity."

"Sometimes," the first man said, "it's a right fine thing to help old Sanford get that crew real quick."

"Yeah," the woman said. "As quick as the crew aboard the hijacked ship got sent to Jones."

Karl had forgotten the Kanddoyd buildings and his mental calculations of energy production. Who were these people? Seemed as if they were talking not just generally, but specifically—and if he understood them right, they were working up to taking someone out.

He looked around, and to his surprise saw three faces watching him.

A woman, short gray hair, big brown eyes narrowed in a mean look, and the strong arms of a cargo wrangler, stared right at Karl, and said, "Patrol might look the other way, but we don't."

The tall, dark-faced man on her right side said, "If Trade Authority won't do something about jacking, then it's up to Traders to keep our name clean."

The man on the left, a squat fellow with red hair and the characteristic powerful upper torso of the Martian colonist, twisted his thin lips in an ugly grin and said, "I'd certainly think twice about fouling the air around honest spacers, if I had bloody hands."

Karl glanced to his own left, and to his right, and he realized that the white noise had completely stopped, that everyone in the place was watching.

The woman said, "Seems like when we're done, we ought to rename that ship, too, shouldn't we? How's *Solar Scum*? Or better, *Killer Queen*?"

Karl realized they really were talking about *him*. A chill of shock twitched along his muscles, followed by anger. Hot, glorious anger.

"You talk about the *Solar Queen*," he said, "you clean up your mouth."

"Then you better clean your hands, jacker," the man on the right fired back.

"Say that again," Karl warned, "and I'll have to clean up your mouth for you."

The woman threw her bulb into the recycler and crossed her arms. "Is 'bloody killer' and 'pirate' nicer?"

Karl didn't answer. There were times when you talked, and there were times when talk would be worthless. He flexed his hands and launched across the table, aiming at the nearest wrangler's throat.

Jellico swung himself up from his desk and hit the door control. Outside his cabin Sinbad strolled, tail high, licking his chops. Since he wasn't coming from the direction of the galley, Jellico wondered where the cat had been begging. With delicate grace Sinbad descended to the lab level, and Jellico followed. He glanced around swiftly when he stepped in. The only person in view was Craig Tau.

Jellico looked down into the sterile chamber the two medics had rigged for Alpha and Omega. One of the cats was batting at a little toy; the other was busy licking her fur. Sinbad hopped up to stare at them, sniffed, then turned away and with a flick of his long tail vanished outside the hatchway again.

"How are Alpha and Omega?" Jellico asked Tau.

"Check out," the medic said. "Whatever hit the crew, it escaped these cats. They are completely clean. We could let them out today, if you want."

"Wait," Jellico said.

Tau nodded, obviously comprehending immediately: better to keep them tanked up until the mystery of their home-ship was solved. Tau looked down at his desk and said, "Want an update on the other matter we've discussed?"

"Any changes?"

"Nothing, really."

"It can wait," Jellico said; the last thing he wanted to think about now was long-term effects of strange substances they had encountered on earlier runs. There was too much to think about right now.

The medic turned back to his work, and Jellico backed out the hatchway, stopping when he heard voices coming down the ladder well.

". . . getting into my garden and eating all the fruit." That was Frank Mura, and he sounded angry.

Jellico frowned. Whatever had gotten the quiet, controlled Frank upset was something he'd better know about.

"I can assure you that we have not let the cats out," Rael Cofort's voice came, calm and emotionless.

"If it's not the cats, it's someone human," Mura said. "Someone who should know better. All they have to do is ask—no one has accused me yet of short-rationing the

Queen's crew, not in all the years I've served on her."

"Do you think it's possible," the woman said slowly, "that someone got hungry when you were off-shift—or on leave?"

"I haven't left the *Queen* and I don't intend to," Mura snapped. "The sooner we blast away from this trash can the happier I'll be."

"I promise to keep my eyes and ears open," Cofort said.

Jellico started up the ladder then. A moment later he heard the galley door hiss shut. Rael Cofort appeared at the top of the well, saw Jellico, and backed into the mess so he could finish ascending. He followed her in.

"More things disappearing?" he asked.

She gave a nod, and leaned against a bulkhead. "Food, mostly. And he's also angry because little odd bits of gear have been strewn about here and there." She absently tucked a loose strand of gold-highlighted hair back into its coronet.

Jellico looked away, wanted something to do with his hands, so he drew a hot bulb of jakek. "Runs a clean ship. Matter of pride," he said.

Cofort gave a nod, then bit her lip.

"What's on your mind?" Jellico prompted.

She tipped her chin back toward the galley. "Frank. You know he hasn't been off-ship—"

Jellico said, "Right."

She sighed. "Well, it's obvious he is disturbed by the Kanddoyds. Not surprising, given their looks and the parallel destruction of homelands. And it would be easy to dismiss his annoyance at the little things going wrong on board as hostility against Exchange . . ."

"But you think that's a mistake?"

She gave her head a quick shake. "I don't know what to think. I really like the cylome, and personally, I find the Kanddoyds I've met to be congenial, and even the Shver—those who are willing to talk to Terrans—are interesting. But I get a sense that there's something askew here."

"Like?"

She shrugged. "I can't really say. Different things—even

Mura's missing food. Then there was the way the com center closed up on Dane and Rip so suddenly yesterday."

"You don't think they'd overstepped their boundaries?"

"Not those two," she said with obvious conviction. "I have to admit I've been waiting around here for them to return from today's check—maybe it's just my imagination."

Jellico grinned. "So you've been watching your chrono too?"

A swift flush of color rose in her cheeks, and she grinned back.

For a moment his mind emptied of everything but the curve of her lips, and the merry gleam in her eyes. Did she feel it too, this compulsion like the iron for the magnet?

It was a relief when, this time, she was the first to turn away.

Tang Ya looked again at the numbers on the computer screen.

He'd found it the day before, and had been working ever since, as yet without saying anything to his crewmates. Tang Ya liked to have all his facts at hand before going to the captain and facing Jellico's curt, but always penetrating, questions.

Sleep tugged at his eyelids and the back of his neck seemed to be on fire. He glanced at the array of crushed jakek tubes at the side of his console, and felt a distinct wish for something stronger—like Crax seed.

Though once he handed this data off, his job would not end, and he would not have the luxury of the recovery time a bout with Crax seed required.

Instead, he had to rely on his own adrenaline. So again he typed in the dates.

Computers, of course, had no emotions, nor did the script reflect the operator's emotions unless the operator manipulated the fonts to that end.

Somehow, though, it seemed strange for the bare text to appear in the same bland alphanumerics, picked for their clarity, as more nominal calculations. Still, there it was, the mute evidence at last that something was badly askew here. Unless the comparative timetables for all the registered planets were wrong—which had not happened yet, in all the years he'd used them—the *Starvenger* had officially been abandoned eighteen months ago, Terran Standard.

A year and a half ago.

A year and a half ago the ship was declared abandoned—leaving aboard two cats who, if Craig Tau was to be believed, had been abandoned no more than ten weeks.

He cleared the screen once again, and this time called up the coded log from the *Starvenger*'s hydrogarden. He'd worked at this during spare moments while he was on duty, and during some of his own free time, but he'd felt no strong compulsion to decrypt that log.

Now he felt different.

A little energy flowed into him again. He flexed his hands, swung his arms, and performed the isometrics he'd been taught as a child. He sensed he was on the verge of something . . . if he just kept at it.

"I need more compute power," he murmured, tapping into the ship's computer. He wished he dared to reach through the line connecting the *Queen* to Exchange's compute arrays, for he knew he'd solve the dilemma if he just had an enormous pattern-search space. But he hadn't, which required him to be clever.

He called up the holding matrices he'd set going, and nodded with satisfaction. The genetic neural algorithms he'd bred up had been patiently probing for hidden patterns in the organization of the other computer—and it looked like they were settling toward a solution. He had to know how it was set up first before he could work on decoding it.

Then he glanced at the corner of his screen. The little icon he'd set up as a measure of progress shimmered suddenly, then snapped into a line.

A moment later the screen below flickered, and ordered ranks of alphanumerics appeared. It was still in some kind of code, but he knew how to break codes. The biggest problem had been finding the patterns that would give him clues to the unfamiliar computer's organization.

Flexing his hands again, he called up the sherlocks he'd specifically designed, and set them onto the code. At once they went to work, and again his icon wavered in a foggy line. This would not take long, though, he suspected. He reached for another tube of jakek, flicked the heat tab with his thumbnail as his eyes watched the screen, where his sherlock programs continued their patient unraveling.

He was halfway through the tube when the icon clicked once again into a firm line. He keyed the console, and the codes flickered into readable script.

Paging down through it, he scanned through his blurring eyes, just to make certain it made sense; then he set up some search fields and set them going. This time it only took seconds to scan.

When he saw the results, he let out his breath in a big sigh, got up, and hit the door control.

It was time to dump everything into Jellico's lap.

The subdued booms and thuds of footsteps on the outer lock ladder made both Jellico and Rael Cofort look up quickly. Rael Cofort passed by in silence, going in to the mess. Jellico remained where he was, and half a minute later, there was Dane Thorson's tall, lanky form. Rip Shannon's dark, pleasant face was at his shoulder. "Cap'n?"

"What's the word?"

Thorson spread his huge hands. "Dead space," he said. "Until the Festival of the Dancing Sprool is over—whenever that might be." He frowned suddenly. "Hell! Is that the name of the Shver hibernation period? If so, we're sunk—they hibernate for three months! I'd better check—" He ducked out, and they heard the click of his magnetic boots going up the ladder to the main computer databank.

"What happened?" Cofort asked from the mess hatchway.

"We went back, just as we were told to," Rip said. "But

they told us that we had to continue our business with the Jheel that had begun to help us. And when we asked for him, we were told just what Dane told you—that he'd withdrawn from duty for this festival, and he'd return when it was over. All his business would have to wait."

"No one would cooperate?" Jellico asked, his suspicions intensifying as he walked with his navigator apprentice into the mess cabin.

Rip gave his head a quick shake. "On the contrary," he said. "The other workers who spoke Terran were really apologetic. One woman even tried to help, but she said that the Jheel had put a lock on the *Starvenger* inquiry, so she could do nothing. She said they earn promotions by how many jobs they successfully complete, so it wasn't surprising."

Jellico frowned. "This is not how Trade does business—"

"—in Terran space," Cofort added, from the other side of the cabin.

Jellico finished, "—and we're not in Terran space. Right."

"Three months," came Dane's doleful voice from the hatchway. "They hibernate for a full three months."

"How hibernation can be called 'Dancing' anything, I don't understand," Rip said dryly. Then he turned a serious look to the captain. "I know you and Jan are trying to get us a cargo as soon as possible. Does this mean we have to drop our inquiry as a bad business?"

Jellico was watching Cofort, who stood by a bulkhead, her dark blue eyes narrowed in an expression of abstract concentration. "On the surface it would seem so," he said. "We'll think it over."

Both young men looked relieved, and moved to draw some food from the server. Jellico knew what those expressions of relief meant: they both were confident that The Captain Would Think of Something.

He hefted his tube and moved out of the galley to consider what he had heard. As he started toward his cabin, he saw Karl Kosti coming up toward the galley.

The big man was frowning, which was not in itself a cause for alarm.

"Rough crowd," Karl said as he moved on past.

Jellico turned and watched, wondering what that portended; it was rare for the most taciturn member of the crew to offer any kind of unasked-for comment.

The answer was immediately forthcoming. The intercom tone sounded, and Jasper Weeks, who was currently manning the bridge, said, "Captain?"

Jellico reached for a wall console and tabbed the key. "On my way."

Moments later he was in the bridge, as Weeks, with an apologetic expression on his mild, bleached-pale face, played back the message just received.

A Shver visage appeared on the screen, gray, wrinkled, and glowering. "Am I Lictor of Monitors of Harmony, and the Shauv of Clan Norl. Have I instructions for you, in accordance with the Concord of Harmony. Initiating a fracas, has committed your unit Karl Kosti. Required of you is confinement to your vessel of said unit for the remainder of your stay." There was no further word, and the image blanked.

Jellico reached to hit the com, then pulled back his hand when he saw Kosti standing right behind him. "What's the story, Karl?"

"Wasn't me started that fight," Kosti said. "Riffraff from a company ship, strutting big—"

"You learned how to ignore that kind of talk when you were half-grown," Jellico said, exasperated.

Kosti gave a brief nod, impassive as a rock. "Brag talk is so much noise. Talk about how Free Traders are barely legal thieves, and how they jump ships to claim derelicts—that I couldn't sit by and eat. Especially when ignoring them would have been agreement, in which case half the spacers there were ready to lynch me," Kosti added reflectively.

"So there's talk about our claiming the *Starvenger*?"

Weeks said quietly, "It's to be expected gossip would get

out. How many ships come out of jump and find an empty sitting on their jump point?"

Jellico said, "But if talk is going around about our having pulled in a derelict, then it should mention that our vids of the catch were legit—and accepted by Trade as so."

Kosti shook his head. "All I can tell you is what I heard. It was humans who started it, three cargo wranglers off that Deneb-Galactic ship docked down that way." He jerked his head in one direction. "Monitors pinned the blame on me."

Jellico felt and suppressed a flash of annoyance. No use in lodging a formal complaint with Trade over what might turn out to be a lot of gaseous talk in a bar. "We'll comply, of course," he said. "You may's well take your turn out at the *Starvenger*—replace Thorson. I need him here anyway."

Kosti gave his short nod and moved silently away.

Jellico tapped his fingers on the arm support of his command pod, trying to sort through his reactions. There was too much bad luck here, but it all seemed random and unconnected. He'd be a fool to give in to conspiracy suspicions without some hard evidence of connections—if any.

He said to Jasper, "Carry on," and got up from his seat.

In the doorway to the hatch he met Tang Ya. The Martian colonist's eyes were red-rimmed, his face lined with exhaustion. "My algorithms cracked that code," Ya said, grinning despite his evident tiredness.

Jellico let out a sigh of relief at the first break they'd had since Flindyk had given them the spool to speed along their business. "Good work," he said. "What did you find?"

Ya said, "I think you'd better know this first." He handed Jellico a printout on which he read the date of the insurance quitclaim, registered in local time. Jellico had seen that before. He swallowed his impatience and read on—freezing when he saw the date in Terran Standard.

He looked up at Ya, whose wide-set eyes were narrowed to slits of perplexity. "That's not the only mystery," the comtech said. "The lab record is mostly a kind of diary mixed in with daily reports on the hydroponics. I haven't read it all, only done a couple of searches. One thing I came up with," he said slowly, "is the fact that there's no mention anywhere of the *Starvenger,* or of Olben Kayusha or Nim Miscoigne."

"Odd, but possible," Jellico said. "You could ask how often Frank mentions the ship he's lived on for years—or my name—down in his logs."

Ya nodded quickly. "I thought of that, but none of it explains why the writer of the record called that ship *Ariadne.*"

9

★

Rael Cofort scrutinized the image on the screen: a woman, short gray hair, intelligent brown eyes, weathered skin, age probably somewhere in her seventies. Plain tunic in the Deneb-Galactic colors, its only ornamentation the captain's bars on her high collar. A lifetime spacer, and probably at least half of that life a captain—probably the same personality type as Míceál Jellico.

And there was no mistaking the honesty in both face and voice as she said, "I questioned all three separately, Captain, and while details varied, one common fact emerged: they all had overhead someone discussing your ship and crew. Begging your pardon, they were told that, under the guise of Free Trading, you went about hijacking innocent ships. Though I don't condone their actions, you can understand how that kind of gossip would rile them."

Jellico said, "I can indeed. Act first, questions later. It's happened to my own crew. And they won't stomach space pirates any more than the Company crews."

Captain Svetlana pursed her lips. Her expression was so very akin to Jellico's—a distaste for the necessity of the encounter, but lurking humor at the vagaries of crew members—Rael felt a laugh bubbling up inside her, and controlled it. This incident might be explained, but the situation was only becoming more sinister.

"Did they say who told them this information?" Jellico went on.

Captain Svetlana's brow furrowed slightly. "There is another of the places where the narrative diverges. Corsko insists she heard it from some Terrans up at the gym, but Kherddu says he got it in one of the eateries, from Kanddoyds, and Lu Nguyen swore that he overheard a Shver Monitor pointing out one of your crew—tall? yellow hair?—as a hijacker when he was passing back and forth to Trade Center."

Jellico's mouth was now a grim line, all humor gone.

"I've brigged my three for seventy-two hours for brawling," Svetlana went on. "If you'd like to question them yourself, please come aboard anytime."

"For now, I don't think it's necessary," Jellico said, his words clipped short. "But I appreciate the invitation, and will keep it in mind. Thank you for your time, Captain Svetlana."

"You're welcome, Captain Jellico," Svetlana replied formally, and the screens blanked.

Jellico turned around to face Rael, his eyes distracted. "What do you make of that?"

"She seemed absolutely honest. If she isn't, then she's one of the greatest dissemblers I've ever witnessed."

"That was my impression as well," the captain said. He fell silent, his gaze still on Rael's face. His thoughts were obviously distant as he contemplated this latest twist in what was shaping up to be a strange puzzle.

Rael waited, and presently the ice-blue eyes focused, and saw *her*. And she felt the look, a visceral reaction that quickened her heartbeat and made her want to smooth her clothing and twitch at her hair, and then he looked away. A little wail of rueful laughter ran through her mind: how many times had this occurred since she came on board the *Solar Queen*?

How many times would it still occur?

Many, and many, and it seemed all would lead to nothing.

He said abruptly, "I sent Van Ryke to Trade to run queries on all ships registered with *Ariadne* in their titles. I think I ought to run a double check against whatever records Ross keeps. Do you have the time to accompany me? I confess I want someone to talk this over with."

"I'd be glad to go," Rael said promptly. "Craig is on duty right now. I'm perfectly free, and to tell the truth, if I get any more curious, I'm likely to implode."

"The more I look at this, the more it seems that someone doesn't want my boys to find out anything about the *Starvenger*."

"Are you going to ask Dane and the others to drop the inquiry?"

Jellico stood in the hatchway, frowning. "Finding out the data doesn't matter to me. The past is past. If it turns out there's a wrong buried there, though, it does matter: we owe it to our brethren in Trade to right it if we can. I'm not going to pull the boys back, at least not yet. If we end up having to move to the heavy area to save money, then we will. In fact, when Stotz gets back, I'll have him make the change. Meantime—" Jellico reached for the com. "Jasper, I'm going to run some queries by the legate."

"Aye, Captain," came the prompt reply.

They talked very little on the journey to the legate's quarters, despite the fact that there was little to see.

"Moving to high grav has one other advantage," Rael said.

Jellico didn't speak, but he glanced at her in mute question.

"We'd have better scenery on the ride." She gestured at the gray blur of the tube walls enclosing the maglev capsule.

Maglev routes from high grav cut through Shver territory on the surface, and, as the Shver did not like enclosed spaces, the view on those routes was said to be spectacular.

Ross was there, and he seemed incurious when Jellico asked if he would run a search on ships with the name *Ariadne*. The legate's expression was oddly abstract as he keyed in the search parameters. Silence weighed in the office as they waited for the computer to run its search.

Presently the light flickered green, and Ross scanned rapidly the data on his screen. "Since the legation's establishment three hundred forty-two years ago, twenty-six ships with 'Ariadne' somewhere in their name have docked at Exchange, five in the last ten years: *Ariadne's Web*, the *Diana and Ariadne*, *Ariadne's Star*, *Hellene Line: Ariadne*, and *Theseus-Ariadne*. The *Hellene Line* is here repeatedly, about every six years."

"Any of those reported lost, stolen, or dead?" Jellico asked.

"I've no Patrol flags on any outside of *Ariadne's Web*, which was fined for attempting to smuggle in klifer-dust—an airborne scent which is lethal to Kanddoyd biochemistry," Ross replied. "To find out which have been decommissioned or otherwise taken out of service, your questions ought rightly to be submitted to your headquarters at Trade Central." He looked up, his long face narrowing in sudden suspicion.

"We're doing that," Rael said smoothly. "It's just that our stay is necessarily limited, so we thought we'd do a cross-check here at the same time as our cargo master is at Trade."

Ross gave a nod as he wiped his screen blank. "Your business is rightly Trade's; they ought to be able to give you complete data."

And that was that—dismissal was clear in the man's voice. What was he hurrying to? Rael couldn't help thinking as they walked out of his quarters. Back to designing his holographic rose garden?

"I don't like him," Jellico said as they walked onto a maglev pod. "Seems he's got a cog loose."

"Well, it's the Patrol's job to be suspicious. If we were to tell him that Trade is not cooperating with us, and he hears of those rumors—"

"We're likely to be brigged first, and our ships impounded, and asked questions later," Jellico finished. "Thought of that too." He rapped on the chair arm with his fingers, then said, "Let's go somewhere. Get something to eat, thrash this out."

"All right," Rael said, inwardly amused. His manner was abrupt and distracted—not at all what one would expect of a man asking a woman for her company. He could have used the same tone with Van Ryke or Steen Wilcox, his oldest crew, she thought—except he wouldn't have been so abrupt.

On impulse she glanced at her chrono and said, "Not the concourse eateries. Let's go up to the North Pole. I've always wanted to try the Movable Feast, ever since I heard about it. My treat," she added.

He gave her a twisted smile. "I don't eat my crew's earnings," he said. "I'll pay for myself. Otherwise, lead the way."

Rael talked easily as they traveled up the core of the tower, pausing only momentarily as the capsule made the giddy swing around into the microgravity of the Spin Axis. She spoke mostly about her initial visit to Exchange. Jellico seemed mildly interested, at least enough to distract him from his problems. ". . . so Teague and I went up to the Movable Feast, just to find out that it was closed. It seems the owner, a Kanddoyd named Gabby Tikatik, was molting, and if he can't be there everything stops. Supposed to be quite a character."

Jellico was looking around, interest apparent in his light eyes. The lines of his face were not as severe, and again Rael felt that frisson of attraction, of the desire to protect, to please. She would exert herself to entertain him, to take his mind off his problems just as long as he needed.

"So what's special about this place?" he said. His head was turned; he appeared to be watching the sudden blooms of open space through which the capsule was passing, from tube to spindly truss, across vast tunnels spiderwebbed with light and shadow dwindling in immense perspective. Rael wondered how he could do so without vertigo. "Aside from the fact that it appears to move up and down from the Spin Axis."

"Teague told me the story," she said as the maglev debouched them into a station and they followed a group of glittering Kanddoyd merchants into the Movable Feast. "It's one of the oldest establishments on the cylome—predates even the Concord. Apparently life was somewhat wild and lawless out here—it was an outpost for Traders, smugglers, and outright pirates, no questions asked. The first proprietor, surprisingly enough, was a human, named Gabby Grimwig. It was his idea to establish a fine restaurant here, where the view would be spectacular and the diners could choose their grav levels—or even eat while the grav changed."

"An interesting but repellent idea," Jellico said.

Rael laughed, thinking of the spectacular changes gravity had on some food and drink substances. "The idea was that all the diners would agree on the level and change time."

She paused as a feline biped from the mysterious Enkha System bowed them in, her graceful form clad in a green tunic that floated out behind her in the micrograv. She led the way to a table in a section designed for Terran body types. Rael glanced around, gained a swift impression of comfortable pods arranged in terraced layers in a half-circle. Exotic plants screened each dining pod from the others, but all had a view along the length of the habitat. It was evening, the radiants overhead dimming to a soft glow reminiscent of a full moon on Terra, and the lights of the Shver dwellings far below gleamed softly yellow, lapping up and over in the curving sky to either side like constellations distorted by the gravity of a black hole. The vast towers of the Kanddoyds, lit not with discrete point sources but with gracefully twining tubes of light, shimmered like wrinkled ropes of silk binding a curving earth to narrow heaven.

"Choissess for delectable viandss the exssalted guestss will find here," the Enkhai said in her soft, musical voice, touching the corner console. "Either automated or ssentient sservice available. Dine well!" With a graceful flick of her tail she bowed again and moved swiftly away.

As soon as she was gone, Jellico looked up inquiringly, and Rael continued. "The problems were evident right away. It seemed no matter what kind of beings were in, they always seemed to prefer grav at another level. Traders then being as ready to settle things with fists, teeth, or tentacles, as some are now, there were frequent fights. After Gabby Grimwig's place was trashed one too many times, he made some changes. One, to hire Shver as security. Two, he decided the place would stop at regular intervals, signaled by light flashes, so it was up to the eaters to determine when to come and what grav they wanted to finish their meal in. And three, diners were to eat in harmony. No arguments, no duels, nothing but polite social exchange. Anyone breaking the rules got handed over to him for justice, which he executed in . . . imaginative ways."

"Like?" Jellico regarded her with a fascinated gaze.

Rael suddenly felt mischievous. "Well, one diner had to choose between three unmarked containers, with the understanding that he had to eat everything in the one he chose." She paused, watching Jellico's eyes. Again the habitual hardness had eased; she saw interest, and fainter, appreciation.

"It was full of Hudapi gourds. Hundreds of Hudapi gourds. It took him months, and Gabby made a fortune selling tickets to let people watch him."

Jellico's smile stretched, and suddenly he laughed. "A slime-explosion every time he took a bite?"

"And the spores sprout wherever there's any moisture at all. It took just as long to defoliate him afterwards—when he finished them all he was just a big ball of squiggling green hairs." Rael grinned, then continued, "So the place's success was established—and however things were resolved elsewhere in the habitat, the most hardened pirates were painfully polite if they came here to eat. Sworn enemies would ignore one another by mutual, unspoken agreement."

"I've heard of a few similar places across the galaxy," Jellico said.

Rael smiled. "I'm sure you've been to a few as well. I know I have—Teague has always had a taste for places with unusual histories. Anyway, Grimwig lived quite a long time, and when his successor took over, and made it apparent that the same rules would apply, the name 'Gabby' also stuck. I think there've been three or four Gabby owners since then. Tikatik is the latest, and Teague said he's probably every bit as unusual as the original Gabby."

"Will we see him?"

"Almost assuredly," Rael said, and keyed the menu console. "He supposedly acts like this is a party and he is our host. Shall we order?"

She tabbed the corner idly, looking at the range of printed languages flashing past. Finally she hit the default for Terran Basic, and scanned the astonishing variety of delicacies from countless worlds. When she found a choice, she keyed it in, and looked up to see Míceál tapping in his order.

"Now this is something I've always wondered about," Jellico commented suddenly, pointing at his menu. "Crystalized tulu blossoms in a fresh sauce of pansevny root. Don't tulu only grow on maybe ten worlds, and they only bloom once a century?"

"Look at the price, and answer your own question," Rael said, delighted to see him talking . . . socially.

Jellico gave a soft, low whistle. "Could almost get a ship for that. Upgrade engines, certainly."

"That's exactly what Teague used to say." She laughed.

"And then he'd go out and do it." Jellico's smile was quizzical.

"Well, yes, but that's not to say it's always been success. He was lucky enough to have several great runs right when he started out, but there have been losses as well. Not always the monetary kind—but just as painful." She looked back into the past, then shook her head to chase the sober memories away.

When she looked up again, his blue eyes were interested. "Teague's still solitary."

Solitary, she thought. *Anyone else would phrase it the other way—has he ever married?* "Yes," she said. "He says he can't risk the idea of pairing with someone who turns out to be a dirthugger—or having children who want to stay on one planet. Maybe someday he'll adopt, if he comes across someone who reminds him of the way he himself was when he was small. Until then, he says, just short relationships, entered lightheartedly and ended with an equally lighthearted good-bye."

Jellico frowned down at the table. In the discreetly designed service inset a light glowed green, and two softly steaming drink bulbs appeared.

They had both chosen the automated service rather than paying extra for a sentient waitbeing, fun as it was to have the food artfully presented and the dirty dishes winkled away. This also gave them more privacy.

Did he want to be private? Or had he chosen the automat to save money?

She took a chance, and made the transition from the quasi-personal to herself. "We're complete opposites, Teague and I, in that way," she said. When Jellico glanced up, and she sensed a wariness in him, she laughed and added, "Though you wouldn't think it, particularly if you were to have met me during my university years. We students, particularly when we were pursuing our studies in psychology, were all too apt to get into relationships in which we happily squandered hours and hours discussing and analyzing our every thought, emotion, and sensation. It's amazing we got any work done at all. The relationships certainly didn't seem to last much past the time we ran out of dreams to plumb for meaning, or each other's tastes in music and art to pick apart for what they supposedly symbolized."

"Sounds grim," Jellico said with a thin smile. "I think I'd rather have my teeth pulled out through my toes than sit through that."

Rael laughed. "I think everyone else thought so too—for at least during those years, no one outside our department seemed to be much interested in us but ourselves. It's inevitable, I suppose: we choose companions in our vocations, when we can."

There, it was said—a comment that could be a possible overture.

Again he hesitated, and when the light glowed green again, he turned with a quickness that revealed how glad he was of the interruption.

Rich, spicy smells accompanied the plates of food that they carefully removed from the automat, making certain the fresh peas did not suddenly become airborne. Rael watched Jellico from the periphery of her vision, and saw him staring off as if his thoughts were light-years distant.

She looked up. He seemed to become aware of her stare, and returned his gaze to hers. "Flindyk," he said, tipping his head slightly.

Rael peered through the delicate ferns surrounding their booth, just in time to see a massive figure bizarrely armored in Kanddoyd lineaments bounding with practiced grace into one of the more secluded booths directly next to the huge curving windows. Flindyk disappeared immediately behind a formidable screen of plants.

Jellico frowned, then rose. "He did say we were to come to him with any problems. We've got one now."

"He might not want to do business now," Rael said.

Jellico gave his characteristic curt nod as he said, "I'll just ask him for an appointment." He slid out from his seat, and was gone a moment later.

Rael watched him navigate between the booths toward the more isolated section near the windows. His movements were neat and economical, and occasionally, as he caught at a carved bar and pulled his weight around, there was a hint of the power latent in his lean body. She saw him near Flindyk's booth, but before he could approach the barrier of foliage a

Kanddoyd glided out from behind one of the ferns and stopped him.

The conversation was short. Jellico turned away, and Rael busied herself with her food. He slid in across from her again in the space of a minute, and she looked up in mute inquiry.

Jellico gave a faint shrug. "Was worth a try, anyway. Had a Kanddoyd flunky who was apparently willing to spend all night complimenting me, but it was equally obvious I wouldn't get anywhere. Mindful of those Hudapi gourds, I just said I'd try again during Trade hours and left." He smiled and picked up his fork.

For a time they were silent as they began to eat.

Rael was the first to speak again, praising the excellence of her dish. The talk was natural again as they discussed the meal, ranging through unexceptionable subjects from Zacathan mosaics to O'xyhh music.

They were midway through an excellent blend of rare coffee when a reedy voice caught their attention from the other side of the Terran area. "Ho! Hah! My surprised! To astound!" A cascade of stridulations accompanied this exclamation. "That thou shouldst ask, thou hast woken up without thy braincase, O Lokanadd."

Rael sidled a glance behind her, saw two Kanddoyds at the entrance. One—wearing green ribbons—was not vocalizing at all, but produced an orchestra's worth of clicks, knocks, ticks, hums, and squeaks.

The other Kanddoyd, a small male decorated in flamboyant flame colors, raised his arms high. "But thou knowest as good as thy name—which is Fool—or thine heritage—which is worthless—that my guests do not be troubled with the malodorous threats of yon rubbishing dacoits. Vanish! To displease me no further with thy dire whispers! Hasten, ere your whiskers wither in the blast of mine righteous wrath!"

The Kanddoyd who had not spoken now retreated, his stridulations droning on a lugubrious note. The flame-colored one now whirled into the dining area, circulating rapidly among the tables as he kept up a continuous flow of greetings, compliments, and questions which he scarcely paused long enough to permit of an answer.

"Aha!" he exclaimed when he neared Jellico and Rael. "Most profound greetings, O Captain, greetings also unto you, Doctor, and welcome to the Movable Feast! My inexpressible, your pleasure here to find. Eat! Drink! Merriness unto all; if you are not pleased, my inconsolable! Assure me you shall command my minions to restitute . . ." He danced away, carapace buzzing, to another table.

Rael looked across at her companion, and was surprised to see an odd expression on his face. Her own amusement faded into question.

Jellico finished his drink, then said softly, "It might just be my suspicious mind, but I'd swear that act over at the entrance was some kind of warning."

"Interesting," she said. "I hadn't thought of that. It did seem staged—I thought it was merely for effect."

Jellico shrugged slightly.

"If it was a warning, to whom?" she asked.

He returned no answer, and their conversation reverted to speculations about what kind of cargo they might raise.

But when they left a short while later, the question was answered when the quiet snick of a weapon made both instinctively duck for cover, and a high-velocity pellet whined right past Rael's ear.

10

Someone shot at them again. Jellico's gaze flicked back and forth, then he motioned Rael back into the restaurant towards a flowering hedge, and followed swiftly behind her.

They shoved their way through the thick shrubbery and ran headlong down a narrow accessway, dodging servitors with trays and paying no attention to the mix of Kanddoyd chirps and humanoid yells of outrage in their wake. The corridor terminated in a narrow service exit; just outside, Jellico caught at a decorative pole and swung around and up to the plant-bedecked platform about six feet above them. As Rael watched with interest, the law-abiding captain of the *Solar Queen* placed his booted foot against the rim of a potted tree, and shoved.

The pot tipped majestically toward the doorway they'd just quit, moving slowly in the lower-than-standard acceleration of this level. "Run!" Jellico commanded.

Rael turned and ran. Moments later she heard the smash of ceramic behind her, and shortly thereafter a cacophony of yelps, curses, and squeaks as their chasers hit the dirt pile.

"Humans and Kanddoyds," she said. His lips parted—he had been about to say the same, she realized.

He grinned instead, and flicked a salute.

Shots whizzed by both their heads right then. Rael ducked and began stagger-running, fighting the urge to sneeze. The analytical part of her brain recognized the distinctive burn in her nostrils given off by the pellets: retching agents colloquially known as taste-agains. They were illegal almost everywhere in human space, and with good reason. If the pellet actually hit any portion of their skin, they'd be writhing on the ground in seconds, unable to see or hear, and miserably rejecting the excellent food they'd just eaten.

They dashed deeper into the structures of the North Pole, turning into one of the recreational concourses ringing their end of the habitat, Jellico leading the way. He dodged around passersby with an efficiency that made it plain somewhere in his past he had been trained for action.

Rael recognized the signs, because she had as well.

Together they vaulted over a low bench and a little stream. Then she stopped when Jellico suddenly turned back. Bending down, he dog-paddled water from the stream onto the glassy concourse deck, then straightened up, grinning. She choked on a laugh as they whirled and ran; seconds later they heard the first of the chasers vault over the stream—and let out a whoop of despair, followed by a satisfying crash.

My turn, Rael thought, fumbling in her pocket. She found what she sought, a credit chit, and as they sprinted down the concourse, dodging people and ducking round objects, she saw a row of automats. Putting down her head, she pounded into the lead and skidded to a stop, threw her chit in, and hit a combination.

A moment later into her hands poured a stream of the hard little ball candies that Kanddoyds were so partial to. Cocking her wrist, she threw them back down their pathway, where they bounced and scattered.

Yells and curses rose as people inadvertently trod on the

tiny candies and nearly overbalanced; the runners, barely glimpsed through the crowd, were not so lucky. One, two, three figures flailed arms and shot up into the air, cursing, clacking, and howling. Rael felt that howl down her spine. It was a Shver voice, and the naked fear was probably an instinctive reaction to finding oneself in midair. Shver didn't jump; no one would, in their heavy grav, and habit was too ingrained to make it easy for them to go leaping about even in micrograv. Probably instantly dizzy, she thought, the analytical part of her brain always observing. Shver inner ear arrangements had to be even more sensitive than humans'.

Jellico slapped one finger to his palm: one to you.

He looked around as they curved toward another bridgeway, one that would take them back toward the interior face of the North Pole, overlooking the inside of the habitat. The customary austerity of his face was eased by a curious little smile. *He's playing the game,* she exulted, and waited happily to see what he would come up with.

Zing! Another pellet sang between them, and they ducked, turned, pounded up a bridge toward a smile-shaped slice of sky with strange hook-shaped clouds hanging in it below the dazzle of the radiants. Rael became aware of a slight alteration in the pattern of her run, and realized they were losing gravity as they ran higher. She lengthened her strides, trying to keep from bounding up, and was immediately rewarded with an incremental increase in speed. Soon she'd be leaping and not running at all—but she knew how to run in low grav.

So did Jellico.

The captain ran without slowing straight toward the edge of the concourse, and as she followed Rael saw the deck fall away before them, vanishing under the slender railing that was all that barred them from a sheer ten-mile fall to the distant surface. He altered his step, running now along the edge, the light of the radiants filtered into a green flicker of dappled light across his uniform by the foliage clumped in pleasing arrangements along the edge.

In a flash of curious detachment, Rael took in the awesome view to one side, trying to fight the tendency to veer away from it. The vast green walls of the habitat, curling up and overtopping them like the waves that had whelmed legendary Atlantis, were studded with the huge Kanddoyd towers that lanced up from the surface at the crazy angles made possible by spin gee. The haze of distance blurred the vertiginous landscape into the semblance of impossible mountains.

Then her throat spasmed as Jellico veered suddenly and vaulted up onto the back of a bench like a free-fall gymnast. With both hands he caught the high branches of a tall, thin napuir tree. Scrambling up into its heights, he was obscured by the branches weighted with fuzzy purple fruit. Rael saw the tree shake—he was going up, rather than coming back down, up to a higher concourse!

She looked about, saw not a tree but the fine-mosaic crenellations of an ornamental pillar, no doubt disguising a tangle of cable and piping, and jumping as high as she could, she caught hold and scrambled up.

They both swarmed over the rail above at the same time, and Jellico tossed her an armful of fruit.

Holding her breath, trying not to choke from laughter and a pungently nasty smell, she popped her share of the weird fruit and threw the squashy pulp down on their chasers. Howls of rage came from below the trees—but with it the clatter of fast-climbing Kanddoyds.

"Those Kanddoyds are too good at climbing," gasped Rael.

Jellico nodded, looking around. "We'll have to go down, then." He suddenly seemed to see something and ran forward, deeper into the concourse along a V-shaped gash that bulged the inner cliff edge of the concourse inward here, toward a complex glitter of metal and plasglas with garish laser beams and actinic light points flaring from it.

TORQUEMADA'S DELIGHT, the sign announced. THE GALAXY'S STEEPEST SPINBOGGAN.

"You can't be serious," she said, slowing somewhat.

Jellico glanced back at her, then past her. She shot a look

back along their path: several Kanddoyds were already climbing over the railing.

"There's no faster way down," he said.

And, Rael saw, there weren't any Kanddoyds waiting in
the line that snaked toward the entrance to the establishment. No wonder, she thought, given that the toboggan terminated on the surface ten miles below, in 1.6 standard gees,
intolerable to them.

Then Jellico slowed—he was gauging the timing as they
pushed forward, ignoring protests from the humanoids and
Shver in the line. Then, as one of the iridescent pods, open on
top like a kayak, shot out of an opening and glided to a stop
at the front of the line, he hissed: "Now!"

They dashed forward, pushing aside the two Rigelians
waiting their turn, and dove into the pod. Rael *oof*ed as she
hit the heavily padded interior, cushioning her fall with her
hands and then lying facedown on the humped control chaise.
The screen only inches from her face lit up as she grabbed the
control handles to either side, and she felt the restraints lock
in over her back and legs.

Then the pod rocked under Jellico's weight and lurched
forward; he had taken the forward steering position, leaving
her the even more critical weight-balancing controls. A surge
of pride, of delight, of emotional intensity at his unspoken
confidence in her abilities helped her to orient swiftly and
make ready for what was to come.

The concourse suddenly slipped back as the pod shot forward and the cries of the cheated Rigelians dopplered away
behind them. As it cleared the edge of the concourse it veered
sickeningly to run along the cliff edge for a time, past a series
of restaurants whose tables gave diners a close-up view of the
Delight's victims. She tried to ignore the dizzying perspective
plucking at her peripheral vision over the low sides of the pod
and concentrated instead on the stress and acceleration vec-
tors graphically represented on her screen. A smaller window
within the screen echoed Jellico's screen as he chose their
course: the controls of spinboggans were deliberately set up

to mimic starship navigational metaphors—the trick was to map them to the varying gee field and Coriolis force of a habitat.

Rael had never tried it. She hoped Jellico had; otherwise their ride down would merit the rather sadistic anticipation she thought she could glimpse on some diners' faces when she looked up for a moment.

PING! Rael sneezed again and, after a moment's fumbling, windowed up a rear view. A short distance behind them, two of their pursuers glided along in a pod, the one in the rear propped up on one arm to fire at them.

Their pod slowed abruptly. There was an agonizing pause; then, even though the course plots echoed from Jellico's controls were still evolving, its nose tipped down, bringing the distant surface into view, and the bottom dropped out of the world as the mechanism threw them into free fall down the track.

The wind whistled past the fairing like a chorus of screams—in fact, Rael noted, the edge of the pod appeared to be fluted precisely for that effect. It didn't help her stomach.

At least they won't be able to shoot at us anymore.

They were falling along an excruciatingly attenuated spiral, following a path that precisely matched the effect of the Coriolis force at every point along their path.

KATHUMP! The pod jolted violently.

"Switch point!" yelled Jellico. "Next one we're going inward, gain some velocity before we hit the Toaster."

Toaster? Rael realized she wasn't as familiar with this toboggan as she'd thought. She'd never heard of anything on these rides, popular throughout known space, called a Toaster. She flexed the controls, watching the moiré patterns of stress and acceleration shift, trying to correlate them with what she was feeling.

And soon, with a kind of rarefied delight, she realized that the way a spinboggan worked had more to do with orbital mechanics than she had thought. Grounders never got used to the fact that in orbit, you decelerated by firing your rockets to move into a higher, slower orbit, and accelerated by using your retros to drop into a lower, faster orbit. Here, due to the combination of track friction, the 'boggan's rotational motion, Coriolis acceleration—the tighter the spin, the faster one spun—and varying gee levels, it was the same. She wondered if their pursuers knew this.

PING!

Evidently, they did.

But the pod was gaining speed, the scream of its fairing rising in pitch, mirroring her heart rate. On Jellico's screen echo, their position point inched nearer a huge annular region in the mid-gee levels, crisscrossed by bright lines graduated in yellows and reds.

"Be very careful with the spoilers in the Toaster!" yelled Jellico. "You can pop up right out of the slot if you're not."

Working frantically, grateful that, for the moment, the track seemed sufficient to keep them on course, Rael labored to call up a help screen.

KATHUMP! Her stomach lurched, and not just from the sudden swerve onto a faster track. Gees pulled upwards at her recumbent body, but she hardly noticed, staring in fascinated horror at the readout about the Toaster.

"Here we go!" shouted Jellico as the pod bucked violently. Then the noise of its progress changed to a smooth hiss as it shot into a slot, like a tube open at the top, the opening angled slightly toward the Spin Axis high above. The only thing holding them in the slot was their acceleration; it was up to her to keep them there through whatever course changes Jellico initiated.

Moments later she heard a faint scream, and realized that they were drifting up—the fluted fairing was an audible warning device triggered by its rising above the edge of the slot, not just a nerveracking embellishment!

Then there was no time for thought, only reaction, acceleration, counterreaction, deceleration, in an increasingly dizzy ballet of pursuit and flight.

But their pursuers continued to gain.

"Hold on!" Jellico's voice held suppressed merriment.

"To what?" she yelled back, glad her voice, at least, sounded as unconcerned as his.

"Your stomach!" he called back with a laugh.

His screen echoed a complex twisting maneuver, chosen from among the maze of possibilities offered by the criss-crossing slots of the Toaster. She started to gasp a protest—surely their pursuers would catch up!

But it was too late. With a shattering thump the pod swerved into the first chicane and she compensated frantically as the scream of the fairing rose to a desperate pitch. In her peripheral vision she saw their pursuers in a parallel track, closing in—and their courses were intersecting.

Then Rael saw what Jellico intended. She could abort the maneuver, but she had to trust that he knew what he was doing.

She raised her head, looking squarely across at the humanoid filling her position in the opposite pod, and, with a broad, challenging smile, lifted her hands from the controls.

A look of horror crossed his face as the two slots veered together, the two pods converging at tremendous speed. If they collided, the impact would kill all of them, despite any safety features, and she had lifted her hands from her controls. It was up to her pursuers to decide.

With a wail of despair the other yanked on his controls, and Rael heard the scream of his fairing soar to a shout of mechanical terror as the other pod seemed to shoot backwards, hesitate, and then lift out of the slot into free fall. As it tumbled away towards the approaching surface, she watched in her rearview screen, feeling sick.

Then relief washed through her as a parachute blossomed, to lower them ignominiously to the surface. The unknown crew of the *Starvenger* had probably perished; best that no more die, no matter their motives.

The rest of the ride was uneventful; Jellico steered them through the rest of the Toaster on a conservative course, and then the track resumed, taking them the rest of the way to the surface.

Rael saw the terminus coming up, surrounded by a crowd of excited Shver, and hauled on the brakes. Here on the surface they worked normally, and the pod stopped several hundred feet from its destination.

On the edge of the Shver she saw three others of their race, their aspect menacing. Two were armed with pellet projectile weapons.

"Welcome committee at ninety degrees," Jellico said. "Must have radioed ahead."

Rael nodded. At first she could barely get up when the restraints snapped away, but then she realized it wasn't the weakening aftermath of an incredible adrenaline rush, but the 1.6 gees.

"Let's be quick," she said as the three Shver moved toward them with elephantine grace.

Rael and Jellico toiled as fast as they could toward an exit, and Rael saw that Jellico was familiar with high gee, too: despite their haste he planted each foot deliberately, knees slightly bent to cushion vulnerable knee cartilage.

She was beginning to feel the strain in her thighs when the captain turned aside into a narrow corridor that debouched into a lift station.

There was no one there, and no one in the pod that answered their summons.

With deep, twinned sighs they stood and watched as the crowd of Shver, arriving too late, looked up at them. The pod accelerated, back toward the Spin Axis and the *Queen*.

For a moment neither said anything.

"The napuir fruit!" she gasped finally.

Jellico's smile stretched into a grin, and suddenly he was laughing too. "The candy," he said huskily. "Those arms and legs . . ." He motioned in a windmill shape, and Rael bent double.

"The Toa . . . th-the Toas-s-s . . ." She couldn't get the words out.

They laughed harder, reviewing in gasped one-word exclamations their wild trip through the habitat. Each time Rael thought she was going to stop, she'd remember the howls, curses, gibbering wails of dismay, and gusted into new mirth.

They laughed together. They were alone, or she felt they were alone, walled off from the rest of the universe by the experience they had shared, by their hilarity, by the attraction that had never been so strong.

Still laughing, she chanced to look up, to find his gray eyes—alight with merriment—gazing back at her. And then his expression changed. It was nothing dramatic, like in the vids. A slight widening of the eyes, and a catch of the breath, but she felt his physical awareness ringing through muscle and bones, and watched him feel it in his turn, and before either of them could speak, he took a step, and she reached with a hand, and their lips met in a kiss.

It was an awkward first kiss, half awry, both of them still breathing fast, but the singing of her nerves promised much better. For a moment she leaned against his powerful body, and the kiss deepened—and suddenly he broke away. His eyes were now dark, with passion, with confusion, with wariness.

"We're not safe . . ." he started. His voice was hoarse; he stopped, and faint color ridged his cheekbones.

"Right," she said, striving for balance. "You know 'em?" she asked, when she had caught her breath.

He shook his head. "Not the one or two I saw. You?"

"Nothing from my past," she said. And, glad to have something to look at, she said, "Here we are—change point."

In silence they stepped out of the pod and moved a ways up the concourse toward the maglev that would take them to the docks. Rael had never felt so attuned to Jellico; she listened to the light sound of his breathing, watched the little frown between his eyes, and felt the swiftness of his thoughts.

"Damn," he said presently, indicating the maglev with his chin. "Unless this was random—which I doubt—they know who we are. Which means they know where we dock."

"Which means they might be waiting when we do debark," she said.

Jellico's mouth was grim again. "We chased halfway up into the light zone and I never saw a Monitor. Convenient, isn't it?"

"For whom?" she countered lightly. "We did enough damage to guarantee complaints against us."

He gave his head a shake. "At first I wanted to get their attention, but now . . . it's hard not to see some kind of conspiracy against us, at least passively abetted by the authorities." He squinted up at the alien tangle of cylindrical buildings, all reflecting light in a way never seen on any planet. The weirdness of the place had never seemed so profound. "Well. You ready for another round?" he asked as they walked back onto the maglev concourse. "Or shall we take the long way back to the docks?"

She shook her head. "As you said, they seem to know who we are, so why bother? We can debark almost in sight of the *Queen,* certainly in earshot. If they are waiting for us, maybe we'll learn something this way." She indicated the maglev.

A few seconds later another pod drew up with a hiss, and they went inside and dropped onto a bench. No one was in their immediate vicinity.

Jellico looked about him. He was back in control now, his emotions shut away as effectively as ever. "So you don't think we're in danger either?"

She sighed. "They're either astoundingly rotten shots or else there's something else going on."

"Most obvious reason is that they don't want to risk a capital crime—like using blasters. Pellets are nasty, but they're legal here, and they're also not fatal. If they wanted to kill us, there are plenty of other illegal weapons that won't punch holes in the habitat walls."

"If they really wanted us dead, they'd hire the Deathguard," Rael said.

"The Shver outcasts?" Jellico's brows lifted. "I take it they are nonpartisan about their trade?"

"Whoever pays them the most," Rael said. "Those people after us weren't trained in that kind of thing, or we wouldn't have gotten as far as we did. And those pellets wouldn't kill, just make us helpless."

"They might have wanted to get hold of us," Jellico said. "Though why grab us, I can't guess. We don't know anything that anyone would want, and as for the usual grab-and-ransom, we've got to be the most cash-strapped Traders in the entire habitat."

"Mmmm, just as well they didn't succeed, no matter what they wanted," Rael said. "There are places on Exchange I'd just as soon not visit, not without weapons of my own and a crew of heavies to back me up."

Jellico nodded. "On the other hand, it could be they didn't want to hit us at all, but scare us."

"Into leaving Exchange?" she said.

"And abandoning whatever it is someone doesn't want us finding out."

Rael sighed. "You don't want to go to the authorities?"

Jellico ran his hand through his short hair, and grimaced slightly. "As I said, I don't ordinarily have much patience with those who see conspiracies everywhere. I suppose we can go see Ross again . . . but I think I want to try solving this ourselves. Or at least find out more data as ammunition when we do contact the authorities."

The pod stopped then, and a tall Shver stepped in, sitting on the opposite bench with the great care of heavy-grav beings in light grav.

Rael felt the tension in Jellico, and was not sorry to have the opportunity for talk taken away. She wanted very badly to get back to the *Queen*, to retire to her cabin and think things through. And, she reflected wryly, unless she missed her guess, the captain probably felt just the same.

When they finally reached their destination, Rael braced herself for anything—but no one at all was on the concourse, and no one appeared. Unmolested, they reached the docks and soon were on board the *Queen*.

She was about to go straight to her cabin when Mura called, "Captain?"

His voice was angry. Alarm flooded through Rael; she saw Jellico's jaw harden.

They walked into the galley, to see half the crew gathered there. But they weren't what drew her attention.

Gripped in Dane Thorson's big hands was a small, greenish-blue, raggedly clad being with a webbed crest, now sadly fallen, and thin webbed fingers and toes.

"Found a stowaway," Thorson said.

"And a thief," Mura added.

Johan Stotz put in sourly, "And a saboteur."

11

*

"Mr. Ya," Captain Jellico said, "contact the Monitors."

Dane Thorson felt the little being twitch in his grasp, but it was so small his feet were in no danger of lifting off the deck even though he hadn't magged his boots.

"No thief, me!" it declared in a fluting voice. "I trade, I trade everythings!"

"What were you doing in our engine compartment?" Stotz asked, his eyes flinty. "That was trading?"

"No! I stop you move, me," came the prompt answer in heavily accented universal Trade speech. "No take cable, *turn* it. You not move to heavy zone, far away other side."

The captain sat down in a chair directly opposite the little blue-green person. Seated, he and the prisoner were eye to eye. Dane didn't envy the stowaway's view of an angry captain. Even at his most mild, Jellico looked tough, and he was obviously not in a good mood now.

"Who are you?" the captain asked. "And why are you on my ship?"

"I Tooe," was the prompt answer. "I Trader, me. No thief! Goo," the stowaway added in a sound midway between a cry and a whistle. Its frustration was palpable as it added some rapid words in Kanddoyd and then in Rigelian.

At the latter, Dane saw Rael Cofort's eyes widen. The doctor turned to the captain and said, "I can speak some Rigelian. Would you like me to question her?"

"Her?" the captain said, with a curious smile. "I might have known you'd speak Rigelian."

Dr. Cofort's lovely face glowed with color. "We traded quite a bit with certain Rigelian colonies when I was very small," she said. Then she turned to the stowaway and addressed her slowly in the hissing saurian tongue: "Tell us who you are and why you are here."

Dane understood that much, but none of the answer that spilled at terrific speed from Tooe in response.

No one spoke as the little stowaway talked, sometimes gesturing with her thin webbed hands. Dane watched with fascination as the fervor of her animated movements lifted her off the deck; she merely hooked out a foot under the edge of the table and pulled herself back down with impossible grace—and left her leg cocked up as though the position were perfectly natural. She now stood at an angle to everyone else in the room.

He looked down at the little head with its smooth, faintly scaled skin, colored much more blue than the normal Rigelian green. He saw Tooe's crest flicker, rise, flatten in anger, then fold as she talked. She was obviously a hybrid between a Rigelian and one of the other races seeded by the same saurians millennia ago. The Rigelians did not countenance hybrids; unlike Terrans, who mostly welcomed diversity in the human genome, they were exceedingly purist in outlook, and just as antagonistic toward those with similar biologies as they were toward those of far different backgrounds. He wondered how old she was.

Finally she came to a stop, and Dr. Cofort rubbed her chin thoughtfully. "It's been a long time, and the dialect Tooe speaks is . . . unique, but I think I have most of her story."

"Let's hear it," the captain said.

"She came on board just after we landed, and has been hiding in the cargo area ever since. She brought along a stash of items she thought we could use, and has been leaving them out, one at a time, since she ran out of her own food and had to start using ours. She insists she would have come forward as soon as we blasted out, but it was taking us a long time to do so. She wants to be a Trader, and thinks this was her only chance."

"Does her family concur?"

"She claims her only family is a group of other . . . castaways. They live up at the Spin Axis," Cofort said. "Her age works out to be about nineteen Standard years, which is technically adulthood by Terran law, at least. So she's an independent entity."

Jellico tapped his fingers lightly on the table, then looked up at Dane. "Lock her in the brig for now. We have things to discuss."

Dane gently pulled his prisoner back and turned toward the door; she was so small her mass seemed utterly negligible. He hated this kind of duty, especially when it involved a being so small and flimsy. As he passed by Dr. Cofort he saw her wince in silent sympathy for the little Rigelian, which made Dane feel even worse.

Tooe made no protest as they descended to the brig, Dane keeping a firm grip on her spindly arm. Having seen her performance at the table, he had no doubt that he'd never catch her in free fall.

And yet Stotz did.

He looked at her thoughtfully when they reached the bare cabin that served as the *Queen*'s brig and he had pushed her gently through the door. She drifted across the tiny room, folded down the bench from one wall, and sat upside down under the seat, curling her limbs up into a ball and putting her chin on her knees. Vertigo seized Dane as the utter naturalness of her motions upended his perceptions—now *he* was the one on the ceiling. He magged his boots, feeling himself click firmly to the deckplates, and he breathed deeply, forcing the vertigo away.

She said nothing; big deep yellow eyes looked up at Dane. He hastily closed the door, by now feeling like the biggest villain in the universe.

It wasn't until he got back to the gallery and heard the others talking that he was able to rid himself of the sensation of walking on the ceiling.

"We've been in microgee too long," he muttered under his breath as he ducked through the hatch.

". . . biggest discrepancy in what she was saying," Stotz's voice carried over the others. "If she wanted to blast off with us, then why did I catch her sabotaging my drive?"

Dr. Cofort said, "She insisted it was a measure to keep us from moving up to the heavy zone. She must have been listening when the captain issued the order to prepare for the move, just before we left to visit the legate."

Jasper Weeks said softly, "Have to admit it was clever, to reverse the cable connecting the ignition system to the drive. It would have taken us hours to check all those cables, but it wasn't really damage."

Stotz grunted. "Knows her way around an engine, then."

Mura said, "And these other things she left for me to find. Some of them are odd, but they're not useless."

Jellico looked across at the doctor. "Did she say why she picked our ship?"

"Yes, she did," Cofort answered. "She said it was clean, and the animals were happy. She said she couldn't believe that a ship of villains would be kind to their animals."

"Villains!" Ali exclaimed. "That's a loud one, coming from a saboteur!"

"What I don't like," the captain said, "is the fact that her being here is one more strange thing going on in a series that is far too long for my peace of mind."

Van Ryke pushed himself back down the bulkhead, where he had slowly drifted during the discussion. "But if what she says is true, she got here before things started going sour on us."

"Which was the day we tried to track down the old owners of the *Starvenger,*" Rip said.

Jellico nodded. "Right. But none of you know this: the doctor and I were shot at when we were returning just now. Shot at with taste-agains, and chased halfway back to the docks—and no Monitors in sight."

The crew stared in amazed silence.

"So you can see why I don't like any more coincidences showing up."

"So what do we do with her?" Dr. Cofort asked, frowning slightly.

"I have to admit, if she is a free agent, and if the authorities are corrupt, the idea of turning her over to them sticks in my craw," Jellico said. "But I don't want her wandering around my ship unsupervised. Though she didn't do any real damage up until now, our situation is too ticklish to risk any more problems. And though she claims to be honest, didn't she admit to coming from one of the Spin Axis gangs? I thought that was where the detritus of the three civilizations hid out."

"Behind every being in such 'detritus' usually lies some kind of personal tragedy," Cofort said in a quiet voice. "People, especially those so young, seldom choose a life beyond the law. They are usually driven to it." The doctor shook her head. "Tooe did mention she lived in a crèche when she was very small, but they threw her out for nonpayment."

Jellico grunted. "Rigelian . . . they don't take kindly to hybrids. If her other parent was a spacehound and thought he or she'd make it back, but didn't, that might explain the nonpayment."

"But not why a small child was thrown out to live hand to mouth," Van Ryke growled. "The name 'Harmonious Exchange' seems to fit this canister less every hour we're here."

The captain frowned for a long time, during which no one

spoke. Then he surprised Dane by looking up at him. "What do you think we should do with her?"

Dane rubbed his jaw, trying to think. He hated the idea of any of the others thinking him sentimental, but the more he heard of Tooe's story—if it was true—the more it reminded him of his early years in the Federation Home. Of course no one had thrown him out, but there had been times he'd half wished they would, so bleak was the life there, with the constant hard work in order to strive for the grades that would get one into the Training Pool, and thence to Service, and the constant reminders about how grateful the orphans should be for their free education and board.

He felt that if she spoke the truth, she deserved a fair chance at a decent trade, just like he'd had. So he said, "I'll take charge of her for now, if you like."

"I'll help," Ali spoke up, which surprised Dane. It seemed to surprise the others as well, for there were lifted brows and questioning glances, to which Ali returned a wry smile and an elegant shrug. Dane remembered what little he'd heard about Ali Kamil's past, and realized he probably felt the same as Dane.

"And I," Rip Shannon said, with his easy smile. "Thorson and I dead-ended on our search, anyway."

Jellico grunted again. "That was my next question." He dropped his hands onto his knees; Dane could see the muscles in his leg bunch as they compensated by curling up under the bench he was seated on to cancel the reaction of his gesture. "Well, then, let's try this. You boys take charge of this stowaway. If she offers you any trouble, any at all, or lies to you, then over to the Monitors she goes, corrupt or not. I won't have a troublemaker on board, especially now. But if she seems useful . . . we'll talk again. Maybe she can earn passage elsewhere, at least."

Dane nodded, feeling pleased.

"As for our other matter, it's beginning to look like someone doesn't want us finding out anything about our derelict.

What we need to know is if it's the authorities—or someone else. And Jan and I might be the ones to look at this for now. After you, Tang, get the rest of the data from the *Starvenger's* log deciphered."

"Aye, Captain," Ya said. "I'll get back to it right now." He pulled himself out of the mess and disappeared in the direction of his cabin.

"I'll go let Tooe out of the brig," Dane said.

Frank Mura motioned to him. "Bring her back for a meal," he said. "From the looks of her, it's long overdue."

Dane grinned as he descended to the brig, and opened the door.

Tooe was still under the bench, upside down. Again, vertigo seized Dane; after a brief struggle he accepted the inversion of his world. She looked down at him, her yellow eyes huge. The pupils narrowed into slits and her crest rose in a gesture that looked so hopeful, Dane tried not to laugh. "You're in my charge," he said in Trade, then repeated it again, awkwardly, in Rigelian.

"Speak Trade, me," Tooe said proudly, pinwheeling out from under the bench and flipping upside down to match Dane's orientation. Watching her made his stomach flip-flop. She smacked her scrawny chest. "Learn off vids Nunku get." Then she peered closer at him, as if puzzled.

"Well, you'll need some more practice," Dane said, fighting off vertigo again. What was happening to him?

Then a vivid flash of memory filled his inner gaze: Tooe, interrogated by the captain, surrounded by people all of whose heads were oriented parallel to the same axis. Except hers.

We all act like we're under acceleration, even when we're not. She doesn't. So who was better adapted to space?

"I fast. Very fast . . ." Tooe took her gaze from his face, then hesitated, her pupils widening and narrowing disconcertingly as she looked around as if searching for a word. Then she said, "Zounds!"

"Zounds?" Dane repeated, no longer able to hide his laughter. "How old are those vids you've been watching?"

Three days later, Dane floated into the *Starvenger*'s galley and drew a bulb of hot drink.

Rip Shannon bounced gently against a wall and watched his big, yellow-haired friend maneuvering carefully in free fall. Behind him was a diminutive blue person, miming his movements.

Rip delighted in the absurdity of the situation, but he kept his voice steady as he said, "Good workout, you two?"

Dane looked over his shoulder at Tooe, who had become his shadow during the two days he and Rip had been stationed for their turn on the *Starvenger*. During those two days both men had talked to the little Rigelian, but it was Dane who did the most, sometimes using vocabulary culled from three or four languages. Tooe's understanding of Trade speech was much better than her spoken use of the language, but she was a very fast learner, and her ability to express herself grew noticeably better each day.

"I strong, me," Tooe chirped. "I strong in one grav, like Terrans."

"She can pull a lot of weight for her size," Dane admitted. "She's apparently been working out in high grav for years, ever since she formed her plans for getting into space."

Tooe obviously understood this; her crest spread out at a proud angle above her head, and she grinned, showing a row of sharp, pointed little teeth.

"Everything locked down on the lower deck?" Rip asked.

Dane nodded. "All's shipshape."

"We go back?" Tooe asked, looking from one of them to the other, her yellow eyes wide.

"We're just waiting for the—" Rip paused as a clanking noise reverberated through the ship. "Hey, sounds like the shuttle just reached the lock. Shall we go see?"

Tooe chirped, "I help, me!" She doubled up her feet and sprang from the wall, rocketing through the hatchway into the corridor outside. Rip followed more slowly, just in time to see what looked like a thin blue streak ricochet swiftly from bulkhead to deckplates down the corridor and around the corner.

When he and Dane reached the lock, Tooe's fingers were already busy at the console. Rip bounded toward her, then slowed.

"Will you look at that," he said.

On the screen in front of her the lock icon flashed into a steady green as she initiated the pressure checks.

"All clear, is," she announced proudly.

"All clear, is," agreed Dane and Rip solemnly.

As Johan Stotz and Jasper Weeks emerged from the tube, Jasper smiled in greeting. "How's the new crew member synching in?" He nodded toward Tooe.

Rip saw Tooe glance their way, her crest flicking up at a hopeful angle, and he hid a smile. "Fine," he said. "Learns fast." He faced Weeks and added casually, "Almost looks like home down in the engine compartment."

Jasper's grin twisted a little. "Isn't it starting to look like home all over? Or haven't you hauled over some stuff you like to mess with?"

Rip nodded slowly, thinking of the two little potted rilla-mints he'd brought over. They bloomed so nicely, and their scent did a lot to improve the antiseptic but boring ship air.

"You did," Jasper said with a triumphant grin that was not the least malicious. "Bet you brought some of those lit-tle plants that make the silver flowers. They smell like Terra in the summer, kind of. Or they remind me of my one visit to Terra." His bleached face looked wistful for a moment.

That aroma makes a place home, Rip thought, but he couldn't bring himself to say it out loud. None of them ever referred to the *Starvenger* as a future home, or themselves as its officers. They couldn't; Rip sensed strongly that the other three felt the same. Their own ship, and officer status. No, until it came, best not to jinx it by too much chatter.

He waved a salute and pulled himself after Dane into the tube, followed closely by Tooe. Even though she had made the same short journey when they boarded the shuttle to come out to the *Starvenger,* Tooe looked around just as intently, her crest fluttering, echoing her mercurial emotions. She appeared most fascinated by the silvery, moist-looking walls of the tube, the molecules of which both maintained its shape and healed any punctures by tenaciously "remembering" the stress programmed into them by the lock extruder. Obviously this technology was expensive—and had not been deployed up in the Spin Axis area where she lived.

Dane slapped the lock control, visibly wincing in anticipation. Rip's ears popped slightly as the tube behind them pulled away from the *Starvenger*'s lock and sealed instantly in a mouthlike pucker. As the lock sealed behind them, the extruder reversed its function and began to eat the tube. Rip shuddered: none of the crew could get used to the weird Kanddoyd lock technology.

"Sucks it all up," announced Tooe. "Why it not suck us up, too?"

"Doesn't like the way we taste," said Dane solemnly.

Tooe's crest flattened in doubt, her slit pupils narrowing. "No tongue in lock, and yours is twisted."

Rip grinned at the expression on Dane's face. "She's got you there!" he said.

The hatch in front of them cycled open as the tube shortened behind them and Tooe shot through it, flipping over to bounce off the ceiling and accelerating down through the short cabin toward the control section. Rip and Dane followed more sedately.

"If we intend to be this far out of human space often, we're going to see a lot of habitats," commented Dane, his gaze following the little blue biped.

"Nice to have crew that know them?" During their two days' stint aboard *Starvenger* the big cargo master apprentice hadn't discussed Tooe with Rip, and Rip hadn't pushed him on it, despite his curiosity. Maybe now he was ready to talk.

But Dane merely nodded and pulled himself into the nav-pod—he'd piloted on the way out.

Rip concentrated on his piloting, listening with only half an ear to Tooe's incessant questions and Dane's patient answers. She was picking up the subtleties of Tradespeak now, as shown by her response to Dane's joke.

They didn't talk about anything important on the shuttle; they all knew that anyone who wished to could record conversations. Rip reflected that it would take him ten minutes to check for bugs, but why bother? He and Dane didn't know anything new. Stotz had said nothing, and Jasper had only discussed Tooe and plants when they arrived at the *Starvenger.* This closed-mouth attitude was just as the captain had ordered.

Tooe fell silent as the little shuttle pitched down and the habitat loomed huge before them. They were coming in on an angle from the axis; the length of the huge cylinder dwindled in perspective, rendered into an abstract conic section by the harsh, knife-edged shadows of vacuum. The almost greenish light from the system primary glinted off the dull metallic maze of the huge end cap, a confusion of antennae, sensors, vents, radiators for a variety of energies, and much more that was unidentifiable. At the center loomed the vast mouth of the habitat docking bay, the still center of the visible rotation of the habitat.

Rip triggered the attitude thrusters and felt the tug in his inner ear as the shuttle spun up to match the habitat. The vast construct's rotation appeared to slow and stop. As they approached the bay, the half-phase gray-swirl bulk of the planet it orbited slipped from sight, like moonset.

Looking at Tooe watching the phenomenon with unblinking concentration, Rip realized she had never seen a moonset. Or a sunrise.

They glided inward, joining the incessant ballet of small service vessels and space-suited figures under the terse direction of Dock Control. Tooe's questions started up again as she pointed excitedly at a big Shver freighter newly berthed not far from the *Queen,* but Rip hardly glanced at it, his eyes drawn by his own ship, the *Solar Queen.* Rip studied her length, glowing silvery-gold in the diffuse illumination from the many lights scattered throughout the bay. She wasn't nearly as large as some of the other ships docked along either side, nor as fancy, but she was home. Home. The word brought vividly to mind the *Queen's* crowded galley, the narrow hatchways, his tiny cabin, fixed snugly just the way he liked, and not the spacious home he'd spent his childhood in, with its pleasing view of the lakeside. He frowned, realized he couldn't remember what color his room had been.

A vivid memory intruded then, the tears gathering in his mother's dark eyes. "I'll never see you again, son."

And his own voice, cheery, careless, "Sure you will, Mom!" He could hardly wait to wave good-bye to his family and blast off on his first journey. "The time'll go fast, you'll see."

Well, it had gone fast—for Rip. Had it for his mother, stuck back on Terra, looking at the skies? Though Rip would not change his life for anything, suddenly he was glad his brother and sister had chosen dirthugger careers.

The shuttle clanked and boomed as the fingers of the *Queen's* auxiliary lock seized it. Again it was Tooe's eager fingers that tabbed the controls to verify proper mating and, when the light glowed green, keyed the inner hatch open.

They were soon on board the *Queen.* Mura greeted them, pointed with his chin to the control deck.

Captain Jellico was busy with Steen Wilcox, but when Rip, Dane, and Tooe appeared in the door, he stopped and faced them. "Anything to report?"

"Not a thing," Rip said. "Quiet two days." Next to him, Dane nodded—and a moment later, Tooe nodded in exactly the same fashion.

Rip saw the captain's lips quirk slightly. But all he said was, "There's little to report here, other than Kamil is now confined to the ship. Supposedly he was caught up near the forbidden areas of the Spin Axis—though he maintains he was chased there."

Rip shook his head, mentally promising himself a visit to Ali, to find out what had happened.

Jellico continued, "You two have six hours of leave time, then check back for your orders."

Rip started to turn away, saw Dane hesitate as though he were about to speak. But then he shook his head as though he'd made a decision, and backed out into the hatchway.

"Going down to Ali's cabin," Rip said. "Want to find out what's up."

"I'll check in with you later," Dane replied, which surprised Rip a little. "I have an errand to do first." At his elbow, Tooe's yellow eyes blinked.

Rip felt a cautionary remark forming, and he bit it back. "Later, then," was all he said.

12

Dane frowned as he and Tooe passed through the dock into the main concourse. Had the captain read his mind? Why had he told them that business about Ali?

He sighed, hoping he was doing the right thing. It seemed right, he thought, looking at it from all angles. The Spin Axis was forbidden, and the captain had to officially uphold that ruling, even though everyone on the crew knew there was an awful lot of unofficial and sinister rule-breaking going on at Exchange.

But the habitat was not Terran territory, and the *Queen*'s crew had no influence. Just the opposite, in fact, if someone was spreading bad rumors about them to the other spacers. Dane would have liked to explain his idea to the captain, and get his okay—but then that placed the burden of the decision on the captain. Dane couldn't do that. So he was going to have to take this risk on his own.

He looked down, saw Tooe watching him, her crest half-raised at a hopeful angle. "Lead on," he said.

They zapped through the dock tubing to the access lock, but instead of bouncing their way down the concourse, she looked around carefully, then said, "We go this way, us." And she retreated toward an area jumbled with cables and cranes. Again a look, then she slipped behind a monster automated loader. Dane squeezed after her, cursing to himself when he klunked his head against an unseen pipe. That wouldn't have happened in normal grav. *But here, it's all too easy to launch yourself fast enough to knock your brains out,* he thought sourly as he pushed after his charge. *And maybe that's just what I need.*

Tooe kept looking back, her yellow eyes bright with a chatoyant glow, as she picked her way past a jumble of outdated equipment. Then she clambered up onto a pipe and jumped into an open air shaft. Sighing to himself, Dane followed.

The microgravity of their level had made it easy to follow her up the shaft at first, but after they had climbed for a while Dane found himself losing all sense of orientation. He realized they were now in the Spin Axis proper—that area of the habitat where the gee force was too small to influence the human vestibular canals sufficiently to give any sense of up and down at all. He wondered briefly if the boundaries were different for Kanddoyd and Shver, or how their physiology worked.

They came out on a deck canted at a weird angle, and vertigo tugged at Dane. He shut his eyes for a moment, then hastily opened them again. That was worse: without vision to orient him, free fall was just that—an endless fall that made his monkey hindbrain gibber in terror. He tried to force himself to abandon the concepts of down and up. Now he had six directions to choose from, instead of four. The deck wasn't canted; he was.

Again Tooe launched into a dark hole. Dane pushed after, his heartbeat accelerating. Was this going to be the stupidest—and the last—impulsive decision he'd ever made?

At first Tooe led him through abandoned air shafts and service hatchways cramped with poorly lashed, corroded cargo pods and other ancient junk, all dimly lit by random console or emergency exit lights. Dane frowned at the sight of one particularly large tangle of pipes and reaction vessels—perhaps an autochem or something—that was fastened down so loosely that Tooe's impact on it when she changed direction sent it slowly toward the bulkhead. That kind of carelessness killed people, he thought, then grimaced as he remembered where he was. On a ship, yes, badly stowed cargo could be a death sentence for ship and crew, but anything that hit the habitat hard enough to make this junk move would open the habitat to space and kill everyone on it long before shifting junk up here had any effect.

As he followed the little hybrid, he thought over the last couple of days. All his instincts favored Tooe, but he realized now that that might just be because she was so small and flimsy she didn't seem to constitute any kind of threat. But that was aboard the *Queen,* in their territory. Here in this weird hinterland, she could always get a lot of small creatures together, and they could do what they wanted with an unarmed spacer.

Suddenly his breath caught in his throat as the space around them opened up abruptly to a vast cavern, with huge spokes reaching off at thirty-degree angles, their shadowed depths dwindling in impossible perspective. He realized they had to be at the top of twelve of the Kanddoyd towers—down the center of each spoke was the slender tube of a maglev, bedizened with the strange liquescent light-lines favored by the insectile aliens. The maglevs came together in a twelve-pointed star; suddenly, to Dane's already stressed perceptions, the sight suggested nothing so much as some immense denizen of undersea with twelve luminescent tentacles, and he half expected one of them to curl towards them with feral intent.

But Tooe spared the spectacle not a glance. Instead she pulled herself gracefully along the interstice between two spokes and thus across the cavern, taking care to stay under the structural bracing—out of sight of inimical eyes, no doubt. Following her maneuver more clumsily, Dane put his hand on a pipe and yanked his fingers back with a hissed curse. The insulation was tattered and the pipe was bitterly cold. Only then did he note the ideograph denoting inert cryogenics. Probably nitrogen, he thought, then dismissed the thought, resolving to be more careful. He saw many more pipes like it, carrying different gases and liquids, some quite dangerous, and realized with mild appreciation the wisdom of the design: the emissions from any ruptures would tend to stay localized in zero gee, giving more time for repairs.

They traveled through air shafts for a while longer, finally emerging into an intersection off which led five dark tunnels. The sixth was closed behind steel doors. Fog drifted out of one of the tunnels, veiling the faint lights that illuminated the open space and further confusing his sense of orientation. Dane's danger sense prickled at the back of his neck. Where was the fog coming from?

Tooe paused, and when they saw a slight movement in the shadowy alcove just beyond a pool of light, she whistled quickly, a complicated series of notes, then rapped her knuckles on a loose piece of sheeting. It boomed softly; Dane noticed the center of it was shiny and dark, as if from years of steady use.

His ears caught the sound of movement, no more than a scrape, but Tooe swiftly followed up her whistle with another pattern, then visibly relaxed when from the shadows came a rapid clicking noise.

She gestured quietly to Dane, pushed off, and rocketed into the dark hole from which the fog was drifting. As they flew through the tunnel, Dane heard a faint hiss and saw the source of the fog: a leaking pipe. *This must be a very old part of the Spin Axis,* he thought; and indeed, as they went on, there were more and more leaks.

Occasionally Tooe would stop and whistle, or call, or tap some kind of signal, and on receiving a signal—usually from unseen watchers—she'd go on. At first Dane tried to memorize the trail, but had to give up before long. At the end, he was fairly certain they had doubled back.

He was about to ask what was going on; then an unsettling thought occurred to him: he'd been so busy wondering whether she could be trusted, he'd forgotten how Tooe must be feeling, taking a stranger to the place where her group hid out.

After what he'd heard over the last couple of days, Dane had a pretty good idea how life was in the Spin Axis. In the mostly abandoned space away from the area where the mysterious and sinister Shver Deathguard claimed, there were plenty of hidey-holes where various gangs lived, and none of them particularly liked or trusted the others. Sometimes there were fights—bad ones, since there were no Monitors to stop them. Mostly, though, the gangs seemed to exist in a kind of uneasy truce, lest the authorities suddenly decide to swoop down with heavy weapons and flame the place clean.

There were those groups that made their living from theft, or worse things. Tooe's gang bartered.

"Nunku find we young," Tooe had said. "Teach us! We learn data, we learn machines, we trade. Get away from Spinner. I Tooe, go to space, me," she'd said proudly.

So Dane resigned himself to following a torturous path to Nunku's hideout—when a piercing whistle echoed up from somewhere.

Tooe caught hold of a thin cable and stopped.

The sound came again, a high, weird note dropping down to another. Dane felt his neck bristle, and he flexed his hands. Now his danger sense was going into hyper—and from the looks of Tooe, it wasn't just his imagination.

The little Rigelian darted to one of the adits, her crest flattened out in anger mode.

"That our call," she said quickly. "Danger—Shver hunt!"

"Shver hunt?" Dane repeated.

Tooe paid him no attention. She was very still, head angled to listen.

The sound came again, fainter, and this time Tooe sprang to a half-blocked shaft, and sped up inside.

She was going off to the rescue, with no weapons, no aid

but Dane. Cursing himself for not having gotten a sleeprod, at least, he pushed after for a few seconds, his mind rapidly making and discarding plans.

A sharp turn in another old shaft and the Spin Axis opened up around them again, into a complicated space filled with angular cargo pods lashed to a confusion of pipes and tiedowns. Here too was the fog, and the air was cold. The whistle was suddenly very near. Tooe flicked out her skinny arm, and she and Dane watched as a squat being scooted by, ricocheting in terror-inspired grace off the cargo pods. As the victim disappeared from sight, there was a rumble of deep voices, and eight or ten Shver appeared, wearing some kind of jet-packs. In the dim lighting Dane could see that these Shver were young, and wealthy, and they all carried vicious-looking force blades. Anger burned inside him: eight heavy-weights against a small being scarcely larger than Tooe!

"You stay." Tooe's voice was reedy with fear. "My nest-mate Momo, I help—"

"Wait," Dane murmured. "Can you get us ahead of them somehow?"

She whipped around and stared after Momo and the chasers, as if figuring a vector on the probable path. Then she nodded, her crest flicking into hope mode.

"Then get me there ahead, and we'll have a little fun, if I've figured this right," Dane said, scanning the pipes running through the chamber.

Dane never did figure out how she did it; perhaps the adrenaline of the chase effaced the memory, but in a very few minutes, after a dizzying flight through interstices he would have sworn were too small for him, they were back in the foggy tunnel. He could hear the whistle of terror from Momo coming closer, and, fainter, the brutal laughter of the pursuing Shver. Dane pulled himself along as fast as he dared, scanning the tunnel walls until he spotted what he'd hoped for: the leaking pipe from which the fog was billowing. Fortunately, it was inert cryo again, for there was suddenly no time left as Momo rocketed past and, with no further warning, the Shver were upon them.

The bulky beings stopped, nonplussed. He saw them squint, trying to see through the fog veiling him and Tooe. Then the one in the lead smiled, evidently seeing easy prey. It jetted forward slowly, waving the others back, its force knife humming shrilly as it pointed the weapon square at Dane's head.

Dane didn't move, and noted approvingly that Tooe didn't either. He flexed the toes of his right foot very slightly, checking that his foot was still firmly hooked under a cable.

"Vanish you, or be prey," the foremost Shver growled, his posture arrogant.

Dane didn't answer. Instead, as the Shver lunged at him, he twisted down and aside by pulling up his right leg, and, as he rocketed down, chopped savagely at the leaking pipe with his left hand and yanked sideways on it with his right, pushing hard against the tunnel wall with all the strength in his legs.

With a shrill screech of tortured metal the pipe ruptured and the liquid nitrogen jetted out straight at his attacker, the roar of its release suddenly augmented by a basso scream of agony from the Shver.

"Now!" shouted Dane, and they flew off down the tunnel. As they swung around a corner he looked back and bile suddenly spurted into his throat. Out of the boiling fog that veiled the confused panic of the Shver a small object looped toward them: a severed hand, frost covered, the force knife still humming in its rigid grasp. As he watched, frozen with a mixture of horror and triumph, the hand hit the bulkhead a few feet away and shattered into dust.

Dane felt a tug at his arm. "Trounced rascal knaves, you," she crowed; then her crest flattened as she saw his expression. She shook her head. "Won't bleed, him. Saw freeze wound once—lots of time, medic fix."

Dane pushed off and followed her, shocked less by the

sight than the violence his actions had revealed in him. Then he thought of the *Ariadne*. What if the *Queen* had been attacked? The thought made him feel a little better, but he was still subdued when they caught up with Momo.

The little being was a kind of humanoid Dane had never seen before. He was small, squat, and his skin was red—almost crimson; Dane wondered what influence in his environment could have created that. At first Momo was sobbing, and Tooe made consoling noises. When Momo was able to gulp back his tears, he and Tooe held a rapid conversation in Kanddoyd, snapping and tapping their fingers in complicated rhythms to accentuate their speech.

Dane followed along behind, doing his best to follow the flow of words. The Kanddoyd they spoke seemed highly idiomatic, or else had been adapted over time for the benefit of physiologies different from Kanddoyd.

Suddenly they both turned to Dane, and Momo said in Kanddoyd-accented Terran, "Gracious and forever gratitude to Terran visitor, my honor to give to you." He lifted both hands to his head and covered his eyes with his thumbs, flickering his fingers in a gesture which Dane recognized as an analogue for the respectful clacking of Kanddoyd mandibles.

"Glad to help," he said, feeling awkward.

"We conduct honored rescuer to Nunku," Momo said.

Dane bit his lip. Wasn't that where Tooe had intended to take him all along? For a moment his suspicions rose again, to disappear when he realized that the two were taking him on a straight route, rather than the circuitous one Tooe had embarked on at first.

Warm air and the deep droning of vast engines, more a vibration than a sound, indicated they were somewhere in the vicinity of the great motors for the ventilators that kept the air moving in the Spin Axis. The air smelled slightly metallic, but was fresh enough, and unlike the still air in the abandoned storage areas, this ruffled gently across his skin, making it clear that someone had seen to circulation.

They passed a jumble of ancient hull metal and other discarded parts of spaceships. Twice Tooe made calling sounds, but there were no answers this time. Warnings, Dane thought. Before, she was signaling for permission to enter other gangs' territories, and now she was letting her own gang know she was coming.

I wonder if the signal says anything about me, he thought as they floated down into a vast circular room, well lit from an astonishing variety of lighting equipment scavenged from several centuries' choices of styles.

At once eight or ten beings appeared, ricocheting down with bizarre grace from the network of catwalks and cables stretching everywhere, all of them raggedly dressed in ill-fitting spacer castoffs. They represented biologies from an astonishingly wide range of systems, all humanoid, but that was the only common bond.

The one that drew the eye was a very weird creature indeed. Her head seemed much too large for her body, but Dane realized after a second look that her head was normal in size. The thin, strangely elongated body inside the tattered old robe was not. It was as if a child's body had been stretched out to ten or twelve feet. Such a person would have to live in free fall, Dane realized as Tooe eagerly drew him forward. She could never stand on her own in normal gravity.

"Dane Thorsen, here Nunku," Tooe said.

A pair of wide china-blue eyes regarded Dane gravely from under a tangle of lank light-brown hair. "We thank thee for thy help," she said softly.

Tooe and Momo then launched into a stream of talk, mixing together words from six or more languages. Mostly they spoke Kanddoyd, but here and there were Terran words. At the end, there was even one Shver: "Golm."

Dane looked up sharply, and the others reacted with startled glances.

Dane felt his neck and ears burning. "Sorry," he said.

Nunku shook her head slightly. "Clan Golm," she murmured. "Thou knowest of them?"

Dane shrugged, feeling stupid. "It's just that there was one of them—called himself the Jheel—who . . . made things difficult for my shipmates," he finished lamely.

Tooe whistled, then said, "Golm Jheels, all three, bad, Zoral very very bad. Zoral hunt Momo," she finished.

Nunku said, "It is an old clan, and powerful. The young ones do not act worthy of trust. They want more power."

Dane said carefully, "The Jheel I mean works in the Terran Trade communications office. Do you know something about this Jheel?"

Another fast conversation in mixed Rigelian, Kanddoyd, and other languages, this time with other figures coming forward to participate.

At last Nunku nodded, and it was Momo who said, "Thou art my rescuer. I trade data. What needest thou?"

Dane sighed. How to explain? Ought he to explain?

He looked from Tooe to Momo to Nunku, saw them waiting expectantly. He had come because Tooe wanted him to; she kept talking about Nunku and the others like . . . like he would the crew of the *Queen*. Like they were family.

"Well, here's what's going on," he began.

13

Craig Tau ruffled Omega's ears and stroked the sides of the cat's muzzle, smiling at the resultant loud purr. Alpha head-butted his other hand, and he knelt down and for a time did nothing but pet the cats.

It felt good to empty his mind, to just play with the animals. They lived so much in the moment, without worrying about missing ships, or lying rumors, or vanishing credit—or personal problems among their crewmates.

A scratch on his arm brought his attention round to Sinbad, who batted him again. Now he had three cats to stroke. He reached down and scratched Sinbad's wedge-shaped head, watching with a grin as the notched ears went flat and the eyes narrowed with pleasure. Sinbad's rusty-sounding purr was twice as loud as the others'.

"Well, old friend, what should I do?" Tau addressed the cat.

Sinbad licked his lips and purred louder.

"That's what I thought," Tau said with a wry laugh. "Keep my mouth shut."

Alpha jumped up onto his knee and tried to settle into a loaf despite the microgravity. Claws pricked through Tau's trouser leg as the cat pulled itself down into his lap, making him wince. He gently lifted the cat down, hooking his calves under his seat to keep from drifting forward off the chair. He threw a couple of the toys he'd fashioned, and watched all three cats leap after them, their tails stretched behind them in the stabilizing position of a free-fall-acclimated animal. Sinbad lagged behind, not yet as adept in microgravity. Another clue to the identity of the *Ariadne*'s crew: they'd evidently spent a lot of time in microgravity, which meant outside of human space where habitats were common.

The two new cats seemed healthy and happy, and Tau was glad he'd decided to let them out of isolation. Sinbad had been more forbearing than he'd dared to hope, for a cat who'd had the entire ship as his own territory for so long. Or perhaps he knew he'd be no match for the two newcomers under these strange conditions they seemed to know so well. Of course the two had not ventured out into the ship yet; they seemed content, for now, to stay in the lab.

Tau straightened up, his gaze on the three cats. If only it was that easy with humans, he thought. Of course, with some people it probably was that easy. But he'd served as medic for a shipful of reticent individualists for years now, and he wasn't sure if he should break habit—no, *tradition*—and get the two on his mind to talk, or to just keep his own mouth shut.

It didn't help when one of the persons under consideration was the captain and the other was the colleague with whom he worked the closest.

"Laboring hard, I see."

Tau looked up, saw Rael Cofort in the hatchway. She was smiling, looking immaculate as always from her coronet of auburn hair to the neat brown uniform. Tau's gaze traveled back up to her face, noted the tired eyes above the smile, and he wondered when he should break that silence.

Perhaps he could better gauge his approach through the relative safety of work. "There's something Captain Jellico wanted me to discuss with you," he said, and watched the subtle flicker in her eyes when he mentioned the captain's name. The captain reacted the same way when Rael was mentioned.

"Have you ever been to Sargol?" he asked.

Cofort looked up from petting the loudly purring Omega. "Never heard of it," she said, smiling. "Except that mention in your records about the plague, and the incident with the drink."

"Good," Tau said. "Then you noted that those who took the drink were the ones who escaped succumbing to the plague."

Cofort nodded, stretching out a hand to Alpha. "And I read your lab reports on the new antibodies in their blood."

"Well, the change in their biochemistry may have gone deeper than we think," Tau said.

Cofort dropped her hands. Now he had all her attention.

"The captain has, as yet, asked me not to discuss it in front of Weeks and the three apprentices, for a number of reasons—mostly to protect them. But it seems they are showing subtle signs of having been affected by the esperite we were exposed to before we landed on Trewsworld."

"Esperite," she repeated in a whisper.

"The exposure was minimalized, and so far none of us older ones have shown any effects, either ill or otherwise. But the young four, the ones who took that drink on Sargol, seem to react to one another's moods without being aware of it. Sometimes they appear to know where the others are, again without thinking about it. Could be coincidence; for the first item, they're all good friends, which would explain shared moods, and as for the second, it might just be logical deductions, for they've all helped each other in duties often enough and can easily extrapolate where the others might be. But . . . it seems to happen rather often."

She nodded, her manner now professional. "But we don't discuss it before the others."

"Before any of the others, actually: as yet only the captain and I have talked it over. Now you know."

She did not make any direct reference to the captain. "What would you have me do?"

"Observe only, for now. If any—incident—occurs you think worthy of notice, get it into the lab reports. I'll show you the password to that particular subdirectory."

She sighed, then straightened up. "Does the captain know you're telling me?"

"No," Tau said. "He's got enough on his mind. But you're a medic, which means you need to be fully briefed."

Her lips tightened, her gaze going abstract, and suddenly Tau took his risk. "As your physician aboard the *Solar Queen*," he said, "I am concerned about you."

Rael Cofort's smile deepened at the corners, and one of her brows lifted with an ironic quirk. "Is there anyone else you are concerned with?"

Craig Tau faced her. "The captain has never been gabby, but I don't remember when I've seen him this taciturn. Both of you have walked around this little ship doing your duties, unfailingly polite, and if you've addressed two words to one another since the day you were chased, I haven't heard either of them. Did you two have an argument?"

"No," Cofort said, pulling herself down into a chair. "We kissed."

Tau whistled.

She laughed softly. "It was a mistake, of course, but I have to admit it was the nicest mistake I've ever made."

Tau expelled his breath in a sigh. "Care to explain?"

She gave a tiny shrug—not enough to bounce her up from her seat—then said, "Perhaps I'd better, if you think it will help. I know Míceál won't talk; it's just not in his nature. I suspect the two of us ought to have talked it out by now— we might even have, had we had the time. But we came back to find the Tooe problem waiting, and then when all that got settled, Kosti's fight, then Ali's . . ." She shrugged again. "The fact is, we're both in love. No, nothing's been said, but I know how I feel, and I can *feel* how he feels. But neither of us is made for the kind of lighthearted fling that Ali, for instance, finds so easy. Love, and leave, and no regrets—no good-byes."

"Then . . . if you do both feel the same way . . ."

"Why don't we do something about it?" Cofort's brilliant eyes lifted toward the lab ceiling, as if she could look through the decking of steel to the captain's cabin. Then her gaze returned to Tau's face. "Because I can feel the conflict in him. For some reason he can't take the risk. And, loving him as I do, if I can't make him happy, I'll try to make him comfortable. If he needs to be loved from a distance, then that's what I'll do. I don't know—maybe there have been too many hard good-byes in his life, and he doesn't want to chance another. I know as well as he does how unstable the Trade life is; I grew up in it. Lost both parents to it."

The light tap of magboots on the deckplates outside the lab made Rael stop. Both doctors faced the hatchway, where Ali appeared, grinning. "Let the cats free?" The expression on his handsome face altered to one of appraisal—and interest. "Did I walk in at the wrong time?"

"Not at all," Rael Cofort said, her poise at least the equal of his. "You're *just* in time to help me recalibrate the chromatographic analyzers."

Tau turned away to hide his grin, and left the lab.

Without any clear plan in mind he demagged his boots and one-handed himself up the ladder. Some idea of finding the captain to assess his appearance flitted through his thoughts, to disappear when Tang Ya shouted down from the control deck, "Got it!"

Tau glanced up the ladder access, saw the upper portion of Ya's broad chest as the comtech grinned down at him.

"Be right there," came Jellico's voice.

A few moments later, they were all crowded into the control area, where Ya could put his data on the big screen. Steen

Wilcox sat with his console lit, the screen glowing with the data that had come with the official transfer of claim of the *Starvenger.*

Ya paged down through the unfamiliar script. Then, as he tabbed quickly, the screen split and data ranked itself in the new screen. Touching his finger to the console, he watched as a highlight bar appeared at a date. Tau noticed it was just a couple of months earlier, by Standard Terran Time.

"Here's the last entry," Ya said. "Note the date."

"Eighteen Standard months after the *Starvenger* was reported abandoned," Wilcox said.

Ya nodded. "Also note the fact that both doctors"—he pointed in Tau's direction—"said that the cats, when we found them, had probably been abandoned from four to ten weeks."

Tau felt the tightening in his gut that indicated danger.

"What's in those last entries?" Jellico asked. "Any indication of what happened?"

"Nothing," Ya said. "Mostly notes on the progress of the hydro, plus notes on her experiments with growing grapes. Our writer was the cook and hydro tech of the *Ariadne.* She was apparently a grandmother—there are references to messages waiting at various stops from her grandchildren—and had been cook on that ship for decades. Nothing whatever about the *Starvenger,* or the names of the supposed owners. Other names show up, but nothing that matches the data from the *Starvenger."*

"So this old date—" Wilcox tapped his screen. "Is it possible that *Ariadne*'s crew found the *Starvenger* and just set up housekeeping on board without bothering to go through channels?"

"If so, then Corlis—that's the cook here—faked up a damn good set of records, going back twenty-seven years. Most of it about plants, and the rest concerning food supplies, meals, eating habits and tastes of the crew, and experiments with growing and cooking."

"A faked set of records, and the other computers cleaned

out," Jellico said. "And the cats, any mention of them?"

"Only once," Ya said. "But it matches what Tau said: one of them had had a litter about a year ago, and they found homes for the kittens on one of their stops."

Everyone looked over at Tau, who nodded. "Alpha was definitely a mother. I'd say within the last year."

Jellico rapped a tattoo with his fingers on the control console as he stared up at the data. "Then that leaves us with one alternative: that ship never was the *Starvenger,* but the name and registry were added."

"Can we take a shuttle and go check?" came Ali's voice from behind, in the hatchway.

Jellico looked up with a grim smile. Next to Ali Rip Shannon stood, his dark eyes narrowed with challenge.

"No," the captain said. "If there's dirty work been done, and the doers are on this habitat, then they're watching just for that. Steen." He turned suddenly to Wilcox.

"Finding it," the navigator said. He'd already started a search, and within moments the big screen flickered, and Ya's data was replaced by the vids of their discovery and capture of the derelict. Steen spooled forward, then enlarged the picture so they could scrutinize the hull where the name and number were painted. There it was, clear and sharp: *STAR-VENGER.* He tabbed the vid forward slowly, but there was no visible trace of any other painting—nothing but that blackened scoring down one side.

"It's got to be under there," Ya said, reaching up to touch the screen. "Though there's no way to recover it."

"Not here," Jellico said. "At Trade there are special stress analyzers and the like to check for that kind of thing. But even if we found it, these people could just say we did it ourselves. We need proof."

"The cats?" Ali asked.

The captain shook his head.

"Could say they were ours," Wilcox spoke up. "Worse, if someone really wanted to make trouble, they could say the cats technically own the ship—"

"But they aren't sentient," Rip protested.

Ali grinned. "Though they seem smarter than some of the idiots we've met of late on Harmonious Exchange."

Some of the others chuckled, but the captain did not crack a smile. "The point is taken, though: if someone wanted to make trouble for us, we could get mired in a legal battle that would ruin us long before anything was decided. No, what we need is some kind of proof—"

"And I think I know where we can get it," said a new voice.

Everyone turned to see Dane Thorson loom in the hatchway behind the other two apprentices, a wide grin on his bony face. "First, though, where's Van?"

"Got a com from someone at the Trade Center," Wilcox said. "Left just after you did."

"Well, I can tell it all over again," the apprentice cargo master said. He pointed down at Tooe, who stood at his elbow. "I went up to her hideout." He paused, sending an anxious look at the captain. Jellico's face hadn't changed. Dane scraped a big hand through his yellow hair, making it stand up wildly. "I know it's off limits, but she kept talking about it, and I had this instinct to go. Strong one. So—well, I did. Anyway, the short version is, her people deal in data trade, and they have a link on what might be the rotten connection in the Trade office. They're looking for data for us."

"And in trade, what do we give them?" Jellico asked.

To everyone's surprise, Thorson's lean cheeks showed color. "Uh, as it turns out, we won't have to."

"Save Momo," Tooe spoke up in her high voice, which reminded Tau of a bird. "Shver hunt, try to kill Momo, Dane save. We get data for Dane," she finished proudly.

"Were you seen?" the captain asked.

Dane grimaced. "I'm afraid so." He explained quickly; Tau winced, remembering his own encounter with cryo once—those burns were excruciating, even without freeze amputation.

"That's bad," Steen muttered.

Rael Cofort, coming up from behind, said, "Not necessarily. Those Shver youths are not supposed to be up there— at least technically—but more important, they won't make a public issue of the fight due to pride."

Dane nodded his corroboration. "That's what I thought as well." He made a face. "Though they'll remember it, and we've already had a kind of run-in with someone from Clan Golm."

Cofort smiled at him, her deep blue eyes bright. "You seem to make a habit of rescuing people."

Now Dane's face was deep red, and he looked down, as if someone had attached a new pair of feet to his legs. "Anyone here would have done it—probably better," he mumbled. Then he looked up. "Anyway, we set up a signal system. One of Nunku's gang will give us the signal if she gets any data."

As everyone began talking, Dane sidled over to Tau and said, "I've got a question about Nunku." Tau listened in growing surprise and pain as Thorson described the weird leader of Tooe's gang. "Do you think there's any way to help her?"

Tau sighed. "I don't have the technology. From what you describe, she probably was taken at a very young age into free fall—"

"She was," Dane said. "Escaped, actually. Taught herself everything, including Terran, since she knew she'd been born Terran." He scratched his head. "You should hear her! All she could get when she was little was a vid-tape of some ancient historical plays, and she learned off that. Didn't know it wasn't current—or true!"

Tau shook his head, trying to imagine one's single reference point to Terra being a piece of fiction about a time a millennium ago. "Remarkable. Well, as for her physiological growth, I'm afraid that's remarkable as well: the living in free fall while still growing, combined with what was inevitably a poor diet, made her bones grow the way you describe. There are probably places that could treat someone like that, probably with some form of electromediated calcium involution, but it would cost as much as our ship is worth for the medtech."

Tooe's yellow eyes switched from Tau to Dane and back as each spoke. Now she said, "No Nunku leave. She stay in Spinner, stay with klinti people, never leave. Knows data, knows console, likes nest."

Tau winced. It sounded like a hellish life to him, but from the sound of it Nunku had found a niche for herself and her gifts. "We won't interfere, Tooe," he said.

As Dane and Tooe started away, Rael Cofort slid up to Tau's other side. "If I can, I'd like to go up there with them and see if there's anything I can do," she said quietly.

Tau nodded. "We can research the syndrome, and make up a packet of mineral supplements and whatever else might be needed—"

"Well," came the mellow voice of Jan Van Ryke.

Tau broke off, looking up as the cargo master bounced in, his white brows soaring.

"Something to report?" Jellico asked.

"Something indeed," Van Ryke said, grinning. "A mysterious person has offered to buy the *Starvenger* from us. At twice the going rate, I should mention. Take her as is, no questions asked, just sign over the papers, take our credit, and run." He paused, looking around at his audience.

"And?" Steen prompted, knowing the cargo master of old.

"And, it seems, our good friend Tapadakk is now desperate to sell us a fine cargo once we come into some money."

"So he knows about the offer, then," Jellico said.

"It seems so." Van Ryke nodded, rubbing his hands.

"Twice?" Frank Mura said, from behind Dane Thorson. "We going to take it, Captain?"

Jellico looked around. The entire crew, except for the two on duty at the *Starvenger,* were gathered around the narrow accessway to the control deck. Tau saw intensity in each face as they waited for the captain to answer.

"Talk it out in the mess," the captain said, pointing below.

With speed born of long practice the crew members dropped down to the galley level and crowded into the mess cabin. With the two missing, there were still twelve, Tau realized as he sat in his usual place, next to Frank Mura. The engine crew usually sat in a group, and the cargo master and his apprentice nearby, Dane standing so his long arms and legs didn't get in anyone's way. The rest filed in. Rael Cofort stood near Tau, and the little Rigelian ranged herself alongside Dane. She pushed herself up towards the ceiling and touched him occasionally on the shoulder with her foot as she drifted down, keeping herself high enough to see over the Terran heads. Tau noticed she now oriented her head to the same direction as the Terrans, unlike her behavior when she was first discovered.

The captain scanned them once again, his hard face impossible to read.

"Who wants to sell?"

The others looked around, then Karl Kosti said, "I do. And I think I speak for Jasper as well. We know what runnin' two crews is like—we did that with the *Space Wrack*."

"He's got a point," Ya said.

"Except there are more of us now—and new crew is not impossible to find," Van Ryke put in. "True, we can't go back to Terraport and trust Psycho to select crew for us, but I'm confident in our own abilities to find people who will synch in. We've had good luck so far." And he gave a gallant bow in Rael Cofort's direction.

The captain did not look up. "Anyone else?"

No one spoke. Rip Shannon's dark eyes were narrowed with suppressed feeling, and Ali rubbed his knuckles restlessly against his other palm.

"If we accept the offer, we drop the investigation," Jellico said. "If we drop the investigation, then we've made a mistake."

"But we haven't," Ali protested.

Wilcox muttered in a low voice, "That's what we have to settle."

Jellico nodded once. "Exactly. We're legally liable if we sell, knowing there's something crooked. And I have to add, we'd deserve everything they throw at us."

Several people murmured, then fell silent.

Jellico smiled slightly. "Now, if you really believe we're chasing space dust . . ."

Kosti said, "There's something stinking about this deal. I admit, my first thought was to get rid of it—let some other poor slob deal with it, and run with the money." He shook his head. "We ought to ride it until it lands—or crashes."

"*Starvenger* or *Ariadne*," Rip said, "they were Traders, just like us. We owe it to them to solve this thing."

Jellico assessed them once again, and his expression lightened fractionally. "Do I have a consensus, then?"

He waited for the "Aye, Captain"s and "Yes, sir!"s to die away, then turned to Van Ryke. "I think it a mistake to turn this down flat. Can you spin it out?"

Jan laughed, and rubbed his hands as he drifted up slightly from his place. "Can I!" he repeated, with every evidence of pleasure. "Nothing would suit me more than to use some of Tapadakk's same techniques on him. Yes, Captain, if need be, I can spin out the negotiations until our Kanddoyd friend goes into his old-age molt."

They all laughed, and Jellico said, "Thorson, brief the cargo master on what you and Tooe learned. Then we'll all sit down and plan a strategy."

14

★

A light tap at the door of Rael's cabin broke her concentration. With a surge of regret, she marked her place in the datafile on blood antibodies and stored it before opening her door.

Outside was Dane, looking huge, awkward, and shamefaced. As always, it was hard to believe that this was the same man who had dashed through fire—facing imminent explosion—to save people, or had had the courage to force his way into a vid station and make a broadcast to all of Terran space, colonies included. Or the same man who had gently earned the trust of two terrified brachs, brought to sentience through the influence of esperite—

Esperite.

Did Dane know how much he had changed since the first day he'd come aboard the *Queen*? Right now he obviously didn't feel any different, she thought wryly as she grabbed up the knapsack of supplies that she and Craig had chosen, using the reaction to push herself against the deck as she strapped it on. At least it wasn't just her. She'd caught the same look of slightly distrustful bemusement on his face when Ali was in his drawling, sardonic moods. It seemed to have something to do with personal beauty—a subject that it just didn't do to bring up when one of the objects of distrust was oneself, she thought with an inward smile as she whisked out of her cabin and tabbed the door shut.

Following Dane and Tooe to the outer hatch, she abandoned her own thoughts and listened with growing curiosity to the rapid conversation between the little Rigelian and the cargo apprentice. They conversed in a mixture of languages with a speed that argued a half-year's acquaintance, and not just a few days'. Remembering what Tau had told her, Rael felt a prickle of awe—and uneasiness. Mindful of his caution, she repressed the urge to question Dane about how he'd managed to understand Tooe so fast.

Tooe led them to a lonely corner of a storage area, then said, "We go now." And she pulled herself into an old air shaft.

Dane demagged his boots and pulled himself after, Rael following. Before long they were in free fall, which made the trip much easier.

What she saw depressed her, the more so as they penetrated deeper into the older parts of the Spin Axis, for Tooe led them through spaces not designed for sentient life, a wasteland of abandoned machinery and cargo and the infrastructure that made life on the cylome possible—for no artificial biome could be as stable as a planet.

But is that so different from a human city? she thought suddenly. *They too have their ugly underbelly.*

But nothing like this. The lack of orientation, the gloom and drifting fog from leaking pipes, the weird ropes and catwalks stretching crazily in every direction, the flickering shadows cast by bulky junk of unknown origin—Rael found herself wishing she could wake from a dream far too like nightmares that had haunted her years ago, of being lost in a world that made no sense. What did this life do to those who lived it?

There were only two of Tooe's group in the nest right then, besides Nunku, who was immediately recognizable. Tooe launched herself straight over to the two members, who were working with fine tools at some kind of complicated engine part, and started chattering in a quick Kanddoyd patois. Dane hovered nearby, listening intently.

Rael's first glimpse of Nunku suffused her with pity. She drew near, and saw the childish head lift on its thin neck. The contrast between head and neck made Nunku's head seem distorted. Rael studied the thin, pale skin, which was almost as bleached as that of the Venusian colonist, Jasper Weeks, the attenuated limbs, and the intelligent, expressive eyes. As yet she made no move to touch her gear.

"Thank you for permitting me to come up here," Rael said.

Nunku smiled a little wryly. "Tooe and Momo clamor prodigiously to adopt yon lanky crewmate into our klinti," she said, using the Kanddoyd word for nest/primary family. "But Tooe also seeketh to adopt into thy ship klinti."

Rael nodded, delighted by the idea of a ship klinti. A brief reflection made her realize that the term actually was more appropriate than not. She thought, *We really are a kind of klinti, at least as I understand the word, just as this group is.*

Nunku's mouth pressed into a line and she added, "I confess, I know not yet whether she sees the dilemma."

Rael drew in a deep breath. She had not considered that aspect of things. For the crew of the *Queen*, the question had revolved around Tooe's trustworthiness, and beyond that, what she could contribute. It was assumed she had no ties of any importance—which was pretty much the way any new crewmate was regarded.

"Once we resolve our difficulties here, she will have to address that," she said.

Nunku gave a little nod, and as a ripple of colored lights

flickered on the console near her, she turned and regarded the complicated, unique computer system she had rigged.

Her thin fingers tapped out a code, the computer hummed briefly, and a chip appeared. Then Nunku folded her hands and faced Rael again. "For what purpose hast thou come?"

"I am a physician," Rael said, having decided in the short time she had observed Nunku to speak the truth. "I will do my best to help you, if in turn you can help me by telling me about your background and permitting me to do a diagnostic scan. The data I gather might in turn help another like you one day."

Nunku nodded again, as Rael had thought she would. "Data," she said. "Another word for it is power. Willingly. What wilt thou have first?"

"I can run the diagnostic right now, if you tell me how you got here, and what made you stay?"

"I am Terran-born, as thou hast probably surmised," Nunku said. "I think I had five years when we came here. I do not remember much about my family; over the years I have gathered bits of information which maketh me conclude that they were a mixed crew of Kanddoyd, human, and other races, and the ship was not a registered Trader, but sometimes a smuggler, operating on the fringes of the law."

Rael listened as she read the readout on her scanner. Profound endocrinological imbalances, a crazily perverse calcium-phosphorus balance, enzymes that the machine didn't recognize—she blinked, amazed at the extent of the girl's adaptations. Any one of these indications would normally be fatal, but together they somehow balanced into life. Rael felt tears sting her eyes at this fresh evidence of the plasticity of the human genome, and the cost of that plasticity.

"That they did exist on the edge of the law is partly proved by the fact that I cannot find anything on them in Trade records, and I have spent much time searching," Nunku continued, evidently not noticing Rael's reaction, or choosing to ignore it. "That is, I trow, a negative proof. A positive one is the last memory I have, which was a great excitement among the adults. I didn't understand it—I have only a bright image in my memory of my father grabbing my mother and saying, 'We got it! We got it! We'll be able to sell it for a fortune—but we have to get away today before they find out.' Then a great deal of activity, including the buying of stores. It was thus I was separated from my people, whilst we ran through a crowd on one of the lower concourses. My memory provideth me with my own terror at all the tall figures around me, all of them strangers. The next thing I remember is being put in one of the detention cells, against my family being found. I surmise now that can only mean that someone had discovered who I was, and what the crime was. Identification has eluded me, alas, for I have not breached the fire walls protecting the Monitor system," she concluded with a wan smile. "I could, of course, but I would probably be discovered in the process." She felt under a neat stack of printouts for a chip, then turned to Dane. "Speaking of which, here is thine access. I've crafted a ferret program that will burrow through the walls in the registry computers. I feel confident that it will bring the needed data—but we will only have this one chance."

"You mean it will trigger counterprograms?" Dane asked.

Nunku waved her hand. "It is so."

"Will that bring the Monitors here?" Rael asked quickly, looking around the nest.

"No, for next I was going to request that thee insert it somewhere. It matters not where, though preferably in the console belonging to some knave who hath done thee ill, for the entry point will be traced. The data will not be directed to thy ship or here, but to a general mail drop down in the Shver area, at one of the rental accesses."

"And if they find out?" Dane asked. "I'll be walking into a trap?"

"Thou must sound the drop first, from somewhere else," she said. "That's easy enough. If they've breached it, you'll know, for I've arranged for that too: you'll only hear this signal if the ferret hasn't been violated. The moment it is, it will self-destruct." She tabbed the audio on her console, and they all heard a bell tone in four distinctive notes.

"So they won't know where you are, but they'll know someone is in the system," Rael said. "And they'll want to find out who."

Nunku nodded. "It's a risk—" She stopped.

Rael turned her head, heard a faint whistle.

"Comes Liuqeeq," Tooe chirped.

Everyone waited in silence, Dane looking soberly down at the chip in his hand. A minute or so later the whistle came, louder, and then a tall, furred being jetted in, spiraling down expertly and stopping himself by catching hold of a tube just above Nunku's area.

"I talk," Liuqeeq honked in a strange version of Terran. "I talk to Fozza, Fozza talk to Zham of Clan Marl, talk to Kanddoyd ally, find out—yes, Clan Golm hire roofnub chase *Solar Queen* captain."

"Roofnub—thugs," Rael translated to herself.

"Clan Golm, eh?" Dane said, with a martial grin. "Well. That helps narrow down the choices for where to insert this thing." He brandished the chip. "Ever heard of baseball?"

Nunku and her klinti all shook their heads.

"Well, it's a Terran game, an old one, but all you need to remember is this: three strikes and you're out. Clan Golm just made three strikes." He spun the chip in the air and caught it. "Now they're going to be out."

"Golm not good," Liuqeeq said.

"Clan Golm get three strikes of fate," Tooe chirruped with immense satisfaction, and she and the others started jabbering in their own language as Dane, grinning, looked on.

Rael turned to Nunku. "Meanwhile, let me give you these mineral supplements, which ought to help you . . ."

Rip Shannon dug into the hot food that Mura had prepared, listening as Tang Ya, Steen Wilcox, Craig Tau, and the captain talked at the other table.

"I probably could design something," Ya was saying. "Or

even Rip over there—he's got a knack with the data-running. The problem is, we don't know the system here, which has to be at least several hundred years old, and it's not human-designed."

"I thought computers ran more or less on the same principles," Jellico said, rubbing the blaster scar on his cheek.

"Bits and bytes," Tau said, smiling.

Wilcox leaned back, his long, somber face thoughtful. "It's true enough when you look at the basics. But past that—and with a computer system as old and as complex as Harmony's doubtless is, you're soon past it—you come to variations in design which can differ as much as languages and customs do. Age adds its own idiosyncracies. Given enough time, someone as good as Ya here could figure out how to crack the system, but we don't have the time."

"Speaking of time . . ." Jellico's hand dropped. "Thorson has been gone too long. I don't like having to depend on these Spin Axis people, for to all intents and purposes they are criminals."

Rip thought about Dane, and as before, he got a brief but vivid picture of his fellow apprentice. "He's on his way," he spoke without thinking.

The others turned to study him. The captain and the other control deck officers merely looked surprised, but the medic's eyes were narrowed in an odd expression.

"How d'you know that?" Ya asked.

Rip shrugged, the image gone. "I don't know for certain," he admitted. "I guess it's just a logical guess: he's been gone long enough."

The odd expression was gone from the medic's face. Tau now looked mildly interested as he lowered his jakek bulb and said, "Maybe Jasper knows for certain. Where is he?"

Rip felt the same flash, and said, "In the lab with the cats." It came out without thought.

The captain looked across at Tau, who smiled blandly, then he grunted. "Hope you're right, Shannon. We need to get moving if we're going to act at all."

They all returned to their meal, no one speaking until the clatter of boots on the deckplates indicated arrivals.

Dane Thorson, Tooe, and Rael Cofort appeared, all of them looking pleased. "Got it," Thorson said, brandishing the type of chip that Kanddoyd computers took. "All we have to do is get it into the system."

Tang Ya gave a quick frown. "I suppose we can do that here, if I design an interface—"

Rael Cofort raised a hand. "No, it has to be somewhere else. Nunku says her ferret will probably be traced to the port of origin."

"So," Dane said, turning to Rip with a grin, "we thought we'd make a little visit to the Jheel of Clan Golm who was so helpful, and start things there."

"But he's gone, isn't he?" Rip asked. "Festival of the Dancing Sprool? Three months' hibernation?"

"Tooe's friend Momo went over there to check, and he's right at his desk," Dane said. "In fact, it's almost all Shver on duty right now."

Wilcox whistled softly. "What arrogance!" he exclaimed. "Did he really think we'd never go back there again?"

Rael Cofort's fine brow quirked ironically. "We Terrans might look all alike to most Shver, but we don't to the Kanddoyds, at least to the ones who work at the Trade registry. I'm sure he has friends among the facilitators who would warn him if the *Queen*'s crew is coming, and then he could conveniently disappear again."

"Either that or just pull the silent treatment again," Rip said.

Cofort frowned slightly. "It does seem significant, doesn't it, this coincidental proliferation of Shver behind the counters at communications?"

"Nobody messes with Shver," Rip said grimly.

"Except us," Dane added, grinning.

Rip liked the look of that grin. It promised action. Rip was very ready for some action. "When are you going?" he asked.

Dane shrugged. "Captain?"

Jellico gave a curt nod.

"No time like the present," Dane said, and he looked up at Rip. "Coming to help?"

"Wouldn't miss it," Rip said, putting his half-eaten meal in the cooler for later.

They managed to get a maglev pod to themselves. As soon as the doors hissed shut, Rip said, "He's bound to remember us. Won't that make a problem?"

"Not if Tooe and I go in first and decoy him," Rael Cofort said.

Rip looked over at her in surprise.

Dane grinned. "She said she wouldn't be left out. And it does make things easier for us. We simply stay out of sight while they distract the Jheel, one of us is on hand to distract anyone else who might see, the other inserts the chip and gets it started, then—" He clapped his big hands. "We're in."

Rip chewed his lip, thinking swiftly. "I think we'd better go in separately as well," he said. "We don't know who talks to who in there, but you're probably right about those locutors and facilitators, Dr. Cofort. We'd better assume that there's plenty of communication behind the scenes."

"Tooe," Rael said, "you speak good Kanddoyd, don't you?"

"Speak perfect, me," Tooe said, slapping her scrawny front.

"Then you can assure all the locutors and other functionaries that we are merely on a sightseeing tour," Rael said. "But—do you know where the communications office is?"

"Yes," Tooe said, her pupils narrowing to vertical slits. "Many, many times Tooe is in Trade place, listen, learn, watch. They do not see Tooe, but Tooe see everything."

"After three visits," Rip said, "I've got the place mapped in my head. We can detour the help and make our way there by a circuitous route."

"Then let's set a time to meet outside the com office,"

Dana said. "Fifteen minutes from entry. Agreed?"

Everyone nodded, and just then the pod slid to a halt outside their stop.

Rip rather enjoyed the next fifteen minutes. Each functionary they met they exchanged compliments with, never giving a hint of their business. Rip exerted himself to outtalk the Kanddoyd talkers, praising every bush, flower, and mosaic they passed. He even stopped once and praised the sight of the elevators moving slowly along the cylinders. The Kanddoyds seemed to be impressed with his wonderful manners.

When it came time to state their business, Dane assured their would-be facilitators that they were there to check the latest monetary exchange rates, but first they just wanted to walk along and chat with other Terrans. Three of the functionaries who accosted them seemed to accept this and went on their way; one also appeared to accept it, but this one's ultrasonic noises tweaked at Rip's nerves and made Dane's ring-brooch glow a telltale blue.

Both men pretended not to notice anything amiss. When the Kanddoyd had retreated, Dane murmured, "Glad our time is up. That one is off to blab, or I'm a Cytherian raptor-slug."

"I don't think you need to grow fangs and start crawling through slime yet," Rip muttered out of the side of his mouth. "I think I just saw our friend duck into the elevator leading to the registry department."

"Warning Koytatik?" Dane suggested. "Interesting thought."

They arrived outside the communications office. Tooe and Rael were just inside; as soon as the Rigelian saw the two *Queen*'s men, she grinned as she pulled a flat case from inside her shabby, loose clothing.

Looking swiftly to see that no one watched, she opened it and divided its contents with Rael Cofort, who accepted her portion into cupped hands.

As Rip and Dane watched from just beyond the doorway, Tooe went to the customer keyboards farthest from the Golm

Jheel's counter, and carefully opened her hands. Then she stepped back and shrieked on a high note.

Business stopped. Tooe pointed and yelled, "Spiders!"

Just then Rael Cofort, who had sidled up to the Jheel's counter while he—and everyone else—was looking in the other direction, opened her hands, and Rip saw tiny black specks scuttle over the counter. Cofort backed hastily and stared up at one of the signs as though her thoughts were parsecs away.

The Jheel turned back to his computer, reached to close it down, then jumped back. He let out a bellow, and a second later there was a stampede of hooming, growling Shver heading for the closest doors.

As the Shver exited, the other customers all started yelling at one another, demanding help, demanding answers, demanding someone find out if the spiders were poisonous. Two people started stomping the ground, and one humanoid scratched at his body through his flight suit, as though something were crawling on his skin. The sight of him sent several more people into a panic.

"Now," Dane said.

Trying desperately to muffle his laughter, Rip followed Dane in and did his best to guard the counter from view as Dane reached over with his long arm and dropped Nunku's chip into a slot on the Jheel's computer, which was still online. He tabbed the ACCEPT, waited for the download light to blink, then he hit the EJECT, grabbed the chip, and backed away.

Rip backed in the other direction, making his way through the noisy crowd for the door.

He dove through a moment after Dane, and they saw Rael and Tooe just passing across a little bridge toward one of the exits.

Rip managed to hold in his laughter until they reached the concourse, but when he saw Cofort gripping the rail above a thousand-foot drop, her hands clutching weakly and her body convulsed in mirth, he gave way.

The four of them stood there for a time, whooping until they had completely lost their breath.

Finally, exhausted, Cofort said, "Well done—all four of us. Now let's go tell the captain that we're in the battle."

15

★

"**We're just about** out of funds," Frank Mura said, coming into the galley mess. "Another day and we'll be dipping into the red."

Dane Thorson, sitting with Jasper and Rip in the corner, exchanged glances with his compatriots. Ali had said once, "When Frank's upset he hides his hands behind his back." Frank stood in the hatchway, firmly anchored by his mag-boots, his countenance stolidly blank as ever, but neither hand was visible.

He wants us to leave Exchange.

Dane felt the thought impact his brain as if someone had spoken out loud. They were all three thinking the same thing, he knew.

"Can they cut off life support?" Mura went on.

Steen Wilcox shook his head. "No, they can't—unless they want to risk breach of contract, and then our debt is nulled. The account is payable when we officially notify them of our blast time and they relinquish life support over to us."

Johan Stotz, who was sitting with a pocket comp next to his food, looked up and said, "But if we can't pay our shot, then we get impounded before we can fire up the jets. Look, Chief, didn't Ross tell you that the head of the trilateral Trade office, this Flindyk, is by-the-books, straight-beam honest? If so, why don't we just go lay this in his lap?"

"Is Ross honest?" Wilcox countered.

"Good question," Kosti growled.

"I've yet to hear of any Patrol rankers being corrupt," Jellico said from his place between the jet man and the astrogator, "but that doesn't mean it hasn't happened. As for Flindyk, I've tried three times to get an appointment with him, but his flunkies fall all over themselves relating how sorry they are to report his unending series of crises that prevent my getting on the schedule. As for Ross, he may not be corrupt, but I think he's worthless."

Rael Cofort glanced up from her seat near the galley. Tau was taking his turn on the *Starvenger,* so she kept busy with a pocket comp as she ran through lab statistics. Her eyes narrowed, and she said, "I've only seen him twice, and that for a short time, but he didn't seem the corrupt type. And believe me, I've encountered plenty of those. He was more . . . detached."

" 'Detached' is a fine way of putting it," Van Ryke said, his mellow voice contemplative. "It seems odd for a Patrol type to stay so silent. I'd thought we'd get a warning after Karl's and Ali's little encounters, if nothing else."

Jellico laid his hand flat on the table. "We'll go to Administrator of Trade Executed in Perfect Harmony Flindyk— and Captain-Legate Ross—and demand a hearing when we have concrete proof. Until we know otherwise, we'll assume that they are honest, and that the trouble is unknown to them. A few enterprising underlings hiding their activities from their authorities."

"I just hope our proof points to something," Wilcox said. "I don't like how the clues, if you can call them that, seem completely unconnected."

"I just hope it's soon," Mura said tightly. "It'd better be, or we'll solve someone's problem, just to end up with our own—in jail, for debt, or free of debt but no ship with which to blast out of here." With that he retreated into the galley.

Mura's departure seemed to be the signal for a general breakup.

Wilcox and Stotz were ready to head down to the one-gee-level gym to work out. Jasper Weeks and Karl Kosti disappeared to engine territory and a project they had going for an upgrade to the macronuclear prefilters, based on some tech they'd discovered on the *Starvenger*. Rael Cofort moved toward the down-ladder, probably to wake up Tooe. Dane knew they were going back up to the Spinner, though he didn't know why.

He also knew it was time for him to head down to the Shver territory and check the mail drop. His palms felt damp. He rubbed them down his trousers, then got up quickly. If he had to do it, best get it over with fast.

The maglev to the surface was nearly empty, though along the way it picked up more Shver, which was not surprising. Dane stayed motionless on his seat, not meeting anyone's eyes directly, and no one molested him. He listened to the talk around him, figuring it was good practice. He rather liked the Shver voices. They sounded like a distant thunderstorm, only pleasingly resonant.

As the maglev sped toward the surface Dane looked out the windows at the gently curving landscape. This, he realized, was where Exchange really got the first part of its name—the Shver had made the inner surface of the habitat into a vast garden. Though there were farms everywhere, the trees, hills, streams, and rows of crops were pleasant to a human eye. If you ignored the up-curving horizon, it almost reminded a person of the unruined portions of Terra.

He was so fascinated he was scarcely aware of the steady increase in gravity pull. They'd reached 1.0 grav while still well above the inner surface. Now, as they neared it, when he moved slightly there was the faintest drag on his joints, a little as if he had some kind of flu. His body felt heavy; he straightened up and accommodated his breathing in the way he'd been taught at Trade Pool years ago.

Heavy grav did not come much in his way. The cost of fuel—and added stresses on the ship—to land on and depart a heavy-grav planet was tremendous, and none of the crew liked the stress on their bodies. But the prospect of a good cargo would cause Free Traders to land anywhere, and Dane had paid attention to learning how to cope in this environment.

The maglev presently stopped at a Shver outpost. Their homes, of course, were well hidden by the forests of trees and cleverly designed hills. But the Shver outposts were nicely designed. Dane liked the huge proportions; it wasn't often he entered a room whose ceiling and furnishings made him feel short.

Moving slowly, he stayed out of the way of the briskly marching Shver, and followed them inside. The air was heavily perfumed with scents from the surrounding plants and flowers, and it felt strange in his nose. He sneezed rapidly twice, which made his head ache. None of the Shver inside, standing at their workstations or conversing in small groups, even so much as looked up at the noise, which had sounded thunderous to Dane. Probably because the air was so dense, he decided—it was transmitting sounds more effectively to his ears.

The front area was for business of various sorts, and Dane passed a few humanoids, and even one Kanddoyd youth, who looked oddly compressed into his carapace.

Dane scrutinized the holographic signs, and recognized the sigils for "Communication." He passed through a high arching doorway into a smaller chamber. The com room was, he was glad to see, fully automated, just as Nunku had promised. He entered his ID, waited, and his heart started pounding when the computer screen indicated he had one e-letter waiting. He got it in print and chip form, paid in cash, zipped both the printout and the chip into his belt pouch, and left.

No one else had come in. No one paid any attention to him as he retreated to the maglev concourse. He restrained himself from touching the pouch until he was safely in a pod by himself. Then he pulled out the printout and scanned it.

The first search field was "Solar Queen," and a listing had come almost promptly, Dane realized, as he looked at the header which gave the time the data had been found. It was within minutes after he had inserted the chip into the Jheel of Clan Golm's system. The name was in a poorly protected security area in the Jheel's own system, and the words were in Shver. Dane puzzled slowly at it, resorting to his belt translator once or twice until he had the gist of it: the Jheel of Clan Golm was ordered, by Prime Facilitator Koytatik, not to deal in any way with crew members of either the *Solar Queen* or the *Starvenger*. And the date in the sent order's header was . . . Dane calculated rapidly, and realized with a flush of indignation that it had to be within scarce minutes after he and Rip had received the official registry claim on the derelict.

He went on to the second field, which was "Starvenger." This file was a very long one.

At first the words didn't seem to add up to anything particularly nefarious or even exciting. It was merely a list of ships lost or abandoned whose quitclaims were duly registered through Trade. The list went back twenty-five years, and the number was a lot higher than Dane would have expected. How high would the number be if the list included those ships lost under mysterious circumstances and not claimed? Scanning rapidly, Dane was reminded yet again how dangerous was this life he had chosen, and he felt the danger weigh in his chest like the pull of the Shver's gravity. But he thrust the misgiving away impatiently, knowing that if he were standing at Pool again, a raw teen fresh from the Home, he would still walk through those doors and ask for training.

He scanned the list again more slowly, and this time some of the components caught his attention. He saw two of Teague Cofort's ships listed. He saw nearly all of one of the lesser-known Company lines, wiped out at once. Plague, he thought, and this time he didn't bother to fight the shiver. All their vessels must have been infected, forcing them to jettison their entire line. Dane didn't want to know what kind of plague would cause a Company to take such a drastic step.

He saw four I-S ships listed right around the time the *Queen* had first run into trouble with some Eysies. Had their attitude caused the problems, or had the problems caused the attitude? Interesting to speculate. He was so used to thinking of the big Companies as all-powerful, he hadn't considered that they could still have problems of their own. He remembered what Dr. Cofort had said: even big Companies are made of human beings. An obvious statement—and easily forgotten.

Dane reached the bottom of the list, and with more difficulty tried to decode the cryptic abbreviations and signs that seemed to indicate the path Nunku's ferret program had taken. Was this really important to anyone but computer techs? he wondered as he looked it over. The end point was Prime Facilitator Koytatik.

Was this a vector? Not really, he had to admit. It was probably well within her rights to have that data. As for the order, even that might be explained, if he and Rip, by trying to insist on contacting the old owners, had inadvertently violated some custom.

But if they had, why hadn't the tapes indicated anything about that custom? He and Van Ryke had done a thorough reading during the dead time in hyper, and Dane knew he'd never seen any mention of this kind of custom.

He sighed, and looked at the last sheet, which was the search for "Ariadne." This flimsy was mostly blank, with a couple of lines of incomprehensible notations.

He was impatient for the long ride back to be over. Not even the gradual lightening of his body as they eased into low grav served to curb his impatience.

At last, though, he reached the end of the journey, and he bounded aboard the *Queen*. He found Jellico waiting, with Rip Shannon. Ya was still asleep, then.

He handed the printout to the captain, and the chip to Shannon, who dropped it into the converter Ya had rigged. A spool of quantumtape popped out, which Rip inserted into the comp.

Within seconds the screen showed pretty much what Dane had already read on the printout.

There was one difference.

When they reached the end, Rip pointed at the screen and said, "Unless I'm totally wrong, what this means is that there are listings for the *Ariadne,* but they are protected behind heavily coded fire walls."

"Will Nunku's ferret break through?"

Rip's dark eyes were considering. "Tang says Nunku is, in her way, a master technician. I expect that, given time, her ferret will break the entire system."

"Given time," the captain repeated.

"Right," Rip said soberly. "These codes here, and here, are reporting having crossed telltale lines."

"Telltales," Dane said. "That means someone knows we're in the system. Though apparently they don't know where, or what we were after, or we'd have been caught by now."

"Right," Rip said again.

Rael Cofort ducked behind a serrated piece of some kind of equipment, peering through a cog hole.

She heard the faint hiss of static, followed by a voice distorted in the way sound is always distorted when amplified through a helmet com. The language was Shver, so the only word she was sure of was "intruder."

The Monitors sped by, the air they stirred smelling faintly of whatever fuel they burned in their gauntlet and ankle jets.

She waited, watching Tooe, who perched motionless behind a huge automated scooping mechanism. Tooe's head was cocked at an uncomfortable angle, her crest flat. Presently the faintest whistle came echoing back, a low, flat note.

Tooe's crest snapped up at a triumphant angle. "Safe!" she whispered. "Now we go."

And she catapulted herself from her perch and ricocheted from the jumble of abandoned farming tools until she had built up speed, then launched through a dark hole. Rael couldn't see what was beyond it, but she launched herself after as hard as she could, her heart hammering in her chest.

The lighting was extremely dim, but Rael got the impression they were crossing a vast space, which left them very vulnerable. She couldn't see, but she knew there were beings who could—and who liked humans only as prey.

She gripped her sleeprod tightly in her left hand, and used her right for navigation as once again Tooe bounced at odd angles down another complicated transition area.

There were no more Monitors—or Spinner habitués. Guided by the whistles, Tooe brought Rael without further incident to the appointed meeting place. She'd hoped that a few of the other denizens of the area might come if she offered free medical care in trade for data.

What awaited her in the weird chamber designated a neutral area by the Spinner people made her stop in amazement.

Perched, lying, clinging, sitting, or curled up was a crowd so large Rael could not count them. No two heads were oriented in the same direction, nor were any of the furnishings— up was entirely a matter of personal choice. And since there were lighting fixtures everywhere, it was impossible to see anything clearly. Monstrous shadows clung to odd corners; elsewhere details washed out in a blaze of light. And the smells! Even her medical training hadn't prepared her for the odor of many beings of radically different genetic backgrounds, in an environment that made washing difficult at best, and even fatal if carelessly approached.

Rael fought dizziness while she looked around, moving her head with painstaking slowness, but no matter how hard she tried she couldn't impose any sense of order on the scene.

So don't try, she thought.

Slowly her vertigo left her; the falling sensation diminished, and she was able to assess her prospective patients. Now she was glad she'd brought the large pack; reflecting that she'd be traveling in null grav, which meant no weight, she'd hauled a good selection of medical supplies, intending to leave them with Nunku for future use. Now, she realized, she would probably use them up and still have people waiting.

She wished Tau was with her, as Tooe started talking in the local patois. Next time, if there was a next time, she'd have to bring him.

As Tooe described the conditions that she and Rael had agreed on earlier, Rael slowly unpacked her kit and set up a kind of clinic. Medicine in null grav, and for races not common to any of her medical books—this was going to be one for a paper, she thought, as the first person approached.

He was Terran, so he didn't need a translator. His age could have been anywhere from fifty to eighty, she realized, looking at the gaunt face and sparse gray hair. Horrible purple blaster burns disfigured a good portion of the left side of his body. He came close, then eyed her, plainly hesitant to speak.

"You understood the terms?" she said gently. "I am not an authority, and have no permission from the Monitors or anyone else but my captain to be here. I don't want your real name or any other details you don't want to give. All I want to know is how you came to be here."

"I'll tell you my name," he growled in a raspy voice that sounded painful to her ears. "Maybe someday I'll get justice— or at least some answers. I'm Kellam Akortu, and I served aboard the *Carthaginia* from boy to man, and then on *Lucky Lucy* for nigh on thirty years. Free Traders, Doctor, like yourself." Rael realized the tattered garments the poor old man was wearing so proudly were the remains of a brown tunic and trousers. "*Lucky Lucy* had a run of bad luck there, back maybe ten, twelve years ago Standard. Old lanes runnin' out of goods, big Companies gobbling up the new stuff. Three auctions we went to, we couldn't even afford Class D planets. So Cap'n Aki says, we're goin' out to new frontiers, out here in Kanddoyd territory, where they are friendly with humans, and might think our stuff worth something."

"Here, just stretch out this way," Rael murmured. "I need to use the scanner to determine the best way to help you. Please, keep talking."

The man eased himself out flat before her; it was evident that even in free fall he moved bent and twisted to accommodate badly healed burns.

"Well, the cap'n was right. We got onto a hot thing. Planet the Shver had left, due to radiation on the surface. Kanddoyds went underground, found minerals galore. Used our mining tools, and we were going to split the profits. Kanddoyds radioed ahead to Exchange, and we went into hyper together, came out together—and the Kandder ship suddenly goes boom!" He gently snapped his fingers. "We all saw it on our screens. Thought it was an engine goin' supercrit or something, their tech being different from ours. But before we could do anything, Cap'n yelled at our navigator to take evasive action, and for crew to stand by in the life pods."

Akortu shook his head slowly. "I was steward, so my station was nearest the pods. I was the only one who got in one before someone commenced firing. Or if I wasn't, I was the only pod got away—though I took a hit." He touched his burned side. "Zoomed off, pod sending SOS signal, and it was a Shver ship took me in. Long range, they got. Big cutter, maybe scared off the pirates or whoever. Anyway, they brought me here, put me in the lazarette, but Trade authorities wouldn't believe my story, said I'd sabotaged my ship, and there I was, no ID, no cred—nothing. Well, with that talk o' sabotage, I could see what was comin', and when I was supposed to be asleep, I snuck out and hid out up here. Better than what seemed ahead. What's that?"

"It's a sprayjector. It won't take the scarring away—you'd have to be lazed for that—but it will suffuse your damaged tissues with a special kind of collagen and give you elasticity again, or at least some. These burns here and here are very deep, and they didn't heal right."

The man lay quiescent, so she proceeded with her treatment. After a minute or so he sighed. "Already feels better," he said. He stirred, was about to push away, then he half turned and muttered, his posture partly hostile and partly shamefaced, "You know what I been doin' since I got up here, right?"

She shook her head. "Existing," she replied. "That's all that matters right now."

He touched her hand. "Thankee, Doctor."

And he was gone, replaced by a tall, feline being who looked like an Arvas. She had a missing limb. This time Tooe translated as the being talked in a sibilant murmur. Rael cleared her scanner and called up the data on the Arvas race, then moved it slowly over the female as Tooe told in her peculiar mix of languages a story that was disturbingly like Akortu's.

The amputated limb could not be helped—it was an old wound—but the being was suffering from a severe mineral deficiency, a mineral crucial to her race but unused by the Shver, Kanddoyds, or humans. Rael had some in her pack, and gave the Arvas a sprayjection, promising to try to obtain more.

The next story was even more disturbing; this was one of Tooe's gang, who were mostly young. This being had been accidentally left behind when his family departed on a Trade run. It was merely a prank, and he did receive a message from the first stop that they were returning for him—but after that his family's ship seemed to have vanished from the universe. Trade insisted they had no record of their movements; meanwhile he was running up a debt that could only be worked off in a work camp—so he panicked and ran.

That had been five Standard years ago.

The stories were taking on some unsettling similarities, Rael thought as she worked tirelessly to mend diseased or battered sentients from an astonishing variety of backgrounds. Even granted that some were lying, it still added up to a statistically impossible set of coincidences.

She worked without recourse to her chrono, until her

back felt like it was on fire and her arms got so tired she could scarcely control her instruments. And finally she ran out of supplies, and got Tooe to promise that they would return again, and she packed up, quietly turning off the recorder she had secreted in her pack.

In silence she and Tooe retreated to the *Queen*.

In silence she boarded. Jellico was suddenly there, his hard gray eyes searching, but he asked no questions, just pointed to her cabin.

She made it down, and meant to shower, but instead she lay on her bunk to rest her eyes, and finally the tears came. She wept because she was tired, because she couldn't possibly help them all, because of some terrible, vast injustice whose cost in terms of the innocent might not be solvable. She wept because the universe didn't seem to care, and when she was empty, she dropped into a deep sleep, and dreamed of a weird chamber, and endless lines of broken, hopeless beings turning to her for succor.

16

Craig Tau stowed his kit aboard the shuttle, and watched as the *Starvenger* spun out of view, bringing the vast bulk of the habitat across the viewport. Beyond hung a gray hopeless arc of light, the marginal planet below that served merely as a spacetime anchor for the orbiting habitats. Just a hole in space, Craig thought, shaking his head. Microgravity was stressing them all—he sometimes wondered if they shouldn't adopt Tooe's disorienting approach, and give up the battle to pretend acceleration. Though he had noted that the four younger men were using their magboots a lot less often than they had on first arriving. The four apprentices seemed to be adjusting the quickest to the stressfully unnatural biorhythms of habitat life and the bewildering amount of strange and new technology surrounding them.

The vast bay of the habitat swallowed the shuttle. Now Craig felt like he was diving up into the maelstrom of ships and lights and machinery and little service vessels, a ceaseless dance of commerce.

But he wasn't watching the activity outside; it was mere backdrop to his thoughts. He'd spent his two days reviewing his initial observations of what he had begun to call the Esperite Effect, and writing up his recent experiences. This was not an easy chore. He was scrupulously careful to report precisely what he had seen and heard, registering his interpretations and hypotheses on another field. At times his text was cluttered with the tiny icons indicating his own views, which totaled three times the wordage of his lab reports. This was fine. It meant someday he might get a clue to what was going on.

It was also preferable to resisting the impulse to reorganize the *Starvenger*'s lab into a replica of the *Solar Queen*'s. He noted rather sadly that the others had stopped taking little items over with them for their two-day stints and then leaving them; he recorded this too, reflecting on how the *Starvenger* had begun, incrementally, to metamorphose into their territory—a process which had halted with Ya's news about the conflicting abandonment dates and the mysterious *Ariadne*.

When the shuttle reached the *Queen*, he went directly down to his quarters to copy his notes into his lab computer, and to make a general status check. The cats were fine, and there were no weird illnesses or nasty accidents recorded in the sick bay log. In fact, there were no notes at all for the past eighteen hours—and, he discovered, a mighty dent had been made in the supplies.

So Rael had made her foray into Spin Axis territory. He wondered how successful she'd been, and went back to check the log for her report. Nothing.

Alarm kindled in him. Had she returned? He crossed the lab toward the up-ladder hatchway just as Rael Cofort emerged from her cabin.

Tau backed inside, frowning at the signs of stress marking her fine skin and expressive eyes. He was about to ask her for a report when she stopped, standing very still, her gaze distracted, and a moment later there was the familiar firm tread of the captain's boots on the deckplates.

"Are you all right?" Jellico addressed Cofort abruptly.

"Of course," Rael said, turning to face the outer corridor.

"Tooe tells us you are planning to go back up there."

"I have to," Rael said. "There's a need."

"Would you obey if I forbid it?"

Cofort smiled, just slightly, but her voice was cool. "I'd have to," she said. "You're the captain, I'm new crew, and not so high in the hierarchy. But before this conversation goes any further, answer me this: would you forbid Craig to go?"

Tau heard a short intake of breath, followed by a long pause. The medic realized first that the captain did not know he was there, and second, though there was nothing personal in the words he heard, the conversation was private.

He was about to retreat back to his lab when Rael Cofort broke it off by turning away from the captain, who was still not in view, and coming inside. After a moment the captain followed, his face impassive except for a tightening along his jaw.

Tau bent to pick up Omega, who instantly began to purr. He straightened up slowly, aware of the magboots imprisoning his feet against the deck. It sometimes took an effort of will not to imagine oneself hanging from the ceiling—there was no sense of one's feet pressing against the deck.

"I'll make my report," Cofort said to Tau, "while you get your update."

Tau turned to the captain, who gave him a terse rundown on the latest news in their mystery. Tau listened to the talk of computer ferrets and lists, but he didn't pay much attention. There were other crew members better qualified to interpret that data. Instead he sifted the captain's words for how the news was taking its toll on the crew.

At the end, he offered no comment, nor did Jellico ask for any. He thanked the captain for the report, then said, "So how is Tooe adjusting? Or should I say, how is everyone adjusting to her?"

Jellico's grim face eased as he gave a slight smile. "She's

divided her time between these runs to the Spinner and sitting in the cargo bay with Thorson cramming data on Trade lingo, and customs, trade, and cargo stowage."

"Could she possibly be a cargo wrangler?" Tau asked doubtfully, thinking of the sinewy Thorson and Jan Van Ryke, whose comfortable-looking bulk hid a very powerful musculature.

"Van and Thorson both insist she knows more about the intricacies of null-grav cargo moving than both of them together. We're used to planetside dealings, and gravity, where size can make a difference. If we're going to push further afield, then we need to adjust to the exigencies of null-grav trade," Jellico said.

Tau, sifting the words, nodded in agreement. "We've access to loading machines if it comes to that. But what I'm hearing here is that they both seem to be in favor of hiring her on."

"At least on a trial basis," Jellico said. "Van put it to me just today. He doesn't want anything said to Tooe yet, though—there's no use in it until we settle our problems with Trade."

Tau sighed. "Right. For a nice moment I'd forgotten that."

Jellico gave a short laugh. "You won't for long. Dane and Ali and Rip will see to that."

Rip Shannon heard a rap on his cabin door.

He opened it, saw Dane standing in the doorway of his cabin across the narrow corridor. Thorson was strapping a sleeprod to his belt. "Ready to go?" he asked.

"You really think we'll need those?" Rip asked as Dane reached into his cabin and pulled out another sleeprod to hand over.

Thorson shrugged. "Nunku and Tang both said that it's inevitable that the ferret is going to trigger alarms, in which case they'll figure out where the data is going. One of these times we're going to find a welcome party waiting for us down there."

"Do these things even work on Shver?" Rip asked as he hastily strapped his to his belt so he'd have both hands free. "With our luck a zap from this will hit them like Dirjwartian Joy Juice and they'll be stampeding after us for more."

"Either that or it just makes them really, really mad," Dane said with a grin. "Anyway, I asked Tau about that. He says these things are a broad-band neural disruptor. They'll deck pretty much any being we've come across—though not for long if they mass a lot, like Shver."

"Long enough for us to show them our heels suits me fine," Rip said. "All right, let's get this over with."

Dane grinned again, leading the way. They left the *Queen* and pulled themselves down the dock. Rip looked around, breathing in the featureless habitat air. If you ignored the weird visual proportions this was like any spaceport: lit at all hours, and busy at all hours. As they moved toward the maglev, Rip wondered if the dock workers lost all sense of the passage of time, or if they had their ways of reestablishing diurnal/nocturnal physiological ryhthms.

The maglev was crowded. Rip hadn't bothered to bring a chrono, since the lack of recognizable (planet-dictated) work-and-sleep cycles rendered time measure meaningless for humans. At least in the Kanddoyd parts of Exchange, it seemed that life went on pretty much round the clock. Though he wondered if they'd inadvertently set out at some generally acknowledged shift-change time, for there were Kanddoyd workers in all of the pods, their fiddle-voices chattering away with the eternal accompaniment of hums, chirps, whistles, taps, and clicks. None of them sat still, but moved about as they communicated.

Rip found that watching them as the pod accelerated was a mistake, especially after the pod emerged from the interior of the habitat's end cap and the interior burst into light around them. The odd horizon out the window and the movement of the pod amid the strangely angled, tube-shaped Kanddoyd domiciles did not accord well with the immediate prospect of Kanddoyds swarming about in zigzag patterns. Dizziness made him clutch at his seat.

He closed his eyes and tried to let the sound pass over him like an audio tide. After a time he had to admit that, so long as he didn't watch the Kanddoyds, their noises were more pleasing than not.

At any rate they did not stay on the pod long; as they started the descent toward the surface and gradually heavier gravity, the Kanddoyds disappeared from the pod, a few at each stop.

For a short time they were alone, then Shver started boarding. Each time Dane eyed the newcomers, his hand straying near his belt. None of the Shver molested them in any way; few of them even looked at the Terran Traders.

Presently Rip's inner ear gave him that steadying sense that one grav affords humans. He stretched out and breathed deeply. All too soon he felt his limbs gain weight, as if his own mass fought against him. He flexed his muscles in some stationary isometrics, figuring he'd turn the experience into a workout.

Presently they started the curve that meant they'd reached the surface, and Rip was relieved. He felt his lungs laboring to breathe; if he tried to breathe too fast, he felt the faintest burning sensation.

He turned to Dane, saw a look that reminded him of Captain Jellico. Dane's bony face was set hard, his jaw grim. But when the pod slid to a halt at their stop, the big cargo apprentice got up with no diminution in his usual speed.

"Walk," Dane said a moment later. "This way."

His voice was quiet. Rip felt his heart rate increase, which was almost painful. He forced his body to move at Dane's pace, being careful to keep his knees slightly bent and to place each foot carefully. He did not want to fall down in this grav—broken or shattered bones were much too likely a result.

"Where's the problem?" Rip asked softly when they were well away from the nearest Shver. He saw the huge, elephantine beings moving about, but none seemed to be particularly menacing.

"Other side of the pod," Dane said, tipping his head back the other way. "A couple of Khelv and a Zhem, all of Clan Golm. I've been learning the clan skin markings as much as I can."

"Where'd you get the data?"

"Here." Dane indicated his eyes. "They won't permit anything written down. But I know what Golm clan looks like now." His deep voice took on a steely edge. "These three were prowling along looking in the pods."

"Then they're onto us?" Rip asked. "Shouldn't we go back?"

"I don't think they are, or they'd be waiting at the mail drop," Dane said. "I'll bet they heard about a Terran Trader being here, which is probably rare enough to put whoever is watching out for that kind of news on his guard. So they're nosing about."

"Khelv . . . Zhem," Rip repeated. "Aren't those levels in the noncitizen rank?"

"Kind of," Dane replied. "It's technically a rank for single beings. A Khelv has only contributed one 'gift' to his or her clan, and they tend to be the hungriest for some kind of score. A Zhem has only one more to make the sacred five; a Jheel has three more. When they reach five, they can find a mate and reproduce, and once they do that, then they get citizenship within the clan, which means speaking rights at clan meetings. They can also be assigned a task in order to advance in rank again."

"Assigned?" Rip asked as they entered the building.

Dane glanced around, as did Rip. To Rip's eyes the Shver seemed peaceable enough; at least they were thoroughly ignoring the Terrans. Dane apparently didn't see the Golm, because he said as he led the way to the communications chamber, "That's right. The group can assign them a task. If they don't like it, or don't complete it, that's it for career advancement. If they refuse out of what the clan terms cowardice, they're cast out."

Rip shook his head slightly, then stopped, feeling his neck twinge.

Both men were silent as Dane tapped his code into the waiting automat. Rip turned his back to Dane and watched the room for any sign of menace.

No one came in. Dane pulled something from the machine and tucked it into his pouch, then said, "Let's move." He was breathing with rapid, shallow breaths, probably from talking so long. Rip could tell that he wasn't put out. In fact there was an instinctive sense, though Rip had no idea where it came from since the big Viking was about as expressive as a sack of coal, that Dane was flattered to have his knowledge sought.

Still, Rip forbore asking any more questions until they were safely back on the maglev. Dane sat tensely, his hand on his sleeprod, until the pod started to move.

Then he relaxed just a little. "There they are," he said, pointing out the window as the pod began to accelerate.

Rip felt the acceleration as added weight, and was disinclined to move far enough to catch a glimpse of the Golm trio. All he saw were three Shver stalking along a grassy path at an oblique angle to the maglev concourse.

"I'm staggering the times of the visits," Dane said. "I wonder how long they've been there?"

Rip had no idea, and did not speak.

Instead, he gazed out the window at the squat, thick-trunked trees that crisscrossed the land in lines, or grew in dark clumps hither and yon. Some of the lines of trees had ditches at one side or another, and Rip remembered someone saying that the Shver were really like the elephants they reminded humans of in that they wouldn't jump. A ditch was as effective as a wall for deterring Shver. At the very idea of having to jump even an inch in the punishing gravity, Rip winced; though the Shver were adapted to their heavy gravity, still, it was a serious business to lift so much mass into the air.

He looked farther, but all he saw was green, and trees, and a few roads. No dwellings were visible, of course, only business-related buildings.

Presently the pod swooped up, pressing them back against their seats, and soon the grav began to ease. The sensation of climbing gave way gradually to forward movement as the pressure on his body dissipated.

Suddenly Dane took a deep breath, and he rubbed his neck. "Whew," he said. "Takes it out of you, doesn't it?"

Rip nodded, gesturing toward his pouch. "What's the word?"

Dane had already slid his hand into the belt pouch, from which he extracted a folded printout. As the pod raced along, Dane read silently. Rip waited, his curiosity increasing as Dane continued to say nothing, just frowned down at the paper.

Finally he handed the printout to Rip. "You tell me," he said. "You're the comtech, and I don't know if what I'm reading is what I'm supposed to understand."

Rip took the printout, and said, "All this stuff at the top is the number and types of fire walls the ferret had to break through, and these are the routes the ferret took to isolate the information."

"Understood." Dane gave a curt nod. "Go on."

"The search field here was the *Ariadne,* as you already know, and—" Rip broke off, scanning the data as the meaning reached him. Names of ships resonated through his skull like a rung bell. Finally he looked up at Dane. "This is a list of all the ships coming through Mykosian space that were insured through Trade, and the insurance codes indicating what the cargo was, in priority order."

"So I got that right." Dane's mouth was a thin angry line. "Did you look at the date that the *Ariadne* was due to arrive?"

"Hell and blast," Rip muttered. "Ten weeks ago!"

"And look whose computer it came from—"

"Our old buddy Prime Facilitator Koytatik. Whatever's going on, she's in it right up to her mandibles . . ." Rip looked up, and whistled softly. "If I'm right—"

"If we're both right," Dane said sourly. "You hit the same rad dump I did—"

Rip nodded. "What we're looking at is hijacking on the biggest level I've ever heard of."

Dane flexed his big fists, as though he was about to go find the perpetrator and effect his own kind of justice.

Just then the pod slid to a stop, and a swarm of Kanddoyds entered.

"Stash this," Rip murmured, handing him the printout.

Dane quickly stowed the paper in his belt pouch, and for the remainder of the journey they both sat in a tense silence, glaring at every passenger who came aboard, their hands never far from their sleeprods.

No one bothered them, though.

When they reached the docks, they bounced out onto the concourse and pulled themselves swiftly toward the *Queen* and Captain Jellico.

17

They were all crowded into the mess cabin—that is, all but Karl Kosti, who single-handedly was watching the *Starvenger*. "Johan and Jasper know how I feel," the big man had said before he boarded the shuttle. "They'll speak for me if there's need."

Dane stood in his accustomed place at the back, where his elbows and knees didn't feel so desperately ungainly. His palms were still sweating, as they had ever since he and Rip had read that printout. He still couldn't really believe it. How could anyone get away with what seemed to add up to legalized piracy?

"So this is what it looks like," Van Ryke said. For once his habitual smile was gone, replaced by a serious expression that rendered him almost unfamiliar. He gestured with his right hand to one set of printouts. "Koytatik receives word that an insured Free Trader ship is coming in, one with at least one high-pri trade item. She sends word to someone—"

"Flindyk," Rip said. "There's a secondary set of ship

names in his computer, time of arrival of messages after the lists Koytatik got. She must be forwarding these ship names to his office."

"So the by-the-books Flindyk is part of the conspiracy?" Stotz asked.

"Possibly," Van Ryke said. "Except he's an executive, and as yet we have no proof that anything sent to him actually gets before his eyes. He could have any number of minions screening his mail—and using his ID to protect them from being scanned by coworkers."

"Conceded," Jellico said. "Go on."

"So the *Ariadne* was reported due in carrying an extremely rare cargo of cielanite, plus some very advanced weaponry that the Shver are always collecting. Whoever is above Koytatik somehow makes certain the *Ariadne* is met out in space, probably soon after snapout—"

Wilcox nodded. "Easy enough to calculate probable jump points, and sit there watching for snapout."

"And a ship is most vulnerable then," Stotz said. "You control-deck jockeys are busy making certain we are where we need to be, while we make certain the engines came through."

"Even if they came out attack-ready, like some Patrol boat, what good if they don't have weapons?" Ali asked. "And how many Free Traders carry weaponry?"

"A few," Jellico said. "Mostly those who either are on the wrong side of the law or else ply their trade so far out on the fringes they perforce are their own law." He gestured to Van Ryke. "Continue."

Jan said, "The pirates fire on the ship to disable, not to destroy—if they can—and space the crew. Take the cargo. Replace it with ordinary stuff from Exchange. Clean the ship, including all logs and computers, space all personal effects. Then they fire on the old registry name and paint in the name of a ship registered as abandoned and claim-released, then they leave it . . ." He paused. "At that point, the probable sequence of events dwindles into mere guesswork."

Jasper said mildly, "Aren't those ships reported as abandoned also reported with coordinates—oh, but those are next to worthless unless the ship is dead in space," he amended.

Wilcox nodded. "And even then it could move, especially if something hits it. Always possible, though unlikely. Mostly ships are abandoned while moving—why spend fuel slowing it down? Sure it travels in a straight line, but what if that line intersects a gravity well? Approach at the right angle, and it slingshots around and zaps off in another direction. You could probably spend the time plotting likely courses of a ship—in fact, that's one of the things we had to do in school—but why bother?"

"These are all minor Traders, with no one in high or influential places to call for big, expensive investigations," Van Ryke said.

"Right." Jellico looked around at all of them. "Two things. We need the name of whoever's at the top, and we need to know exactly what's the purpose behind this switching of ship names. If Jan's scenario for what happened to *Starvenger*—*Ariadne*—is correct, that's a lot of work to go to just to leave the ship as an orbiting hulk."

"They probably wait a certain period of time, then go out and harvest the ships," Stotz said. "For parts, if nothing else. You can get plenty for good engines, or up-to-date refrigeration units, or ship's computers, in the right market. I'm always looking out for a good buy in spare macronucleic collimators, because they have a tendency to blow right after snapout, when we're millions of kilometers from anywhere and moving fast. You can't stock up on too many"—he frowned—"and until now I never thought to ask where they came from."

"Same with the jets and jet parts," Jasper offered, his pale, mild face concerned.

Jellico swung round to face Ya. "Can you do anything to flush out the data we need?"

"I wish I could," Tang Ya said. "I'd need better access to Exchange's computer system—and I'd need time to study its organization. Nunku's the one to oversee it, but even genius that she is, that ferret of hers is bound to crash soon—if it hasn't by now—and she'll never get a second one in there. The system's immune reaction won't permit it. She'd almost have to be on-site to do the delving."

Jellico's fingers were drumming lightly on his chair arm. "All right. Then it's up to us. Let's break, and each consider what we've heard and what we can do. Meantime, Thorson, keep checking that mail drop—but this time I want you to take at least two people as backup."

Dane nodded, surreptitiously wiping his hands down his pants again. He was slightly distracted by the sight of Tooe sliding out of the mess cabin. She probably had to go to the fresher, he thought. She faded from his mind when Rip said, "What I can't seem to get hold of is how could anyone get away with something that big?"

"I think I can answer that," Wilcox said, his austere Scots face grim. "All these ships have been insured through Trade. But except for the *Lucky Lucy* twelve years ago, and the *Ariadne* recently, none have been run by humans. Some are humanoid registered or owned, but they all seem to range from farther outside Terran spheres of influence."

"That would explain the cats," Craig Tau said.

Everyone turned to look at him.

"If the hijackers are used to nonhumans, that would explain why the cats were overlooked. Having ship's cats is a custom peculiar to Terrans," he explained. "Alpha and Omega probably hid when the intruders came aboard, and if you don't know to look for a hiding cat, you won't find one," he finished dryly.

Dane thought of Sinbad, who could make himself scarce when he was of a mind—even though by now there wasn't an inch of space Dane wasn't familiar with aboard the *Queen.*

"And they were in a hurry," Rip said.

"They wouldn't want to risk being a blip on the screens of some ship just emerging from hyperspace, or one moving to its jump point," Jasper put in.

Rip nodded, and continued, "Which would explain their

overlooking that extra little console down in the hydro. It was pretty well hidden by plants, and there was stuff piled all over it. The woman who tended it must have come from a real jungle environment."

"The main thing is that the hijackers are sticking to small stuff. Independents—like us," Dane said.

"Which means even less likelihood of anyone pursuing mysterious disappearances," Ali drawled. "Company ships disappearing would occasion those big, splashy searches Van mentioned. A succession of humans disappearing from well-traveled starlanes might cause a raised brow or two. No one is going to notice a bunch of missing rockrats gathered from spaceports spread across the galaxy."

"Which explains the correlation between the stories I heard up in the Spinner." Rael Cofort spoke for the first time. Dane could see muted pain in her dark blue eyes. "A good many of the people I met were either refugees from unexplained—uninvestigated—ship attacks, or had been left behind for one reason or another when their ships disappeared and didn't come back for them."

The captain smiled very faintly. "So you're ready to do battle on their behalf, Doctor?"

"A system is suspect that deliberately throws away so many people who otherwise would be working happily within the law, utilizing their talents for something besides stealing food and shelter." Her voice was soft, but there were spots of color along her cheeks. Dane looked from her rigid posture to the captain's same and wondered what he was missing. Then he felt a change near him, a kind of mental tickle that made him glance to the side, and he saw an odd expression on Ali Kamil's face.

Ali did not speak. Dane realized that Tooe had still not come back, and he wondered what that meant.

Van Ryke said, "Let us each go our own way for a time, and put our minds to the problem. We all have unique talents, and varying perspectives on tackling problems. Let's use those now."

"We'll discuss this again later," the captain said shortly, and he one-handed himself off his bench and catapulted through the hatchway.

"What's going on?" Dane asked his peers in a low voice as the others were all moving out. "The captain, I mean. And Cofort."

Ali laughed. "The stone and the steel, my blind Viking, the stone and the steel." And he dove out the door and vanished.

"What does *that* mean?" Dane asked Rip, now feeling more defensive by the second where before he was merely perplexed.

Rip just shook his head, and Jasper said quietly, "When the captain decides he wants us to know, we'll know."

Dane sighed, and went off to seek Tooe.

It all certainly seemed to add up, Jellico thought as he pulled himself down in his chair. He stared reflectively at the blue hoobat, who rocked in dreamy slow motion in his cage, making contented noises that sounded like the tearing of metal.

Jellico's mind reviewed the knot of mysteries tangling their affairs. The mysterious disintegration of their cargo deals. The spread of detrimental gossip not just among Traders but Monitors as well. The generous offer to buy the *Starvenger*—sight unseen—by someone who would not meet Van Ryke face to face, but sent a series of mouthpieces whose lies did not match. The postponements, the put-offs, the hounding of his crew followed by official commands to brig them . . . all of these could be viewed as tactics to wear the *Queen*'s crew down, to make them want to leave as soon as they could. Even the postponements, for what that meant was added cost. Jellico had no doubt whoever was in command had a good idea how much credit the *Solar Queen* had, and was hoping they'd decamp and run cargoless—and maybe without taking the *Starvenger,* which could then quietly be made to disappear.

You could almost do anything, if you were working within the law to commit crimes.

Even if the others didn't see it yet, the cold fact was: if Flindyk had commanded the hijackings, and was using his position to mask, hide, and eventually legitimize his actions, then he was going to use his position to stamp out anyone who tried to get in his way.

Ali and the other apprentices were burning for justice for the dead crew of the *Ariadne/Starvenger*; Wilcox and Van Ryke were burning to get their hooks into this villain who would use Trade to hide nefarious actions and thus risk tarnishing the reputation of Free Traders forever; Rael Cofort was burning to solve the problems of the outcasts up in the Spin Axis. None of them seemed to realize that as soon as Flindyk—if it was he—tracked the ferret back to the *Solar Queen,* a squad of Monitors would not be far behind. Locked up in jail and unable to communicate, with the *Queen* impounded, they would not be able to get justice for themselves, much less for anyone else.

Burning with the rightness of their cause, they didn't yet see the inevitability of this outcome. One of Míceál Jellico's earliest memories was the realization that the universe wasn't fair. Though everyone looked at their crossing of the threshold from child to adult in different ways—some merely by age, others by more conventional marks of passage such as graduation from tech training, or making a career choice, or marriage—Jellico's private acknowledgment of his own adulthood was the conscious decision that, though the universe was not fair, he still could be, to the best of his endeavor. He did not expect justice, or mercy, or intervention from an indifferent cosmos, but he did want to be able to know, whenever his life came to an end, that no good person took harm at his hand, and no bad one was aided. Aid in his definition included standing by and doing nothing.

He fully expected Flindyk, or whoever, to come after him. That didn't mean he couldn't make some preparations of his own.

He leaned forward and hit the com. "Ya?"

"Captain?"

"Come here. I've an idea."

"Be right there, Chief."

The com light went blank, and Jellico leaned back again, gently propping one boot on the edge of his desk, keeping the other magged to the deck.

He also disliked cowardice, and the truth was, his refusal to examine his emotions concerning Dr. Rael Cofort could no longer be attributed to expedience—which meant he was a coward.

He sighed and shut his eyes, remembering without any effort at all the intensity in her violet eyes, the determination expressed in every line of her slender frame when she had faced him down in the meeting. So she'd fight for her lost souls at the Spinner, eh?

And he remembered her standing outside the lab, passionate, honest, and completely unafraid, when he threatened to ground her. What she'd fired right back at him was true: would he ground Tau?

He knew he wouldn't.

So if he wouldn't ground Tau, but he would Cofort, then . . . then . . .

He dug the heels of his palms into his eyes.

The truth was that he had found what he had never thought to find, the companion who could keep stride with him, match wits with him, who was as intelligent as he was, and as loyal, and as passionate about doing what seemed right and to hell with the odds against. He'd seen that kind of commitment twice in his life, and both times he'd also seen the terrible grief that resulted when something happened to one partner. That was life in Trade. He'd made the decision never to risk himself that way, never to permit himself to fall in love, but it seemed that the decision had revoked itself.

He couldn't live Rael Cofort's life for her. He couldn't force her to bide in safety and contentment somewhere far from risk, to ignore the teeth of danger when she saw a true cause. If she were the sort who would permit him to hedge her round with the padding of security he would never have fallen in love in the first place.

Ya tapped at the door.

Jellico sighed, and keyed the door open, and—*Coward!* his inner voice taunted him—turned with relief to the problems at hand.

"Now here's what I want," he started.

Dane had been over the *Queen* once, and no Tooe. She'd never before left without telling him, not since she'd understood she was on probation, so he must have overlooked her.

At least that was what he hoped. He decided to be more methodical, starting with the treasure room down in the cargo area, which the crew had left untouched since the Denlieth run—and where she'd apparently hidden during her time as a stowaway.

He was on his way when he felt a twitch of awareness behind him, as though Rip Shannon had called him in so faint a voice he almost didn't hear it. Without thought he turned back to his cabin.

In the corridor between his and Rip's cabins stood Tooe, with Rip. The Rigelian's crest was spread at its fullest, her yellow eyes so wide they seemed to glow. "Come!" she fluted. "Dane, you get help, we go now, Flindyk comp. Quick!"

"What's this?" he asked.

Tooe one-handed herself up the ladder so they were on eye level. She bobbed in the air, held by her webbed fingers on the steel ladder pole as she said, "Nunku says, they find ferret soon. Nunku says, we don't stop now, the Monitors go through Spinner, kill everyone. Nunku says, klinti help now, we go out of Spinner, we go to Flindyk office. You bring help."

"Help? You mean Ya and Rip for computer delving?" Dane asked.

"I think she means for muscle," Rip said with a grin.

Tooe nodded, so violently she bobbed up again, and her crest snapped out flat as she handed herself back to the level of their heads. Dane's mind had been distracted by the way Tooe worked to keep her head oriented in the same direction he and Rip did—as if there was normal grav—and not at the most convenient angle for her next move. She was doing her best to adapt to human ways, and yet she'd left without telling him.

Doubts assailed him afresh. Was this after all another big game, as big in its way as the hijackers'? Was the *Queen* being used by the Spinner klinti to get at the authorities—and had they all been manipulated by those pitiful stories?

Dane shook his head hard. "Wait a minute," he said. "Tooe, why did you leave? You agreed to the terms of your probation."

"Is this the time—" Rip started.

"Yes," Dane cut in. "Right now. She's my responsibility. I have to get this straight."

Tooe's pupils flicked from slits to round, making her eyes dark. Her crest folded back at an odd angle, one he didn't remember seeing before.

"Do you understand my question?" he asked.

"Tooe understand, me," she replied, her voice plangent. "Captain say, 'It's up to us.' Captain want plan. I go to ask Nunku—"

"Why didn't you ask me first?" Dane interrupted.

Tooe's voice went high again as she blurted out a fast answer in Rigelian, then she said, slowly and painstakingly in Trade, "Tooe always talk to Nunku when trouble. Dane always talk to captain when trouble—except when go with Tooe to Spinner, first time."

Dane sucked in a deep breath. He'd never considered she'd observed his actions as closely as he'd observed hers. "Well, what I did was stupid, but I thought it was to protect the captain in case I . . . well, got myself into trouble."

Tooe's crest tilted in a humorous mode, but she said nothing.

"All right," he said. "I can see you had a reason, and I know you want to save your pals up at the Spinner. Except . . . if you're going to really sign on with us, then your first loyalty is going to have to be with us." He tapped his chest, then turned his thumb at Rip and up at the captain's cabin. "You have to think about the *Queen* first."

Tooe's pupils narrowed again. She was still silent.

Dane said awkwardly, "We can talk about it later, all right? Now, what's this plan? We're going now?"

Tooe gave a nod. Dane knew the dangers of attributing too-human emotions to someone not human, but she seemed slightly less energetic, and even her voice was a bit lower as she said, "We go now. Quick, search computer. Find last data. Bad place, Flindyk office, many many traps. Maybe Monitors come, maybe other people." She smacked her palms together lightly. "Try to catch us. You bring help?" she ended on a note of inquiry.

Dane sighed. "May's well." He turned to Rip, who raised a hand as though to say "Count me in." "My first thought would be Kosti—"

"Mine too," Rip said. "No one gets past him whom he doesn't want passing. There's Mura, who is an expert in martial arts. He hasn't left the ship yet—I don't know why—but he might be willing now."

Dane snapped his fingers, then caught at the ladder so he wouldn't bounce. "Go ask him. I've got someone else to ask," he said.

"Let's each grab a sleeprod, and meet at the outer lock in—two minutes."

Tooe gave a chirp of anticipation, and rocketed up the ladder.

Rip followed more slowly.

Dane dove at the down-ladder and hand-over-handed himself down to the engine level. As he expected, he found Johan Stotz at his console, deep in a multidimensional flowchart of the power flow in the *Queen*, from engines out. To Dane it looked like a multicolored sea urchin with a blue-white star at its heart, radiating out crooked, angular spines of light that shaded through the rainbow to red as they tapered out to nothingness. For Stotz, he realized, it was like reading a simple map.

Johan Stotz was a tall, thin, taciturn fellow only a few years older than Dane, though sometimes Dane felt that Johan was closer to Van Ryke's age. He was by nature quiet, and he seemed completely absorbed in engineering; more than once, when Jellico had set down on some pleasant world and gave the crew leave for R and R, it turned out later Stotz's idea of relaxation and enjoyment was to travel halfway across a continent to attend a seminar on "The Macronucleic Interface to Ship's Power: Friend or Foe?"

He never talked about his past—none of them did, really. But Dane remembered very well that first day when they found Tooe. He knew it must have taken some formidably trained knowledge of microgee movement to lay hold of that quick little Rigelian.

"You know null-grav sports?" Dane asked.

Stotz blinked once, his brows rising in mild surprise. "I was pretty good at school," he conceded.

"How good?" Dane asked.

Stotz grinned faintly. "Paid my way through by playing Nuller Rugby."

Dane whistled. That meant he wasn't just good, he was lethal. "That's just what I need," he said, and he briefly outlined what Tooe had proposed. "We're going now, taking a sleeprod. Are you in?"

He half expected Stotz to bow out. He just never got involved in rowdy stuff, at least while Dane had been on board.

But now his slight grin stretched, and with a quick gesture he saved his work and shut down his console.

"Lead on," he said.

They stopped to get a pair of sleeprods, then started up to the outer lock.

There he found not just the captain waiting, but a good part of the crew. Another surprise awaited Dane: Rip, Tooe, and Frank Mura stood on the dock. Mura's face was utterly impassive, and he carried no sleeprod, but Dane noted a short, thin object just outlined in Frank's tunic pocket. Dane guessed it had to be the weird little ultrasonic instrument Frank called a feedle pipe.

The crew watched them go in silence; to all intents and purposes anyone else on the dock would see a group setting out for one of the concourses for some entertainment.

But anyone spying, Dane thought seconds later, would be puzzled by their disappearance. They dropped rapidly through a one-person access hatch that Tooe had shown him earlier, and started along a hidden route.

At a juncture, Dane encountered his third surprise. In the midst of Tooe's klinti members, as though protected by them, Dane recognized the long, fragile form belonging to Nunku.

18

★

Rip snickered to himself as he followed Dane Thorson through a barren service adit, the odd beings in Tooe's klinti methodically zooming ahead, checking in all directions, then waving them on to the next segment of the service transit, just like space pirates in some holovid.

Under the circumstances, the huge sign in three languages and three symbols was more funny than menacing:

AUTHORIZED PERSONNEL ONLY

More than that prompted the bubbling humor, fast and unstoppable as a springtide stream: Ali's lengthy, colorful, and fluent reaction to his being forced to stay behind. The captain had been adamant. Until they knew for certain that the Monitors of Harmony were in league with the enemy, they would keep their promise, and Kosti and Kamil were not permitted to go anywhere but between the two ships.

Another cause for laughter was picturing what Kosti

would say when he returned and found out what he'd missed.

But foremost was the surreal sense that Rip got when he watched the free-fall circus evolving around them. Now he saw Nunku's beauty, an eldritch sort based on economy of line and motion: an eel-maiden moving in a sea of micro-gravity that was slowly drowning him, the earthbound one. Not only did he feel like he was in a holovid, now he was living a fairy tale.

Rip fought back a snort-spasm of hilarity. He knew that he should stop laughing, that he was probably closer to hysteria than he realized, but he just couldn't. Luckily none of the others paid him the slightest attention; Dane was concentrating on the whispered reports in some other language that the klinti made from time to time, and Mura just ignored him. Stotz gave Rip a faint smile once, then he too ignored him, instead moving with a speed and control of effort that inspired instant admiration in Rip. He'd been amazed when Dane showed up with Johan, of all people, but now Rip could see why he was along—though how Dane had known to ask was still a mystery.

They traversed a good portion of the dock area before stopping behind an adit at one of the maglevs that stayed in null grav. His antic mood was wearing off, eroded by the occasional disorientation of free fall and the strangeness of the Spinner. Now that Nunku was just a weird girl with spidery-thin arms and legs protruding from a ragged robe, some of his humor dissipated. But the obvious respect the others treated her with made it apparent she wasn't just a mutant who hadn't a decent change of clothes, or access to enough water to launder what she had. It was hard to look at her—and harder to imagine what her life must be like.

A closer glance at that pale, mottled skin sticking out of the tattered, old-fashioned djellaba made Rip wish suddenly for wide spaces, fresh air, and gravity.

The fresh air and wide spaces, at least, they got. After the scouts had watched for several long minutes, finally they signaled the all-clear, and the assault circus (as Rip privately termed this odd combination of beings) hastily emerged from the adit.

In quiet, law-abiding form they boarded the maglev.

Beings, mostly Kanddoyds, crowded on and off the maglev for the few stops they needed to make. Just before Rip and his party debarked, a group of Traders came on, several of them saluting the *Queen's* men before one of them scrutinized Dane and nudged one of his partners. A quick whisper, and the other Traders moved with more haste than necessary to the other side of the pod, studiously avoiding looking in their direction.

Though Dane didn't react, this effectively killed the remainder of Rip's sense of humor, his conviction that what he was doing wasn't real, and filled him with an anger-laced sense of purpose.

After waiting a few seconds he, Stotz, Mura, and Dane followed Tooe's group off, so it wasn't immediately obvious they were all together, and they drifted down the concourse, looking off at the winking chains of lights along the Kanddoyd buildings.

By a circuitous route they approached a fine building with a fern garden carefully tended round it. One by one they followed one another behind a sheltering scree of ferns, and ducked into another service adit.

This one was narrow, with pipes and conduits lining all the walls. An aggressive antiseptic smell didn't quite cover the dank odor of waste on its way to the recycler.

Rip's sense of purpose got an adrenaline boost when one of the scouts stopped, listening to a wrist com, and chattered to the others.

"Fast!" Tooe squeaked. "Fast! Fast! Monitors changing shift—"

They bounded from wall to wall, zooming up the narrow accessways. Rip was immediately completely lost, for the accesses bent and twisted at odd angles. Someone knew where they were going, though.

Finally they came to a halt, and again the scouts used a

tiny peek-through to ascertain when the hallway just beyond
their hatch was empty. This was in null-gravity territory,
which meant people came and went at all hours, which
summed up Kanddoyd life. The Shver followed simulated
sun cycles when they could, but the Kanddoyds had bred the
diurnal rhythms out of their life cycles uncounted generations
ago.

When the corridor the scouts had chosen was empty, two
of the klinti came forward. Rip saw that they had donned the
plain gray coveralls of maintenance personnel. As they slipped
out the hole, a third carefully handed them a canister. Puzzled, Rip pushed himself forward; then alarm thumped in his
chest when he recognized the glowing hooked orange trigram
indicating biohazardous contents.

Tooe closed the hatch almost all the way. From the darkness beyond, the rest of the group crowded around to watch.
The two workers stood waiting quietly, one with his clawed
fingers on the latch of the biohazard container.

Noises sounded; a group of chattering Kanddoyds appeared around a corner. Rip, peering down at an awkward
angle, just barely glimpsed them before one of the workers
pushed against the other, let out a yell, and next thing they
knew the canister was open and zillions of tiny shapes
swarmed out, spiraling into the corridor.

The Kanddoyds screeched like overtuned strings, clacking
and whistling in supersonic ranges that brought up goose
bumps on Rip's neck.

One of the workers hooted something in High Kanddoyd,
to which the beings responded with total panic.

Soon shrieks echoed back, one of them human: "EVAC-
UATE! APYUI VAMPIRE FLIES!"

Apyui vampire flies? Rip backed away in horror lest any
of the black shapes still darting about in the hallway slip
through the service hatch still cracked open. Everyone knew
about Apyui vampire flies, an insect harmless to the Fifftocs
but deadly to every other race. Every space farer knew the terrible story of the Plague of Athero. Just a couple of the flies

216   *   **Andre Norton & Sherwood Smith**

had gotten aboard a Trader that stopped in Fifftoc space and were inadvertently carried to a human system, where they rapidly bred by feeding through soft human skin. They didn't just suck blood, they paralyzed their victims first with a potent chemical that spread through the nervous system, making the victim think he was dying by fire. Most victims died by suicide in their efforts to stop the pain; the few who lived were paralyzed for life.

"We'd better—" Rip started nervously.

Tooe's webbed fingers grabbed his shoulder in a surprisingly strong grip. "Move not! Not Apyui flies. Ekko-tree mites. No harm."

Rip realized what had happened, and drew a shaky breath. "That's brilliant," he muttered.

"Sneaky, but brilliant," Johan said wryly.

Dane grinned, then tabbed the hatch open and motioned them out. "Building has to be empty by now. Let's get to it."

"Won't they seal and gas the place?" Rip asked as they bounded down a hall passing doors above, below, to the sides, always squarely in the middle of walls.

"Gas won't harm anyone but Jharzhakiu there," Dane said, pointing to a being with two sets of arms, one that ended in claws and the other in tentacles. The claw arms were busy pulling a breathing apparatus over a very weird face. "All we'll smell is cinnamon," Dane added.

"Here," Tooe said. "Move back."

As she opened the hatch she tossed through it an automated doll with something strapped to its back. Dane sensed a flicker of response. Moving with feral grace, a boneless tentacle of gleaming metal lashed down from above the door and transfixed the doll as it scuttled frantically into the room, adhesive glands holding it firmly to the deck. As Rip watched, there was a bluish electric flash, and he saw a pulse zap back up the tentacle. A moment later a weird hum he hadn't previously been aware of ceased.

Moving with practiced efficiency, several klinti moved in, teasing out the other traps and stings.

Dane said, "How would Flindyk have time to activate that stuff? The entire building must have been evacuated in half a minute."

"Remote activation," Rip said. "Easy enough to rig, if you've plenty of money and power."

At last the klinti indicated it was safe to move. Inside they found the mute evidence of hasty evacuation. Flimsies lay everywhere, chips had been dropped; here and three were floating bubbles from drink tubes that had gotten smashed somehow in the general exodus. There were four live consoles, each with projects suspended. Rip watched Nunku float from each to each, studying the keypads as though there were something to be read there.

He knew he was supposed to be backup muscle in case they were discovered, but he was a navigator by trade, which meant among other things learning computer tech, and he couldn't take his attention away from her.

Signing to Dane, who was gently guiding wobbling fluid spheres out of their way, he said, "Yell if you need me. I want to watch."

Dane nodded and returned to his chore.

Stotz took up position by the main door, stationing himself just inside at an angle where he could see out but not be immediately seen. Mura made his way to another door and waited there, watching with blank face as the klinti moved about the room picking up chips and flimsies.

No one touched the consoles.

Nunku gestured toward a door cleverly hidden in a fabulous mosaic, and two of the klinti sprang to it. This time they tossed a diaphanous veil of teased-out Rackney silk, triggering an apparently solid image from its fluorescent fibers with a juiced-up toy holobeamer. The response was more subtle: Dane saw a flicker of motion and the image sheered sideways and disappeared as something snatched the silk from the air. Different klinti moved in; this time clearing it took longer.

Inside was the garden room, just as Rael had described to the crew. Rip gave an appreciative glance at the wealth that had gone into the office's design. Could a Trade official earn enough to afford this stuff—even a fellow saving for a hundred years?

He shook his head and turned to watch Nunku.

Meanwhile, she had been moving cautiously behind her boobytrap scouts toward a touch console inset into a desk. There were very few keytabs but those were extremely costly porcelain, gold-painted.

Nunku cast a quick glance at Rip, gave him a surprisingly shy smile. She altered her posture so he could see better as she removed a chip from her tattered clothing and dropped it into a slot. The screen lit up, but only swirled in a fractal chaos that parodied the beauty spinning overhead.

"Mine chip hath released a nofratu," she said in a soft, sibilant voice. "Very dangerous, quite forbidden. There are no inherent constraints on its reproduction."

That voice, the odd accent, like his grandmother's almost, and her childish moon face above the long stick body made him feel curiously adrift, as if reality had turned inside out and left him stranded in a dreamscape. "There is very little it cannot dissolve," she said as the movement of the patterns on-screen accelerated.

He realized she was happy to explain, that this odd, pitiful person was a born teacher.

Abruptly, the screen cleared to a maze of symbols and glyphs.

"What is that?" he asked, his finger drawn to a particularly complex ideograph.

She grabbed his wrist in a surprisingly strong grasp; he noticed for the first time how large her knuckles and wrist were in proportion to her fingers and arms. "It is something the varlet Flindyk would most straitly desire thee to touch," she said without heat.

She released him as he pulled his hand back. With an attenuated finger, she touched the screen gently. The pattern folded in on itself, swallowing ranks of data. Rip had the sense of something focusing and wondered how Nunku saw it.

"A twisted web indeed he spinneth," she said. "But I shall pluck out the treasure at its heart." She touched the screen again, this time with a complex pattern of several fingers. Again the evolution, the sense of something evolving from blur to image. Nunku was once more the eel-maiden, this time swimming in a sea of data, with its own predators and beauties.

The unreality of the scene was intensified when Rip heard someone sneeze a few times in the outer chamber, and moments later he smelled a sharp odor rather like cinnamon and burned straw. The maintenance people were flushing the supposed vampire flies—they'd be in soon.

Nunku had to realize it too, but her face was merely absorbed as with delicate touch she tried various patterns of pressure and rhythm, watching the screen ripple through simpler and simpler patterns of symbols.

Finally the screen flickered and Rip saw data ranked in the Kanddoyd language. Moving swiftly now, Nunku pressed a keytab and at once the status light for a download shone a steady green.

"It returneth, its appetites sated, and with it our data."

It took only a few seconds, then Nunku pulled the chip out and the screen flickered to the fractal display they'd first seen.

"It should have erased my tracks," she said, "at least on the surface. A direct probe would reveal what we have done, but I do make no doubt I left nary a trace to raise the suspicions of yon miscreants."

"Then we'd better go," Rip said.

Until now she'd moved slowly; now she placed one of those impossibly thin feet on a surface and shot through the door to the outer room.

Very swiftly they all exited, the scouts reversing their process of entry so the pitfalls would be intact. Rip knew that the interruption would show up on some computer somewhere, but it couldn't be helped. They could only hope that if the room seemed to be untouched no one would check—

at least until they were safely out of reach.

They shot into the service adit just moments before a vanguard of maintenance people moved slowly down the hall, ostensibly looking for pests. One of Tooe's klinti left the hatch open a fraction, just enough for them to see that the maintenance people were followed by two fully armed Monitors.

Someone closed the hatch, and in the dim indirect light of the service tunnel they moved swiftly back through the building's crazy angles and curves until they emerged once again behind the protective screen of huge ferns.

Again they progressed in twos and threes onto the concourse, the last of the klinti being the two who had meanwhile shed and stashed their maintenance clothing.

This time, however, they did not go to the maglev. Instead, Rip and his companions from the *Queen* followed the others in an evasive pattern that led to the Spin Axis.

Rip was fascinated by the increasing strangeness of their surroundings as they approached the Spinner. Their route became ever more crooked, compressed by the micrograv shifting of forgotten cargo and junk over the centuries. Several times he saw where automated buildbots had evidently just chewed through everything in their path, bracing abandoned machinery to the walls merely as support for the new pipelines or data paths that transfixed them. No wonder there were so many leaks. It was almost like the Kanddoyds expected their cylome to be no more permanent than the planet that had rejected them.

From out of the fog and shadows came a hooting call, another in the series that had followed them, as unseen but ever-present klinti monitored their progress and their intentions. Of course they were tense, he thought, perceiving now the fragile network of relationships that kept the various factions and territories from deadly strife.

We've fractured the peace here—everywhere on the cylome, he thought. *If this doesn't work, if we can't prove this conspiracy, we won't survive. Everyone on the habitat will have been turned against us.* Watching Nunku, Rip realized that the klinti knew this, and knew they would not survive either. They had made their choice: an irrevocable one.

The klinti nest was so bizarre that it gave Rip the sense of being the source of all the weirdness of the Spinner, rather than its effect. Not only was there no sense of up and down in the vast chamber, it seemed to have been designed using these elements of the klinti habitations with ferocious intent. Spidery latticework tubes—the free-fall equivalent of cat-walks—webbed the space at all angles, swollen here and there with homes like galls on an oak branch. Between the thinner strands of the web were cables, ropes, and even some vines, which the inhabitants used to change direction on their grace-ful flights between catwalks. But when he saw two klinti meet and pass, each upside down to the other like an old Terran print he'd seen once, Rip saw how much more space that gave them. For a moment he flashed on how the *Queen* must look to Tooe, its wasteful, almost pretentious insistence on nonex-istent acceleration, with almost half her space sacrificed to a cramped up-down orientation.

Nunku seemed to have no objections as Rip followed her to the strangest console he had ever seen. At a glance he knew that it was completely self-designed and built, and as he scanned it more slowly, his fingers unconsciously flexed as if they wanted nothing more than to get at those keys.

Nunku settled in place and inserted her chip, and moments later the screen reflected the same data that Rip remembered seeing on Flindyk's screen.

"What I have," Nunku said, "are the payroll records. All of them."

Rip whistled to himself. That would be uncountable gigs of data. "Search on the ship names?" he asked.

Nunku nodded. "I do not think we shall find any ship names here," she said. "But of course we must examine for them first."

"You mean rule it out first," Rip said with a grin. "It won't be that easy."

A rare, sweet smile transformed Nunku's face for a moment into something . . . almost human. Rip felt a wrench of pity for this young woman who was, after all, human, and who had been forced into this nightmarish form and existence through no fault of her own.

Her fingers tapped softly over her screen, tabbed two keys, and she said, "Nothing."

"How about people?" That was Dane. Stotz—of course— was busy examining the vibration compensators rigged on the junction with one of the catwalks. "The ones we suspect: Koytatik, Flindyk himself, and anyone from Clan Golm, but especially the Jheel."

Nunku's fingers danced rapidly across the screen.

After a time, she said, "Here is Koytatik. They are paid by the piece, so this will be difficult." She pointed at the screen. "Here is Trade Authority—these are all ship Companies. Here's one for a starfaring Shver clan."

"Is that suspicious?" Dane asked.

Nunku said, "We are right to think anything suspicious, though the piece of work seemeth straightforward enow: registry of an upgrade in engines, and the addition of another energy weapon for far-range work . . ." She paused and checked something swiftly on a side console, then nodded. "As I comprehended. Clan Shren is known for frontier exploration and mapping."

"We can mark it for later perusal," Rip said, "but I think that's a dead end."

Nunku nodded. "We should, I believe, assume that most of this is perfectly legitimate business."

"So how do we find what isn't?" Rip said, watching as Nunku scanned swiftly through endless items of business.

"Vector," Nunku murmured.

Rip knew that, but how to find what to triangulate on? He turned away, feeling more frustrated by the moment. If the data was in a language he knew, and on a computer he could operate, he'd figure out an attack pattern for shedding the unnecessary data. Not to be able to read what was on the

screen before him made him feel like he was trying to grasp
and hold water.

"I shall try a search on common providers that Koytatik
and Flindyk and the Jheel have." She tapped, they waited in
silence, and she laid her hands on her console. "Nothing."

"Take Flindyk out," Rip suggested.

This time they had too much information. The Jheel was
connected with Koytatik's office in certain capacities, so it
wasn't surprising that a myriad of businesses showed up.

They tried other combinations, until Rip, who'd stopped
watching the screen and was resting in midair, pretending that
he had his own computer before him, imagined a vector that
he would follow.

"Go back," he said, opening his eyes. "To the Jheel and
Koytatik."

Nunku moved back, and looked up inquiringly.

"Now, how about finding out who's behind each of the
businesses? Strip out Trade departments, of course."

Nunku nodded slightly, her fingers working. Her face was
absorbed, not at all surprised, and Rip suddenly wondered if
she hadn't already thought of it, but out of an innate cour-
tesy listened to his ideas. *She's a leader,* he thought, watching
her. *She makes all these weird beings feel needed and valued.*
A good trait, he realized, for a captain.

"Ah," she said, with that sudden smile, and he knew he'd
been right—she'd initiated a search right from the start because no computer was that fast. "I have done inquiries on
each of the ownership combinations furnished by the Exchange listings, and of them, there is one that is registered as
based here, but the owners . . ." She paused, and in a light-
ning move sent yet another probe into the system. "Zounds!"
she exclaimed. "As I surmised. Sphere Eleven Startraders, a
limited partnership. These owners were once individuals, but
all are deceased."

Dane clapped his hands, ignoring the laugh from Tooe and
some of her friends as the movement sent him into an inad-

vertent somersault. "Run the dates of payments from Sphere Eleven Startraders for a month before and after each of the ETAs on the insured ships."

Once again Nunku's fingers sped over her screen, and then she sat back and smiled. "There it is," she said. "The Jheel is on the listing after *Ariadne,* but no others. Koytatik, however, is listed after . . . five disappeared ships, each a month after the ETA."

"It's good," Rip said, rubbing his fingertips to get rid of the tingle of the computer tech who is on the scent, "but it's still not proof. The last connection—"

This time Nunku laughed, a lovely, merry sound. "The trail of credit from Sphere Eleven to whoever is providing the money."

Stotz came forward and spoke for the first time. "That probably won't show up," he said. "If it's Flindyk, he's so entrenched in the system he knows how to ride it and how to blind it. I'll stake any sum he gets some goon to pay cash, anonymous source, into the Sphere Eleven accounts at intervals that have nothing to do with the payouts—"

"And in amounts that won't match withdrawal sums or dates from his own funds," Rip said. "Yup. I'd do that too, if I were setting up a hijacking empire. Make sure your flunkies are paid promptly, because they don't care where it comes from, but make certain the source is sufficiently fuzzy for the random legit auditor, who does care."

"Then we're stopped after all?" Dane asked, looking annoyed.

"I shall see if I can break through the guardians of Flindyk's own accounts," Nunku said quietly.

"Look, Viking," Rip said. "Let's take what we have and give it to the captain and the others. We can't expect to get it all at once, but what we have here ought to be enough for quick brains like Ya's and Van's and Wilcox's, not to mention the Old Man's."

"Right," Dane said, but without much enthusiasm. He turned to Nunku. "Thanks for your help, We'll report back."

"Momo and Ghesl'h'h shall see thee safely out of the Spinner," was all she said.

All four men were silent on the long journey out.

Just before they returned to the *Queen,* Dane said, "Why don't you take this data to the captain? I'm going down to Shver territory to see if our ferret extracted anything more. We obviously need every scrap of data we can get."

"Bad idea," Stotz said. "Didn't someone say Flindyk has to be onto that ferret by now?"

"It's going to burn at me until I know," Dane said. "Look. I'll do it just like before, nice and easy. If there's anything suspicious, I won't go in."

"At least sound it first," Stotz said.

Dane and Rip shook their heads at the same time, and Dane grinned before saying, "If the ferret's discovered, the sounder will be too."

Rip said, "Then I'm going with you."

"Maybe we should all go," Frank said.

Dane shook his head. "In that grav, if you try to block a Shver's hit your arm will shatter. And Johan, your nuller skills won't be much use in one-point-six gravs."

Stotz grinned. "All right. Besides, I think this"—he waved the chip Nunku had given them—"better get into the captain's hands right away."

They stopped at a maglev concourse, and before separating, Mura said, "If you're not back right away, we're all coming after you."

19

★

"**Promise me one** thing," Rip was saying as he and Dane rode the maglev down.

"What's that?" Dane took in a deep breath. It was good to be in one grav again. Strange, the almost overwhelming sense of rightness. *Almost* worth the rest of the journey, he thought wryly.

"If you see any of those Clan Golm jokers, we're smoke. Any," Rip repeated.

Dane grinned. "Already decided that. They have to know we're onto them, which means—"

"If we do see them, they're there to make trouble," Rip finished.

Dane laughed. He had a suspicion that Rip's emotions were much like his—anticipation, impatience, a weird mixture of fun and fear.

And a desire for justice.

"One more piece, one more clue," Dane muttered. "That's all we need. Let it be there."

After a few moments, during which the acceleration gradually increased, Dane felt a kind of twinge in his mind, like a bad memory that hadn't quite surfaced. Puzzled, he glanced at Rip, who was sitting back against the seat, doing heavy-grav breathing.

Rip looked up right then, and said, "Just had an ugly thought: what if it had been us?"

"You mean instead of the *Ariadne*?"

"Could have been," Rip said, his dark eyes narrowed. "If we'd found some kind of rare mineral on the Denlieth run, or something else we could have made a big killing on—"

"And we would have radioed ahead to Trade for insurance," Dane said, continuing the thought.

"And these slime buckets would have been sitting on our jump point, waiting for us. And the *Queen* would be orbiting in Mykosian space now, empty, with some other name painted on her side."

Dane flexed his hands. How good it would feel to grab some hijacker by the neck and fling him out a lockhole into space! No Free Trade ship should have to go through that again. They simply had to win. They had to.

Rip sighed.

"Winning, right?" Dane asked, humor leaching back into his thoughts. Anger in high grav didn't feel good; it was as if a big Shver foot stepped on his heart every time it beat.

"And Tooe," Rip said. "First I was thinking about how right our cause is. That any crew would feel the same. Then I thought of Tooe and her . . . what do you call it again?"

"Klinti," Dane supplied.

"Let's imagine that everything miraculously clears up and we don't end up brigged here forever, and we're ready to blast off. Do you think she's going to be able to leave those people?"

Dane shook his head. "I don't know. It's been on my mind all day today," he admitted. "Until she took off to warn Nunku—and I understand why she did it—I thought there was no problem. But she really does seem to need to see how the klinti is doing, to talk to Nunku, to get her ideas. Makes me wonder if all her work with me is a kind of game." He shifted position to ease a cramp forming in one leg. "Well, Van says whatever happens with her, it's good practice for me. I guess I'd gotten so accustomed to things as they are I half thought I'd be an apprentice forever."

"I guess we'll see," Rip said. "Hoo. We have to be almost there—I feel like somebody dropped a spaceship on my chest."

Dane glanced out the port just in time to see them grounding. The maglev whizzed along the Shver countryside, through forests of great-trunked, spreading trees, toward the stop now familiar to them both.

The nature of Shver building made it impossible to scan ahead for dangers; they did not like their domiciles in the open, the buildings were never more than one story—not surprising for a race that couldn't jump—and even the general-purpose establishments were fairly secluded. Dane noticed, as they slowed, that once you were on the surface you did not even see roads. Was being witnessed traveling as big a taboo as public eating? Or was it merely prudence on the part of a people whose culture was unabashedly militant?

No one to answer that, Dane thought, leaning forward carefully—the last thing he needed was to strain an abdominal muscle by jerking his body forward just to scan the concourse as the maglev pod gently braked toward its stop.

Shver were about, but none of them bore the clan marking of Golm.

He looked with care on both sides before nodding to Rip. Walking with caution, they disembarked from the pod and started toward the building.

Shver came and went, but except for a curious stare from a pair of small Shver, no one paid them the least heed—overtly.

Dane felt he was being watched, and attributed it immediately to the knowledge that Nunku's ferret was bound to have been discovered. There were no signs of danger, and he kept ceaseless watch, though it meant turning his head and slowing his step so that he did not risk losing his balance.

They passed inside and went straight to the communications chamber, where Rip took his turn at watching while Dane keyed in for messages.

There was nothing.

Alarm now burned in every muscle, intensifying the pull of the heavy gravity. Something was wrong; Rip did not speak, but the wariness in his gaze and his tightened jaw indicated he felt it as well.

The two men moved just a little apart, in case they had to defend themselves, as they started their retreat. No one waited outside the com chamber. Relieved, they sped up just a bit, until they reached the outer door. There was the pod, not fifty meters away.

Dane wanted to keep his gaze on the relative safety of the maglev pod, as though that would vouchsafe their reaching it, but he forced himself to turn his head from side to side, scanning.

No one was in sight—no one at all.

Bad sign.

"Hurry," he breathed, the word coming out in a *whuff*. Ignoring the protest of joints, muscles, and lungs, he quickened his step, and Rip did the same beside him.

Twenty-five meters . . .

Twenty . . .

Fifteen—

Shadows appeared on the periphery of his vision, spiking his adrenaline. Crouching slightly, he turned—and his hand encountered the ceremonial weapon of a huge Shver.

Pain lanced through Dane's knuckles. The Shver—a first-rank citizen, a part of his mind noted hazily—had moved with preternatural quietness right up behind him.

More Shver appeared, hemming in Dane and Rip.

The Shver whose weapon Dane had inadvertently touched

began to speak, his low voice sounding like thunder in a distant valley.

Rip stayed silent and watchful, until the Shver suddenly turned and departed as silently as they had come.

"I got that last," Rip said, as they eased themselves into the pod. "Something about Monitors?"

"They're reporting to the Monitors," Dane said, shock ringing through his head. "All nice and legal," he added bitterly. "Flindyk wins again—a legalized murder."

"What?" Rip exclaimed, then gasped for air. "Murder?"

Dane said, "I've been challenged to a duel."

Craig Tau watched Jellico's impatience steadily increase until at last he laid his hand decisively on the table and said, "I can't wait any longer. The Kanddoyds might keep all hours but Ross doesn't, and I don't want to risk talking to whoever sits in his office when he's gone."

"We'd just get referred to the Monitors," Van Ryke said.

"Or picked up by them," Wilcox muttered.

Jellico gave one last glance at the chrono and shoved himself gently up from the table, catching hold of the hatchway. "If they're not back in . . . half an hour, Wilcox and Stotz, you go get them. Ya, I want you on the com. Cofort, are you still going up to the Spin Axis?" He looked across the mess cabin at Rael for the first time during the discussion.

"Yes," she said. Craig felt her tensing beside him—as if she were bracing herself for an argument.

But he gave a short nod and said, "Weeks, if you go with her, maybe the two of you can shorten the time you're needed up there. You've helped in the sick bay before—just do what she asks you to."

"Glad to help," Jasper said with his shy smile.

Jellico jerked a thumb at Jan Van Ryke. "I want you along with me, Van. I need your assessment of Ross. Something's missing, and I can't put my finger on what. You too, Craig, for the physician's point of view."

His hard gray gaze lifted, as if by chance, to Rael's face again, and he hesitated, as if about to say something, but quite suddenly he turned and vanished.

For a time Rael stood where she was, watching the hatchway. Tau was also still, observing. He could heard the captain's voice in the corridor outside, giving orders to Mura and Ali Kamil, and then he was gone.

Rael Cofort flexed her hands, then suddenly looked up to meet Tau's gaze. He didn't say anything, or look away. There was nothing to say. She did not try to hide her emotions; she understood that he knew what was going on. She also understood his compassion—and his determination not to make the mistake of trying to interfere.

She smiled, gave a slight shrug, then she too vanished through the hatchway.

A few minutes later Tau propelled himself through the outer lock after Van Ryke and the captain, then pushed off to sail down the corridor to the maglev halt. With some amusement he watched Van Ryke's big form maneuver with grace around the corners and up the last corridor.

They settled into a pod, Van Ryke's bushy white brows soaring as he scanned around them. As might be expected, the pods were all full of a variety of spacers all determined to get some kind of business done before the last of the diurnal emporia closed—either that or were about to embark on what passed for an evening's conviviality in a habitat.

Unfortunately it also precluded any kind of private talk. Tau wanted to find out more about what the captain wanted him looking for—though he decided as they sped along that maybe observation without any previous expectation coloring his views might be the most valuable.

There was no one in the Way of the Rain-dappled Lilies; this was where the highest Kanddoyd officials lived. Tau looked forward to the spectacular view of the inside of the habitat that this particular area was said to offer.

Ross was present. Tau had heard about the Rose Garden, but at least by the time the Kanddoyd who greeted them had ushered them inside the legate's domicile, he was not to be found studying his holographic plants.

The office was recognizable as a standard Patrol captain's office, right down to the regulation desk. Nothing was out of place, nothing looked amiss. Even the windows were blocked, giving the room an atmosphere of focus and efficiency. Ross himself was seated behind his desk, neat in the black and silver uniform of a Patrol officer, his long face alert.

"Captain Jellico," he said as the three *Solar Queen*'s men walked in. "I'm glad you're here—it saved me having to request an interview." He looked down at a flimsy. "I've received a surprising number of complaints, mostly rowdyism and illegal trespassing, about your crew. Can you explain that?"

"It's why we're here," Jellico said, handing Ross the printouts that Tang Ya had prepared, plus a tape spool.

Ross set the spool in a slot, where it could be automatically downloaded, as he perused the printout in silence. When he looked up, he frowned slightly, but otherwise there was no expression at all on his face. "How did you get this information?" he asked.

"Illegally," Jellico said.

Ross dropped the papers, which took a long time to settle to the desk. Tau watched them in fascination as the legate stared at a point in space midway between his visitors, then looked up again. "I can stop the transmissions—in fact, I will send a coded 'gram to HQ . . ." He halted.

Van Ryke said, "I am assuming that if what we've found out is true, even your secure line has probably been compromised."

"And the message will never get there, yet I'll receive an acknowledgment," Ross said. For the first time there was some animation in his lean countenance. "If that is so, it would explain a number of anomalies that are side issues to what you have here. But that can wait. What I'll do, then, is send a spool up with the next guard rotation, and it can be radioed not to HQ but to the legate at . . . Sheng Li." He named a system on the space lanes between Mykos and Terra. "They'll send it from the Patrol ship. I'll have them jump out to some random coordinate outside Mykosian space before they send, to be safe."

"We've probably been seen coming here," Van Ryke said with his easy smile.

Jellico said, "You might send one from here as well, just in case."

Ross blinked, then said, "Yes. Just an order to stop the transmissions of the lost and abandoned lists. I'll send a message to Trade HQ about the insured ships as well." He gave a slight, wintry smile. "As there's been nothing to do here for the past number of years, my appearing to perform the minimum required of my post will seem in character."

"How long have you been stationed here, Captain, if I may be permitted to ask?" Tau spoke up. "I thought regulations were specific about rotating people in and out of hostile environments. A habitat would be listed as hostile, wouldn't it, as it is so alien to our kind?"

"Four years," Ross said. "That's reg. But I've been here almost sixteen. They apparently don't get to us this far out as often as they ought to."

Tau nodded, but he made a mental note to do some checking in the public records.

"Back to us," Jellico said. "What are our chances of demanding an investigation?"

"You can," Ross said, "but I can't, acting alone. A court of inquiry at this level must involve all three races, according to the Compact of Harmony."

"So," Jellico said, "we do it."

"You can," Ross said, "but it'll break you. In fact, I strongly suspect that if all this is true, it is the single reason why you have not been dealt with more summarily until now.

If Flindyk really is the . . . mastermind of this conspiracy, then he would like nothing better than to fight you in court. You don't have proof of his culpability, which means investigation."

"What's wrong with that?"

Van Ryke raised a hand to pinch the bridge of his nose. "I should have thought of the obvious."

Ross gave that slight, pained smile again. "I think you see it. Shver justice is summary. Kanddoyds, who oversee most of the civilian cases, can take years to solve the simplest case."

"Wouldn't the investigative committee be made up of all three races?" Tau asked.

Ross turned to him. "Yes, but you have to understand that anything to do with the Kanddoyds is going to take ages to resolve, by the most complimentary, indirect methods possible. Everything is done to save face—I expect the decision is probably arrived at and accepted before it's actually heard."

"Of course," Tau said. And suddenly from his studies a chilling analogy emerged from memory: that both Kanddoyds and Shver culled their defective newborns, as did many races with population problems. But while the Shver were plain about it, making the decision and quickly carrying it out, the Kanddoyds made an elaborate festival of it, calling it the Time of the Celebration of the Perfect-Born. It amounted to the same thing, except where the Shver injected the cullees before the family, so at least it was painless, the Kanddoyd culls were borne away in silence and quiet, so no one ever knew who did it or what was done.

Tau felt his guts gripe at this unexpectedly sinister side to the seemingly friendly race. *And Flindyk has reputedly become more Kanddoyd than human,* he thought.

Jellico said, "If we request the investigation, then we'd be required to testify, wouldn't we?"

"Correct. You'd have to stay at your own expense, unless I arrested you and impounded your ship."

Van Ryke shook his head. "Flindyk could easily spin this out ten years if he wanted."

"Meanwhile we're stuck here, and not necessarily safely," Tau said. "So what can we do?"

Ross tapped together the printouts, and laid them in a sealed file. "You may be certain that I shall do my own investigating, though it will have to be slowly and with care."

Jellico gave his curt nod. "Thanks, Captain. If you need us, you know where to find us."

He flicked glances Tau's and Van Ryke's way, and in silence the two officers followed their captain out.

No one spoke until they reached the maglev concourse. This time they waited for several pods until they found one that was empty. As soon as it started to move, Jellico turned to Tau. "Your impressions?"

"I want to check the Patrol's public records to make certain, but I'll just bet that this man was not the kind to interfere if things seemed fine on the surface."

"You mean he's part of it?" Van Ryke frowned.

"No, I don't think so at all," Tau said. "Of course I could be wrong—I've been fooled before—but I do think he's by nature a depressive personality, a trait worsened by this habitat. When humans first tried to live on them, there were numbers of people who developed adverse psychological conditions."

"So if you look at the record what do you expect to see?"

"That his predecessors who were very active spent their four years here and rotated back, and those who were more hands-off stayed longer. I'll further wager that Flindyk has enough control over com to see that Ross's requests for transfer have never gone through."

Jellico nodded. "From what I know of Patrol regs, after the four years in a hostile environment, a request for transfer would get high pri. This far out, though, if there was no request—or even a request to stay on—nothing would be done. It's expensive to send a ship out this far."

Tau watched his captain, saw the characteristic drumming of his fingers—lightly, so that there was no reaction in the micrograv—which meant that he'd reached a decision.

Van Ryke looked up expectantly. "And so, Chief?"

"If Ross can't solve this," Jellico said, "we will."

20

★

"You've been *what?*"

"Challenged to a duel," Dane said.

They were crowded into the tiny space between Dane's and Rip's cabins. Dane backed into his room, snagging ahold of his bunk to keep from bouncing gently against the wall. He looked out at the three faces: Tau's unbelieving, Van Ryke's mildly surprised, and the captain's angry.

"That's it," Jellico said, his gray eyes lambent points of silvery light. "Get all our crew together. We're blasting out."

"Can't, Chief," Van Ryke murmured. "Can't pay our shot."

Dane watched the captain's jaw work as though he were aching to say, "Watch me."

Another silence ensued, this one more tense than the first one after Dane's announcement. Dane knew the captain could get them out of the lock; with his piloting, they could probably outrun those unwieldy Shver dreadnoughts they used as Monitor Patrol ships—but once they were outside, they wouldn't be able to run up to jump speed before the defense guns could blast them into atoms.

Which was probably just what Flindyk was hoping for.

Jellico gripped the ladder so hard his knuckles went white, but when he spoke again, his voice was utterly emotionless. "I will not stand by and permit that scum to annihilate one of my crew." He turned his head, pinioning Dane with his cold, hard gaze. "You did not provoke this."

It wasn't even a question.

Dane knew that if he had, he would have been given at least a fair hearing, but nevertheless he was glad to be able to shake his head. "Came up behind me. I didn't even know he was there until he started spouting the ritual challenge at me."

"He what?" came a new voice.

Everyone looked up—or what they were used to thinking of as up when they were dirtside—to see Ali Kamil hanging by his knees from the ladder to the next level, floating with his arms wide, a curious grin on his handsome face.

"Thorson," he said, "how about some details? What exactly happened?"

Dane shrugged, repressing a spurt of annoyance at Ali's drawling assumption of superiority—as though he had all the answers. He'd do that before a firing squad, Dane thought with a faint return of his old amusement. Out loud, he said only, "Nothing to report. Rip and I checked the mail drop, found nothing, started out, saw no one. Suddenly this Shver is behind me—I feel a bump on my arm, and he starts in with the challenge. His brethren were with him, and they hemmed us in, or we would have tried to get away, and hang 'honor.' "

"I don't see much honor in one of those two-ton heavyweights taking on a human who can barely walk in their cursed heavy gee," Stotz said sourly from his perch in the ladder well to the lower level.

"It's a frame-up," Tau said, frowning. "We all know it. Why should Dane have to go out there at all?"

"Because it's a legal requirement," Ali said from above. "Same as being arrested."

Looking quickly from Stotz to Ali, Dane felt his sense of up and down shift; suddenly they were at either end of a room, and he was lying on the floor. Vertigo tugged at his guts, and he had to lean against the wall and force himself to orient again.

"So what do we do?" Rip asked from his doorway. "We can't let Dane go back there and get murdered."

"If you all will grant me a few moments"—Ali's drawl was more pronounced than ever—"I believe a solution is possible." He waved his arms grandiloquently.

Wilcox made an impatient movement copying Ali, and said, "Well, enlighten us!"

The others laughed—except for Van Ryke, who sighed, looking up at Kamil as though at an erring child. He was about to speak when Jellico said suddenly, "Get down here, Kamil. Or at least orient yourself the same way so that smart mouth of yours is below your eyes, where it belongs."

Ali grinned and with a careless flick of his feet loosed himself from the ladder and floated gently to the deckplates in the midst of the little group.

"Here," Van Ryke said, opening his door. "We'll have another meter of space if we step this way."

They moved to his cabin, some going in and some standing just outside. Ali perched on one of the cargo master's tape storage bins, crossing his legs. "Now, Viking," he said instructively, "begin again, from the point at which your challenger touched you—or, more correctly, forced you to touch him, however inadvertent it was. What exactly happened?"

Dane shook his head. "I felt a pressure on my right arm. Turned, saw that big long knife that the Shver citizens wear. He'd bumped against me with that knife—"

"Bumped against you, or hit you with it?" Ali asked, his posture still relaxed but his gaze intent.

"Made it so that I hit him."

"Was it still in its sheath, or out?"

"Sheath, I think," Dane said, after a moment's thought.

Rip nodded corroboration. "I would have remembered if it'd been out, with that serrated edge—"

Ali waved this away with an airy, impatient gesture.

"Dane, my innocent," he said, "a new lesson I am about to follow myself." He raised a long forefinger.

"Cough it out, Kamil," Steen said with a pained look. "Quit the playacting."

"What is it," Ali addressed the air in patently fake sorrow, "about navigators that makes them so distrustful of their fellow beings—particularly the very engineers who propel the ships they guide?"

"We'll debate philosophical etiquette later," Wilcox said with a grim smile. "Get on with your solution, or are you just gassing?"

"Not at all," Ali said, becoming slightly more serious. "When we first got here, I downloaded what I could find about dueling, as I thought—things being what they were— if any of us were to be challenged, it would probably be yours truly. I felt I owed it to my crewmates to be prepared for any contingency. When I found myself confined to quarters, I pursued it further, this time out of interest. Our friends the Shver are a very interesting culture. Within the context of their militancy, they can actually be quite subtle."

While Steen and Ali had been talking, Van Ryke had called up some files on his computer. Jellico divided his time between scanning those and watching the talk. Now he gave a faint nod.

Ali grinned. "I can save you the search—what's going on is this. Deliberately crossing into another Shver's personal space is a dueling offense—as would be expected from even those used to a heavy world. Gravity is gravity, and stopping, starting, and especially falling are no light matter—"

Rip groaned. Van Ryke coughed, hiding a laugh.

Ali continued as if sublimely unaware of the reaction to his pun. "—so they are careful to stay out of one another's personal space unless they have to fight for some political or social or familial reason that cannot be aired in public. Hitting someone with the shauv knife is the usual means of challenging someone for reasons that the challenger cannot, or does not, want to explain."

"Ah," Van Ryke said. "Now I think I see . . . Go on, my boy."

Ali nodded. "Now, there are further refinements. To hit someone means something different from permitting oneself to be hit, if you see what I mean. Hitting someone means you have a legitimate grief. To permit oneself to be hit is a little more mysterious; it can mean that the challenger has been forced into the duel."

Dane nodded slowly, faint hope entering his tired brain for the first time since that dreadful trip to the mail drop. "I see, and there's also the sheathed blade and the bare blade, which I do remember reading."

"Right," Ali said. "Hits with bared blade mean to the death, no questions asked."

"I thought all duels were to the death," Rip said.

"Well, technically they are," Ali said. "Here's where the Shver get subtle. Let's suppose that someone is forced by the clan to challenge someone else to a duel, someone the individual has no quarrel with. He lets the person know in much the manner that Dane received his challenge, and this guides the combatants in their choice of weapons. If the fight is declared satisfactory to the challenger, whether there's a death or not, then the insult can be declared dead, and they leave the best of friends."

Rip sighed. "Except these guys can choose their own weapons before the duel. At least that's what Dane told me while we were coming back up here. Though blasters and fire weapons that could breach the habitat walls are forbidden, anything else goes, right?"

"Right," Ali said, grinning.

"Then that oversized elephant can show up with a twelve-foot-long force blade big enough to take on an entire Patrol platoon if he wants, and Dane can't do a thing about it—and the only weapons *we* have to choose from are sleeprods and . . . and . . . Frank's ultrasonic feedle pipe!"

Ali had begun to laugh, but he stopped, a strange look in his eyes.

No one spoke for a time. When the silence began to seem protracted the captain's quiet voice was heard. "Ali?"

"I have to admit, I had everything figured out except what kind of weapon Dane might take," Ali admitted. "But I think . . . I have it."

"We can't get our hands on any illegal weapons now," Steen said, his impatience making him sarcastic. "The duel is in less than an hour!"

"Won't have to, if I'm right," Ali said.

Van Ryke frowned. "This isn't a game, my young friend," he murmured. "Dane has to go out there and face whatever weapon this fellow brings. He'll be in heavy grav against someone who is bigger, stronger, and masses three times what he does, and has been trained in fighting since birth. I'd say he's facing a terrible risk."

"He faces that risk no matter what," Ali said. "We've been forced into that much of a situation. But think of this: that Shver is not a Golm, has never been near us before. He caused the duel in the most neutral manner he could—"

"He *has* to face Dane armed with something deadly, or he's declared a coward and an outcast," Rip said.

Ali nodded. "Right. So Dane has a choice. Either he's more deadly, or . . ." He looked up. "Steen—you and Dane and I need to have a talk."

A piercing whistle on five distinct notes echoed through the dim tunnels of the Spin Axis.

The sound had become very familiar to Rael Cofort. She looked over at Jasper Weeks, who was already packing up their gear.

Rael's heart thumped warningly but her hands stayed still as she used her thin immune-probe to restimulate the ill-healed muscle tissue of the man lying against the wall before her.

As soon as she was done Jasper dropped a healpak over the reddened flesh, now responding again to the memory, deep in bone and sinew, of the original injury. Healing would go to completion. The patient twisted slightly and pushed off with his feet; moments later he was gone, diving through a narrow crack in an old lock.

"Come! Come!" Tooe shrilled, grabbing the gear from Jasper's hands.

They could hear the sounds of the Monitors clearly now; Rael's heart was pounding as she rebounded after Tooe, shooting through a maze of abandoned air ducts in which ghostly fronds of ancient dust fluttered lazily.

When they were safely away, Jasper veered close to Rael. "Fifth one," he muttered. "I wish I knew what was going on."

"What's going on is easy," Rael replied as they reached a dim chamber full of immense, flaccid sacks on the walls, dim and bulky in the reddish light—Rael was irresistibly reminded of enormous fungus. In this case, she thought, fungus marked with the sigil of chemhazard. Whatever had leaked out of them was long dissipated.

Then they dived down into what seemed to be a dark well. Blackness closed around them and Rael flew along with her hands out. They bumped into a corner, another, and then saw light—and her orientation snapped into a new alignment: now she was ascending toward the light. "The Monitors are out in full force," she continued, now that she could see Jasper. "What we don't know is why."

They stopped at a nexus obviously well known to Tooe, and waited until, ever so faintly, a signal was heard. Tooe whistled back. After a long space of two or three mintues another whistle came, equally faint.

Rael did not know the meaning of these particular signals,

but that one five-note sequence would probably feature in nightmares to come, she thought grimly as once again they started off. *Flee! Monitors coming!*

The signals being sent back and forth now were most likely the regroup points. Tooe led them on a wild flight through the endless ducts and abandoned chambers; Rael knew she could have been led through the same area again and again and not notice, the whole was so alien to her.

But at last they stopped, this time in a long, thin room with what looked like a threshing machine at one end. Rael looked at it, and at the bare walls leading to it, and was glad that no one could turn on the grav and force them into it.

Then she forgot it as, once again, patients of all ages and races began drifting in. She and Jasper unpacked their kit with practiced speed, and with no words wasted motioned the first person to come forward.

Before, they had gotten well through at least a few patients before the alarm came. This time, though, Rael was just about to activate her scanner when the first two high notes sounded, faint and far off, but no less frightening for that: all around them people stiffened, alert, then bounced off the nearest surface and zoomed away through an opening.

The alarm came again, clearer, now the room was empty; it was a five-note series, but different.

Tooe turned glowing yellow eyes to Rael. "Deathguard!" Her voice was shrill with strain. She whirled about, then froze again, her crest flat and quivering.

Another high note sounded, so high Rael knew what she had suspected before, that the Spinner people communicated in the ultrasonic range.

"Truce," Tooe said. "Conference—"

"What does that mean?" Rael asked, as Jasper once again began packing the gear.

"Tooe not know, me. All those Monitors—Deathguard blame us, maybe. Monitors look for us, Monitors look for them, who knows? Maybe they know."

"Do we have to go to this conference?"

Tooe's pupils went wide and black. "Oh yes." She nodded vigorously enough to make herself bob gently against the wall at her back. "Or they come to us."

Rael felt the cold grip of fear at the back of her neck. Jasper was looking at her, plainly waiting for her to decide.

"Let's go," was all she could think of to say.

A long, crazy journey later, Rael Cofort floated, hands loose at her sides, behind Tooe and Momo. Jasper was just above her, one hand hovering near the sleeprod at his belt, though his pale face was mild and polite as always.

The neutral place was brightly lit and bare, affording nowhere to hide for those with treachery in mind. The air was warm and redolent of a faint metallic tang, and Rael felt more than heard a deep, ambient hum.

Positioned around the circumference of the chamber were four clumps of people, all poised near a flat surface in wary readiness for action.

Rael half-listened to the steady rise and fall of voices. Nunku and two other Spinner gang leaders spoke a strange mélange of languages that she couldn't make out at all. They all three faced the black shrouded figures against one wall; as yet none of these had spoken.

The followers of the Spinner gangs kept absolute silence, including Tooe and Momo, so Rael and Jasper were also quiet.

She was just as glad of the chance to watch, to reassess. She moved slightly, partly to get a clearer view and partly to ease her aching neck—and saw one of the sinister dark-clad beings across the room flick a glance at her from inimical-seeming eyes. She kept her hands wide, palms out, in the universal gesture of goodwill.

Working in null gee was just as tiring as laboring in gravity, she realized as she watched the conversation, for one had to constantly brace oneself against the reaction of one's efforts; one couldn't rely on weight to absorb the energy of push and press—and one's mass had very different meaning here.

Despite all those interruptions a greater crowd than the first time had appeared, causing her a strange emotional response midway between exhilaration and despair, the latter because she knew she could not help them all. Her supplies would give out, or she would.

A change in the speakers' postures broke her thoughts. The three facing the black-shrouded figure were stiff, still, wary; a tense silence fell, and then a deep Shver voice growled something from inside the black cowl.

The three whipped around and Rael found herself the focus of their attention. Someone spoke. Tooe touched Rael's arm and said, "They have questions."

Rael felt Jasper move restlessly at her side.

She sent him what she hoped was a reassuring glance, and pushed away from the wall she'd floated near.

Everyone's heads were oriented in one direction—a concession to the Shver, she figured.

The dark-cowled one spoke, and Nunku said, "The Deathguard wisheth to hear thy story from thine own lips."

"What story?" Rael asked. "How we found the derelict, or what has happened since we arrived here?"

"Everything," Nunku said. "They say that those from the *Solar Queen* have brought the Monitors into the Spin Axis. This changes what hath been accepted for lifetimes."

Rael heard the threat implicit in her soft voice, and felt danger clamp her insides. She knew very little about the Deathguard, other than that they were Shver outcasts and assassins—and that they had nothing to do with anyone outside their numbers, unless they were paid. These Shver outcasts would not have any interest in the plights of the other inhabitants of the Spinner, so they certainly would not care about justice for the *Starvenger* or the *Ariadne*.

She took in a deep breath, cast her mind back to Denlieth, and started to talk.

21

![star icon]

Rip Shannon was not surprised when every present member of the *Queen*'s crew expressed his desire to accompany Dane Thorson to the site of the duel.

"Right," Captain Jellico said. "There are ten of us who want to go."

"Five is an important number to them," Van Ryke said.

"As well," Jellico said. "We'll pick lots, then. I want half here to guard the *Queen* against any other tricks that Flindyk might concoct."

Frank Mura produced some fine tiles from somewhere, some colored white and some blue. He mixed them all up in a bag, and as each man picked one, the captain said, "White goes, blue stays."

Rip didn't say anything, but he was relieved when the tile he pulled out was white. He wanted to be there for a number of reasons—partly guilt, because he still felt that he ought to have talked Dane out of the fruitless errand to the mail drop in the first place, but also out of an intense desire to see if Ali's plan would work.

He thought grimly to himself as he handed his tile back to Frank and bounded down to get his sleeprod that he also wanted to be there to help in case Ali's plan blew up in their faces. He wasn't going to stand by and watch some planet-sized Shver warmonger munch his crewmate. Rip was very ready to prove that humans could fight—well—when they had to, and he could see in Kamil's bright-edged gaze and challenging smile that he felt exactly the same, even though he was staying with the *Solar Queen*.

Surprisingly, Frank had chosen a tile, and as it was white, he had silently produced his feedle pipe before he took his place with the others.

Steen Wilcox had drawn blue. As he frowned at his heir-loom, discreetly stowed in a sturdy bag in Dane's arms, Jan Van Ryke, who had also gotten a white tile, said, "Wilcox, we can swap if you like. You can keep an eye on your prop-erty."

Steen hesitated, then gave his head a shake. "Better not," he said. "If there's a problem, you'd be better at talking us out than I. If they come here, there won't be any talking." He smiled grimly, then nodded at the bag in Dane's hands. "As for that—my being there or not isn't going to make a parti-cle of difference. But it's been safely through many a battle, so I'll hold to the faith it'll come through one more."

Jellico said, "It's time. Let's get this over with."

Rip followed the others into the lock tunnel. Behind, he heard Ali and Steen talking to Stotz, Tang, and Tau, planning their defensive strategy. Their voices very soon dropped away as the five bounded their way to the maglev access.

The five got half a pod to themselves. Rip had half ex-pected either emptiness or stares, as if news of the duel had somehow gotten all over Exchange—demonstrating Flindyk's far reach. Except that Flindyk wouldn't want it publicized, he realized as he noted a group of Kanddoyds buzzing and clack-ing away in a corner, utterly unconcerned with either the knot of humans at the other end of the pod or the four Arvas spacers at one side, who spoke together in a sibilant language of their own.

He looked across at Dane, who was fingering some mysterious lumps and bumps pressing against his bag.

"You know what to do with that thing?" he asked.

Dane gave a short nod. "Steen showed me when we went down to his cabin to get it." He grimaced slightly. "Not that there was time enough to show me how to really operate it. But I know enough to . . ." He stopped, then shrugged. "Succeed or fail."

Jellico had been conversing in low tones with Van Ryke. Now he glanced up, assessing the other occupants of the pod, and Dane and Rip. He didn't say anything to the apprentices, but Rip decided to drop the subject.

As the grav increased, Rip became aware of a faint breathing sound coming from somewhere. He looked over, fascinated by the sight of Dane breathing into the bag, eliciting a soft wheeze from whatever was in it. It was changing shape, flattening into a kind of ovoid with odd bumps poking at intervals along one end. It reminded Rip unpleasantly of some asymetric sea creatures—was it some sort of biological construct? His stomach lurched. The use of living weapons was forbidden throughout Terran space, but out here . . . ?

Captain Jellico didn't seem concerned. The last of the passengers on the pod hurried off, sending odd looks toward the Terrans.

Dane didn't look back at Rip, hunching instead over the bag as if meditating. Was he imagining the impact of Shver weapons on his weaker frame? And how did that feel to someone who'd probably gotten used to—or become resigned to—being bigger than everyone else?

As they reached the one-gee level, whatever was in the bag had distended to a hard-looking mass; Rip could hear its coarse breathing, edged with a weird, honking whine, and the odor of its breath, a kind of rank, greasy sweetness, filled the maglev pod. What kind of bioweapon had Steen Wilcox been secreting in his cabin all these years? All Rip knew was that he had several heirlooms from his Scots ancestors, and that Ali had somehow found out about them. And he remembered a Scots word—"haggis"—that he'd overheard a spacer mention once with a look of great horror on his face. Was that what Dane had?

As the grav increased, the wheeze faded away, and Dane straightened up as the bag flattened out into a completely incomprehensible and utterly sinister shape. The haggis—if that's what it was—was silent. Was it dead? Dane didn't seem upset. Rip was no advocate of violence—or he'd be wearing the black and silver of a Patrol officer now—but the menace of the thing in that bag was comforting just at this moment. Rip firmly hoped a haggis was much more deadly, and fast, than whatever the Shver would face him with.

Soon the familiar vise squeezed slowly on his heart and lungs. Rip knew they were near the surface; he hoped he'd never have to feel this pressure—or see this place—again. *Just let me leave alive,* he thought as the maglev trundled its way slowly toward the place the Shver had told Dane they would be met.

They passed the mail drop building, and proceeded deep into Shver territory. At the proper stop, a group of five Shver waited, silent and impassive, for the Terrans to debark, which they did slowly and with care. The Shver waited without speaking until everyone was on the concourse, then the lead Shver made a slight gesture, touching hand to chin.

It was a neutral gesture of respect.

Jellico responded with the same gesture. Rip noted the only sign that the captain made of the effort it took to match the speed of the gesture was how his muscles tightened up his arm and shoulder.

"Come you this way," the lead Shver said.

He turned and started walking. The other four stepped out to the sides, closing in around the others as they proceeded in silence down a pathway past some thick, rubbery-looking shrubs that effectively curtained off the countryside around them.

Rip found himself paced by a tall female who, if he remembered aright what Dane had told him, was wearing the sign of a Khelv. Curious, he tried without moving his head much to scan the signs of the other four; they all wore different signs. He recognized one of them, the sign of a Jheel.

Again, a neutral signal, in that their company ranked one from each level. Five Zhems would have been an insult. Five Khelvs comprised an honor guard.

The path led downward, and Rip felt his thigh muscles protesting at each step. He did not look forward to walking back up that hill—if, of course, they lived through whatever was coming next—but at least it would agonize a different set of muscles.

At the bottom of the hill again they passed a line of boundary shrubs, and found two ground cars waiting. They were motioned into one; Jellico hesitated, and Rip could see how much he hated trusting their lives to these Shver. The leader of the group climbed in with them; as soon as they were seated, the plasglas opaqued to a deep blue, and they moved forward.

No one spoke at all during the ride. Rip listened to the roar of the engine and the deep, thrumming growl beneath him that he finally realized was the sound of wheels moving over ground.

When they stopped, the door opened onto a flat area made of flagged granite with obscure patterns worked in different minerals. The field of honor was ovoid, screened off all the way around by the thick waxy-leaved trees.

Waiting in the center of the ovoid was the Zhem who'd challenged Dane. He was not alone. Stationed round half the perimeter of the field was a great number of adult Shver—probably most of his clan, Rip realized.

Was this a bad sign? It was too late to do anything about it now.

Dane walked out into the center, still holding his bag. Rip felt a corresponding burst of adrenaline, as though he were the one walking out there. No time to pursue that empathic reaction—obviously his vivid imagination.

The Shver had something long and shiny lying at his feet; he bent and hefted a sword at least six feet long, with a wickedly curving blade. Rip didn't know whether to be relieved that he had not chosen a force blade—an energy weapon would at least afford a cleaner death than being hacked apart one limb at a time by that sword.

The Shver stood ready, speaking no words.

Dane carefully worked his bag loose, then tossed it behind him. What he held looked just as sinister as it had sounded in the maglev pod. Rip blinked at the great bladder, covered with cloth of a faded geometric pattern, transfixed by a number of black tubes protruding from it. His preconceived notion shattered: the haggis was some sort of sonic weapon, like Frank's feedle pipe.

For a moment no one moved. Rip saw the sheen of sweat lining Dane's brow.

The Shver then gripped the sword and swung it in a swift, humming circle to one side, then the other. At the same time Dane drew in a deep, rasping breath, and his face purpled as he put his mouth to one of the tubes and blew.

Everyone watched, Shver and Terran alike, as the great bladder filled, and then, without warning, Dane punched it viciously! The haggis screamed, droning in weird multiplicity as Dane's fingers danced spasmodically on one of the tubes, a groaning, wailing, urgent cacophony that tore at Rip's ears and filled his heart with fierceness.

Clang-g-g! The sword hit the stones barely two centimeters from the side of Dane's left boot. He stood his ground, squeezing the bag with his arm as he drew another breath. Rip could see sweat rolling off his purpling brow.

Clang-g-g! The sword's edge caused red sparks to fly scarcely a centimeter from Dane's right boot.

The sword raised high above the Shver's head, the vast,

powerful muscles bunched under the gray hide—

And Dane took a third breath, blew, and this time the rudiments of a tune tweedled out of the droning voice of the haggis.

And suddenly the Shver flung down the sword, opened his mouth, and out came a mighty "Hoom, hoom, hoom."

He was laughing.

Around the perimeter the Shver hoomed along, like some kind of musical thunderstorm.

The sound ceased as Dane tucked the bladder under one arm, fighting for breath, grinning slightly.

Ali was right, Rip thought. At least—so far. *And won't he crow,* came the rueful after-voice, but then Rip thought: if we get out of this alive, then as far as I'm concerned he can crow about it until Sol goes nova.

The Terrans did not make the mistake of moving. They waited until the Shver stopped laughing.

In the center of the field, the challenger said, this time in Trade, "Performed you brave, Terran. Quarrel have I none with you." And he made the gesture of respect. "It is dead."

Dane returned it with his free hand, and though he was still gasping for breath, he growled out a short sentence in Shver tongue.

This time the Shver answered in his own language, slowing when Dane half-raised a hand and said a word.

They held a short exchange, then Dane made a speech, not long in words, but it took him some time, between the cost to his lungs and his fighting for the correct words.

But when he was done, it produced a profound effect. This time the Shver in the watching circle made different sounds, growls so low Rip felt his feet thrum and his back teeth vibrate. Danger thrilled along his nerves, and he fought the impulse to clutch at his sleeprod. He forced himself to stand still, not even wiping his sweaty palms; he'd take his cue from Captain Jellico, who had not moved an inch the entire time.

The Shver spoke a little longer to Dane, and then something surprising happened: a tough-looking older Shver stumped forward, her great legs like animated tree trunks. She spoke just a couple of words to Dane in Shver, but then she too made the gesture of respect, turned, and left the field through a hidden access in the shrubbery.

Her clan followed, all except the original guard, who motioned Dane and his crewmates back to the ground car.

Rip was certain within half a minute that they were taking a different route back, but just as alarm was again squeezing his heart, they drew up directly next to the maglev pod.

Relief flooded through Rip's aching body as he lowered himself gratefully onto the bench in the pod. The others sank down around him, and the otherwise empty pod started to move slowly.

Dane leaned back and closed his eyes, sighing.

"Here's Steen's carryall," Frank Mura said, holding it out. He poked cautiously at the deflated bladder clasped under Dane's arm, its tubes dangling, and said, "What is that thing, anyway? Some kind of ultrasonic torture device?"

"It's a musical instrument," Van Ryke said, his voice husky with laughter.

Rip stared. "That weird noise was—*music?*"

Everyone laughed.

"It's called a bagpipe," Dane said, trying to catch his breath. "When I started blowing it up on the pod—Frank told me it's airproofed with some sort of oil and molasses and the bladder walls tend to stick together—well, I knew I was in trouble. Playing it was a nightmare." He laughed softly and somewhat painfully. "Well, it's bound to sound better when played by someone who knows how. Steen just had time to show me how to cause the notes to play, and Ali and I roughed out the first section of melody of a Shver triumphal air. Then it was time to go. But it worked."

Van Ryke shook his head. "It wasn't the song—if they even recognized it. What they liked was the way you stood your ground and played that silly thing while that fool of a Shver minced the stones around your feet."

Rip said, "What I want to know is, what did they say?"

Dane sighed again. "Just a minute . . . I don't feel like I'll ever breathe right again . . . whew!"

"Rest," Jellico said, clapping him once on the shoulder. "You can talk when we get to micrograv. You did well back there," he added, which praise—effusive for Captain Jellico—made Dane's bony, long face turn a fierce red.

Rip tried not to laugh, and instead looked out the window as the pod raced up into lighter grav. The pressure eased slowly from his body, leaving a pins-and-needles sensation in his joints. He massaged his shoulders, noting the others easing necks and elbows and knees.

Finally Dane said, "Much better. And Ali was right, all the way down the starlane. The citizen told me I'd acquitted myself with such honor he couldn't believe I would dishonor the blood or block the path."

"What?" Van Ryke exclaimed, his white brows rising.

"That's what they were told."

"This is of the Blood, the Path, and the Conquest to Come," the cargo master said softly. "The formal statement of Shver honor."

Dane nodded. "So I guessed. He said it was a . . . I guess the easiest translation is 'a family obligation'; but it was an insult to them to have to challenge riffraff like us. Kind of like cleaning up the trash," he said with irony. "But he had to, or disgrace his family. And guess who forced them into it."

Rip and Van Ryke said together, "Clan Golm."

No one laughed.

Dane gave a grim nod. "That's it. They disliked the duty enough to believe that we might actually have a case, and so they chose the neutral approach all the way."

Van Ryke shook his head. "And except for Ali, we might have misread it to a lethal degree."

Dane said soberly, "True. All I could think of was fighting—and losing. I never could have lifted any weapon in that gee. Just holding this and blowing into it nearly killed me." He touched the bagpipe. "Anyway, by doing what we did, we made it clear we had no gripe with them, though I have to say, I was just as glad to be half fainting, when that sword came smashing down like that." He grimaced. "Anyway, now they say they owe us, and that's when I told them all about Flindyk and the derelicts. The talk of hijacking got right to 'em."

Rip, remembering that deep growling, said, "It sure did."

"He said that Golm has been gaining influence through the office of the Administrator of Trade, more and more to the detriment of the other trading Shver clans."

"Interesting," Van Ryke said, steepling his fingers together. "Very interesting."

"And so?" Jellico prompted.

"And so we are to call on his clan if we want any help." Jellico nodded slowly.

The others started talking over details of the duel, and how they'd reacted, and how the others would react when they heard about it. When the pod reached microgee, Rip felt as if his heart had lightened along with his body. Everyone was in a celebrative spirit as they made their way back to the *Solar Queen.* Only Captain Jellico was quiet, his gray eyes distant as if he was deep in thought.

When they reached the others, the whole story had to come out again, but this time it was properly celebrated in the galley with delicacies that Frank broke out, having saved them for just such an occasion.

Rip couldn't help noticing that the captain still stayed silent, except for sudden private talks first with Tang Ya, then Jan Van Ryke. He was going to shrug it off as not his worry when he noticed Tau watching the captain as well.

Time slipped along, and several crew members decided to call it a day and rest. It had been a long day, Rip realized; though the eternal lighting was the same, his body—strained the more by two trips to Shver territory—clamored for respite.

Something was wrong, though, he could sense it. But no one said anything, and at last he got up and swung himself through the hatch to go below and sleep. Dane had already gone, and Ali was just in front of him.

He'd gotten about four steps when he heard the crack of a hand against a bulkhead, and the captain's voice. "Craig, if they're not back in an hour, I'm going up to the Spin Axis to bring them out."

The Spin Axis. Rael Cofort and Jasper.

How long had it been?

Rip looked around for a chrono, and felt his head swim. He knew then he'd been awake too many hours.

Dropping his feet through the hatchway of the down-ladder, he pushed gently with his hands and prepared to catch himself at the bottom when there was a blue flicker at the edge of his vision.

With two fingers he snagged the edge of the ladder and halted his drop. Lifting his head, he watched Tooe zoom through the outer lock, rebound off the deckplates, somer-sault without losing an iota of velocity, and rocket straight up to the control deck.

"Captain!" she shrilled in her fluty voice. "Captain! We come!"

Rip's eyes were still at the level of the floor; he felt a pres-ence behind him, looked, saw Dane emerging from his cabin. "Tooe's back," he said.

In silence the two apprentices ascended as Jasper Weeks and Rael Cofort sailed through the hatchway, clutching their gear, both looking tired and tense.

The captain dropped down from above, landing on the deckplates before the two, one hand keeping him motionless. "Why are you late?"

"The exigencies of events," Dr. Cofort said. Her hair was tousled, and there was dust smudging her face and clothing, but her eyes were alert, bearing a hint of challenge. "Do you not trust us?"

"It is the exigencies I don't trust," Jellico returned.

"Sa-sa," Ali whispered, coming up behind Dane and Rip. "Another duel, eh, me hearties?"

"Shut up," Rip muttered.

"Freedom," the doctor said, unsmiling, "to a degree."

Jasper gave her one odd look, and the captain another, and silently Jasper pushed his bag of gear toward the hatchway where the other three apprentices were watching. They made space for him to drop below, but he just sent his gear out into the air and turned to watch as well.

The silence between the man and woman stretched until Craig Tau appeared from behind the captain, and murmured a few words to Cofort. She bent her head to listen, then her expression changed, and she said, "I'm sorry. I have a lot to report."

"So do I," the captain said.

"Then do it over a meal," Frank Mura spoke from the galley hatchway. "You both look like you need it."

They disappeared into the galley, and the apprentices turned to hand themselves down to the decks below.

Ali gave them a wicked grin before he dropped to the engineering deck. "Brace up, friends. The final confrontation is nigh."

No one asked him which confrontation he meant.

22

"Wake up."

The voice seemed to come at Dane from the sky. He tried to look up, realized he was at the bottom of a well. A deep well, and he was buried from the neck down . . .

"Thorson!"

The voice was insistent, jerking him out of the darkness into which he'd drifted.

"You can't sleep—none of us can. Captain said this is it. Dane, *this is it.*"

Dane made a tremendous effort—and opened his eyes.

He was not in a well, but in his cabin, and the big, booming voice dwindled down to Ali Kamil, for once not drawling, or grinning, or lounging.

"I'm awake," he croaked. Even in microgee, it took an effort to move.

"Here. Frank sent these down with me," Ali said, holding out a drink bulb.

Dane took it, flicked the heat tab, and smelled real coffee.

"We have just a few left," Ali said, some of his old humor coming back. "But it seemed the time to issue them."

"How did you manage to stay awake and chipper?" Dane asked, trying—unsuccessfully—not to sound cross.

Ali lifted one shoulder. "Napped a little while you were dueling. Slept my way through most of the action so far, truth to tell. Next time, it's my turn."

"You could have had mine for the asking." Dane sighed and swung himself to his door. Ali drifted after. "Jasper? Rip?"

"You're the last of us," Ali said. "Tau's been waking the officers who were on alter-shift."

Dane nodded, realizing then that the captain had called a meeting of the crew. A few moments later he sailed into the mess cabin.

". . . go right up there, haul the jerk out from behind his desk, and pound the truth out of him," Karl Kosti was saying.

Dane wedged himself in among the apprentices, and realized that all of them were there, for the first time since their arrival at Exchange. So the *Starvenger* was empty. Somehow this more than recent events or Ali's words made Dane realize that the end had really come.

"I'd like that," Captain Jellico said, his face grim. "I'd like that very much. But we have to be realistic. He has tremendous power, and I doubt we'd get far past his door."

"Then we waylay him outside his office," Johan Stotz said.

Jellico negated this with a quick wave of his hand. "Then we've broken the Concord, and we're liable for arrest, and don't think he wouldn't be ready for that. No . . ." He paused and looked around. "What we're going to have is a peaceful confrontation. But we are going to pick the time, and the place. The time," he said with a faint, unpleasant smile, "is now."

He waited for the sounds of approbation to die down, then said, "And the place is . . . over dinner."

It was so unexpected, so incongruous, that half the crew thought he was joking, and laughed.

Jellico's faint smile was still there, but he did not laugh. He merely waited until the mess was silent again, so silent that Dane could hear the quiet hiss of the air circulators.

Craig Tau then said quietly, "I remember Flindyk generally eats at the Movable Feast after his duty at Trade, if it's high enough—he masses quite a bit. But I also remember seeing him in splendid isolation, which means no one is permitted to bother him."

"And I remember what happens to people who try to cause trouble in that place," Johan Stotz said. His long face crinkled in a grimace. "I wouldn't want to test any of those rumors—apparently the Gabbys are all picked for their imaginations as well as their abilities in the cookery line."

A murmur of agreement rose from the others.

"Why there, Captain?" Rip asked. "Do you think he'll talk to you?"

"I think we have to take the risk," Jellico said. "It's the only place where we're on roughly equal terms. But we do have to play by their rules. You have to remember that the Concord, imperfect as it is, is *all* there is between three very different races. It's also very fragile. The contradictions like the outcasts at the Spin Axis, and the Shver duels, and so forth can be looked at as fairly regularized methods of dealing with the cracks in the Concord's structure. What we have to do is avoid breaking the Concord as we address what might turn out to be the biggest crack."

Tau glanced at the chrono. "Time, Chief."

Jellico gave a decisive nod. "Flindyk just got the trade authorities to call for us to pay our shot on some pretext of going over some limit in our debt. This is his last attempt at trying to get at us through legal means. The time limit for paying up has just passed, and a squad of Monitors is most likely on its way to arrest me now. I won't be here. I'll be on my way up to face Flindyk off in what I am counting on being neutral territory: the Movable Feast. It's in low-gee right now, and Trade has just closed up their offices, so Flindyk will be there."

Again there was silence.

"I know you'd all like to be there, but I'm only taking four with me. The rest are to stay, one team on the controls, and the other on defense. If the Monitors pull anything, your first job is to save the *Queen*."

Again, no one spoke.

"Cofort and Van Ryke, you come with me. Tooe, you as well, in case we need translation. Thorson, you're the one who started us off in the investigation, so it's right that you should be in at the kill. Let's go."

Dane followed silently. Behind, he heard Steen Wilcox say, "All right, Tang, you're the key, so take your place at the com and wait. Frank, you take charge of the defense team. Now, this is how we'll divide up . . ."

Tooe darted ahead up the lock tube, then came scudding back, her crest wide and her eyes glowing. "Monitor! Pod coming—two tens of Monitor."

"Good work." Jellico gave Tooe a quick nod. "Take us by your short route."

Tooe grinned, her crest flicking up proudly. It didn't take any great powers of observation to see that she was pleased to be called upon.

With a racketing, sometimes heart-stopping speed, she led them through the outer byways of the Spinner. Dane recognized a landmark here and there, but he still would not be able to get around, he realized as they zoomed down an ancient air duct. Tooe only whistled once, and the answer came prompt and clear. So there was at least one person watching their progress unseen. The big, dark spaces no longer seemed empty; feeling a little unreal, Dane couldn't decide if that was bad or good.

They whizzed around a corner. Dane felt sudden coldness in his face as they dove through fog from one of the countless leaking tubes. An unwelcome memory of that frozen hand flying at him flickered through his mind, and he wondered why he had never heard anything from that particular clan again. Had they considered honor to be satisfied?

Or were the Golm biding their time against a more propitious moment—like now?

As they progressed, Dane became aware of odd noises here and there. Nothing profound; the clack of an old door, or the sudden whir of an ancient elevator. He realized then that the silent follower—or followers—were matching their pace.

When he had a chance, he caught up with Tooe and whispered, "We're being followed."

Her crest flattened.

"Bide easy," she whispered back. "For now, all Spinner is klinti."

"You mean united?"

She gave a flick of her crest that signified agreement.

"Including the Deathguard?"

"No," she said quickly, stealing a quick look around. "They choose no side. They stay away—watching."

Wondering if that was the worst threat of all, Dane dropped back as Tooe led the others down the last portion of space.

They eased out on a maglev leading from one of the Kanddoyd towers. As they boarded a pod, Tooe pointed a webbed blue finger through the window, and Dane saw the memorable landmark nearby: they would be at the Movable Feast in mere moments.

Still, he found himself holding his breath every time the pod stopped.

By the last stop the pod was crowded. Dane felt that people were staring at him as he followed the captain off the pod. The unpleasant sensation made him scan every face he passed; luckily he was tall enough to do it, for the sensation sharpened into conviction when he saw a Kanddoyd veer out of his path and dart, clacking and keening, through the crowd to a Shver. Dane peered after the Kanddoyd, trying to see more.

A sudden surge in the crowd hid him, but a moment later there was a gap and Dane recognized the Jheel of Clan Golm.

The Jheel recognized him as well, baring great teeth. His gray head bent: he was giving orders to the Kanddoyd.

Dane took two fast steps to catch up with Jellico. "Captain—"

"We saw," Jellico snapped. "Let's hustle."

Moving as swiftly as they could, the *Queen*'s crew glided along the path. Dane was careful not to step in anyone's way, or cause undue attention. On the periphery of the concourse crowd he could see figures darting here and there. The Golm leader was mobilizing his gang, Dane realized.

Once again he had safety in view, but this time he wasn't fighting against the pull of nearly two gravs. He wished they'd learned the low-grav lope, which used far less energy, but he, at least, kept flying off the deck every time he tried it. Sliding his feet in the shuffling walk they all adopted in low-gee, he lengthened his steps.

Ten meters . . .

Outcries from the crowd made him hurry: they were closing in.

Five . . .

Tooe dashed ahead, palming the doorway. She shrilled admonitions to hurry; the captain gripped Cofort's arm, and together they went through. Van Ryke looked about—Dane heard heavy Shver breathing behind him, and gave one great leap—

And he was in.

He somersaulted to his feet, saw the Jheel himself standing directly outside the restaurant. Five or six sinister figures crowded in next to him, but as one of Gabby's green-tunicked workers waved them away, they disappeared into the rest of the tourists.

"Now for it," Jellico said.

No one spoke as they made their way inside. First, through the garden area that marked off the section of the restaurant where the Shver liked to eat. Dane glanced about curiously, but all he saw were high walls of carefully trimmed ivy dividing off cubicles. The next couple of levels down were where humans and humanoids customarily ate. Why were the Shver above, he wondered, in inversion of the layout of the habitat? The prickling of his back as they descended told him: above, the Shver could see but not be seen.

Dane tried to shake off the awareness of many eyes, glancing in casually at various cubicles, catching whiffs of inviting aromas. Jellico looked straight ahead, leading the little group past and down another level.

Here the Kanddoyds had their area. It was mostly open, like the human area, so diners could see one another if they wished, though the tables were set at different levels, some facing the wide windows through which they could see the splendid towers and the liquid glint of the light strings. At the higher levels, certain booths were marked off, mostly by banks of exquisite ferns that blocked the view from above. It was straight toward one of these that Jellico made his way.

A Kanddoyd glided smoothly from behind a tall tree bearing fragile blossoms, and his course intersected theirs. "Gentle Traders?" he asked, bowing.

Van Ryke bowed back. "A fine evening, in a very fine place," he said genially. "We wish to avail ourselves of the rare opportunity to join a fellow human in the evening meal."

"A compliment to your generous impulses, O Terrans," the Kanddoyd said, ticking and clacking rhythmically; Dane felt a visceral warning in the pattern. "Alas, in this direction are only those who wish to imbibe in solitude."

"Ah," Van Ryke said, bowing again. "One must always respect the wishes of one's fellow beings. One also must respect promises made by those who make them. Flindyk honored our captain with a specific request, and now is the time for the captain to heed the request."

Dane felt his neck gripe. He didn't have to look at the ultrasonic reader on his ring-brooch to know that the Kanddoyd was broadcasting loud and clear.

Van Ryke smiled, knowing they had won. The Kanddoyds

would have never promised any such thing, but Flindyk was human, even after all those years of taking on the guise and habits of another race, and that empty promise he had made Jellico and Cofort on their only visit to him had been a very human thing to do.

The Kanddoyd had one more try. "It is my pleasure to acknowledge the rightness of requests being honored, and vows kept, but this is not a place of business. The strains and stresses of the business hours are now past. The rules here are strict, so that all beings may enjoy their delectable viands in a harmonious atmosphere."

Van Ryke smiled, gesturing in the mode of Pleasant Discourse, with a little flutter of Surprised Inquiry.

"What else could we have to do with our fellow being from far Terra, but compare the beauties of these herbaceous borders to those fine gardens we left at home? Now, can you not tell me the names of these attractive gymnosperms here?" He gestured behind the Kanddoyd, and as all of them pressed forward, Van Ryke kept up an admirable stream of questions about each plant they came to. The Kanddoyd clacked and squeaked increasingly but was forced to answer these direct questions, and so, plant by plant, step by step, they closed in until at last Flindyk was visible through a frame of delicate fronds. Amazingly, his cubicle, despite the greenery, was open to the levels above. Was he so sure of his power?

Flindyk saw them almost the same moment Dane saw him, and for a moment he went rigid. Then, as at last the *Queen*'s crew rounded the last obstacle, he sat back, his fantastic carapace gleaming richly in the reflected light from the levels towering above them.

"My very dear captain," he said suavely, opening his hands. "You honor me! If you have come to settle your affairs, I shall be most happy to terminate my free time early, and expedite matters for you."

"There is no hurry," Jellico said. "Please, continue your meal. We shall discourse upon the pleasantries of life on the Garden of Harmonious Exchange."

Through the green of the ferny border, Dane saw two of Gabby's workers just visible, one a tall being in a green tunic, another a Kanddoyd wearing green ribbons.

Flindyk sat back, a huge figure in his carved and gilded armor. Dane realized suddenly that that was, in fact, what he wore; he wasn't just an old, obese human pretending to be a Kanddoyd; he was armored. He thought narrowly, *I'll bet my life's pay that stuff he's wearing is blastproof.*

Flindyk smiled slightly, and raised a fine cut crystal goblet full of amber-colored wine. Dane noted he didn't use a bulb, which meant he was sure of his control over the liquid. "You shall enjoy my hospitality when we depart this place," he said. "That is also a promise."

Van Ryke moved slightly as if he were about to speak, but Jellico flicked a glance his way. Dane watched the cargo master nod and return to the posture of the observer.

Jellico's was not the first (or even the tenth) name that would have come to Dane's mind if he were to count up the *Solar Queen*'s crew members who were able to talk in the flowery, roundabout manner of the Kanddoyds. Apparently, though, the captain could employ that kind of language when he needed to.

"If you wish," the captain said, "but you will permit me to provide the entertainment."

"Alas," Findyk said, holding the goblet up to the light. Dane was fascinated by the ocher glints and sparks thrown off by the fine crystal. "Alas, though your intentions are . . . sincere . . . yes, we shall honor them for their sincerity, if not for their perspicacity. But to resume. Though your intentions are truly praiseworthy, I would regret deeply being a passive witness to the diminishment of your sadly limited means."

Flindyk smiled as his fingers played with the crystal goblet. Dane forced his attention away from the odd behavior of the liquid in the wineglass, which never quite came close to spilling. Instead, it bulged up in an odd bubble above the lip of the goblet, held together by surface tension and the wetting action on the crystal. Seeing how deadly aspirated liquids could be in free fall, it was a powerful statement of confidence.

It's a hint, Dane thought, feeling tension pound in his head. *He's showing us how he's playing with us, and how he still retains control.*

Just then a slight movement on the periphery of his vision caused him to glance to the side to see that the ferny border of the booth was dark with witnesses. Dane saw the gray of Shver skin, black-clothed, and the tension accelerated into danger. Deathguard! Had the Jheel managed to bring his group of toughs in, then?

But then a subtle change in the light from above drew his gaze upwards, and there, far above, the balconies of the highest level were lined with Shver staring down in silence, their martial ornaments glinting in the pinlight illumination they favored.

Flindyk sensed it too, revealing this by the barest flicker of his eyes.

His smile increased, full of confidence and false bonhomie.

Before he could speak again, Jellico said quietly, "Though the means may be limited, if the story is compelling enough, the entertainment will fascinate the widest audience."

"Perhaps," Flindyk said, finishing the wine at a toss, then setting the goblet down. At once his Kanddoyd servitor refilled it. "But at the end, the audience wakes up, and leaves, and knows after all that a story is just that: mere fabrication."

"Only," Jellico replied, "if you overlook the holographic arts. Through them we can review the acts of history. I assure you, they are very entertaining."

Flindyk's eyes narrowed sharply, then he smiled, and steepled his fingers. On the periphery Dane saw movement again, this time a flicker of red.

It was Gabby.

Dane put his hands behind his back and gripped them tightly, determined if anyone made any move toward the captain, they were going through him first.

"Alas for the fact that audience as well as performers are equally aware that holographic representations can be manufactured, just as are the stories our actors mouth out upon the stage."

Jellico smiled. It was not at all a pleasant smile. "When the actors believe what they are saying, the performance can be remarkably convincing."

Flindyk considered the keen gray eyes, the hard face creased down one side by a blaster scar, and leaned forward. For the first time Dane saw just a trace of doubt visible on the man's face. "You haven't enough actors for this play," he said in his mellow voice. "And when it is done, and you are gone, the . . . effects . . . of it remain with the actors for the rest of their lives."

"It already has," Jellico returned. "And there are plenty of actors for the story of Sphere Eleven Startraders. More than you think."

The ferns on the periphery rustled, and several figures stepped forward. Dane looked up, and it was then he realized what Jellico had gambled on: that the word would spread, through all the Traders, and not only were two Spinner gang leaders there, but Dane recognized the Shauv of the clan he'd had his duel with, and three Company ship captains—including one from I-S—and a cluster of Kanddoyds.

"More than you think," Jellico repeated.

Flindyk's thin lips went white. With one hand he fumbled at his belt, then he leaned back. "You may have gotten these fools to believe your bluff," he said quietly, dropping all pretense of politeness. "But you forget I still hold this station, and too many owe their livelihoods—and their lives—to me."

Both of them glanced aside; as yet Gabby had not moved.

Jellico said, "I think the time has come for you to confess the truth: that you have committed piracy, theft, murder, and barratry, and have profited therefrom."

"The time has come for your life to end," Flindyk said, all suavity gone. "Which will occur as soon as you step outside these doors."

Jellico nodded at the people ringing the booth. "I believe I can make the same threat."

"Then we wait here," Flindyk said, smiling cruelly. He stretched out his wrist, and pointed to the handsomely carved platinum chain there. Set in its midst was a jewel, not unlike Dane's ring-brooch.

"Alas for your loyal crew," Flindyk said. "I've just caused some modifications in life support for the *Queen*—of which, you know, the cylome docks have total control. Their air, my dear captain, is being contaminated by carbon monoxide." He smiled again, showing his teeth, startlingly feral against his babylike cheeks. "It's a painless death," he added unctuously. "I am minded to be merciful in honor of our common heritage."

"They will take care of themselves," Jellico said steadily. "You've been in a habitat so long that you've forgotten how common combustion engines are on planets. We're familiar with cee-oh poisoning."

"How about drowning in sewage?" Flindyk snarled suavely. "I can mix in some live steam, if you like."

"Then my comtech will have time before he dies to issue one last com: we sank a bitbomb into the communications system, and every file we have will be spammed all over the starlanes."

"You have no proof of anything," Flindyk said softly.

"But someone with time, and money, and power will undoubtedly come who will get proof. There's enough there to interest someone, don't you think? Ya's orders are clear: as soon as anyone does anything to my ship, that com goes out. And meanwhile, we can sit here until the restaurant descends. How long has it been since you experienced one grav, much less one-point-six?" Jellico went on. "I endured it today and lived. Can you say the same?"

"Many hours will pass between now and then," Flindyk said. "You will have no crew to return to."

"That is the risk I take," Jellico said. "The cause is justice for a greater number than six."

Flindyk started to fumble at his wrist communicator again, and no one moved to stop him.

However, not everyone was still. Flindyk himself realized something had happened, and looked up, then froze.

Gabby had raised one hand, his carapace droning a weird threnody of stridulations. He made a gesture, and the lights in the restaurant flickered—not once, but three times.

And Dane felt a gentle lurch in the pit of his stomach that rapidly grew to dizziness. The restaurant was dropping! Whispers, toots, keens, hooms, all sounded around them as the apparent gee force slowly declined toward zero as the program Gabby had set in motion gradually released the restaurant into free fall. Far below, the surface began to expand slowly as they plummeted toward it.

But his attention was wrenched around by sudden movement from Flindyk. A ring winked brightly on one fat finger and there was sudden movement among the Deathguard. They drew their weapons, serrated short swords intended for low-grav combat, designed to snag in the rent flesh of an enemy to enable the combatant to change vector easily after the stroke. Dane could see their huge muscles bunch under the black cloth that shrouded their forms.

From far above, in vast recapitulation of his tweedling bagpipe in the duel, the ancient triumph music of the Shver pealed out, brass and drum and shrilling hydraulisynth, electronic echo of the bloody Shver past. The crowd of witnesses shouted, screeched, keened, and tooted in shock as the bulky Shver leaped off their balconies, floating down with elephantine grace, brandishing the same type of swords. Dane saw that every clan was represented, all by Shver of the highest caste.

The Deathguard halted, frozen in a posture of pure menace, ready for anything as the Shver from above landed between them and the Terrans. Dane could hear the click of their magboots fastening to the deck. The eldest Shauv hoomed and rumbled at the Deathguard; Dane caught only one phrase, but it made his skin prickle.

"This is of the Path and the Conquest to Come."

Dane translated rapidly to himself, and realized what had been left out of the ancient phrase: "The Blood."

A frisson gripped his spine as he realized what had happened: the Shver had spoken to the outcasts, not welcoming them back—they were no longer of the Blood—but acknowledging that they too walked the Shver path.

"This is of the Path," said the lead Guard, whose face was invisible in its black cowl. "And the Conquest to Come."

Abruptly, the other members of the Deathguard relaxed. They did not step back, but their menace subsided. After a moment the Eldest Shauv sheathed her sword, followed instantly by high-caste Shver and Deathguard alike.

Now the restaurant was falling free. Dane noticed the klinti, however, did not allow themselves to float up into free-fall disorientation. They knew there would be acceleration again, if the Movable Feast were not to plummet through the inside surface of the habitat and out into space.

In confirmation of his thought, Flindyk's wrist communicator bleeped suddenly and then shrieked in a high voice: NECESSARY DECELERATION AT BOTTOM WILL EXCEED TWO GEE IN NINETY SECONDS!

Flyndik paled. At the rate they were accelerating toward the inner surface, the braking needed to stop them would shortly exceed even the 1.6 gee Shver enjoyed. Dane stared at Gabby: that acceleration was dangerous for Kanddoyds.

Suddenly the fat man sat back in his carapace, the reflections on it of the light tubes favored by Kanddoyd writhing like bright snakes as its surface flexed slightly against his weight. He raised his wineglass to them as he gave a great sigh.

"I salute you, Terrans," he hissed, and raised the goblet to his lips.

Without warning, a flick of his wrist sent the wine bulleting out of the glass straight at Rael's head. It was a deadly assault, Dane knew, for the normal human reaction to such an attack was to draw breath to prepare for combat—an action appropriate on a planet, but one that would choke and drown you quickly in free fall.

But just as quickly Jellico launched himself forward from the planter he'd been braced against, diving between Rael and Flindyk with one cupped hand extended. His hand shot across the path of the bulleting wine bubble and gently pulled it into a different vector with a graceful sweep, using its surface tension to gently divert it without bursting it into a deadly cloud of choking microdrops. The wine bubble shot past Rael's head, ruffling her hair before it burst against a column. Several klinti lunged out of the vicinity as a Kanddoyd servitor appeared almost instantly with a vacuum canister to remove the danger.

Flindyk looked into the empty goblet. His old, wrinkled face was set in lines of bitterness. "All right," he said, looking up at Jellico, now anchored on the deck next to Rael. "You win—though see what it'll get you."

A vast creaking thrum announced the return of gees as the restaurant began to decelerate, and Flindyk's breathing became harsher and the acceleration began to flatten out his huge bulk, compressing his lungs. But his comlink was silent—he would survive.

"It'll get your debts cleared," came a new voice, dry and dispassionate.

Everyone looked up to see Captain-Legate Ross standing there, formidable in his neat black-and-silver tunic, a blaster strapped to his side. At his shoulder stood the lictor of the Monitors, the Shauv of Clan Norl. And on Ross's other side an ancient Kanddoyd decorated with lacelike patterns of silver—Elder Councillor Doydatakk, the highest Kanddoyd official.

"Flynn von Dieck, you are under arrest for breaking the Concord," the Elder Councillor said in a reedy voice. "Lictor, please take the administrator into your custody. Cancel all his commands, and secure his comlinks."

"That's it," Jellico said, as all around them noise broke out—discussions, questions, arguments, pleading, defending.

Dane watched the captain reach out a hand, and after a moment Rael Cofort slid her palm against his, and their fingers intertwined, gripping tightly.

Cofort didn't speak. Jellico said, "Come on, let's go home."

23

Rael Cofort watched Karl Kosti bounce through the outer lock, an anticipatory grin on his craggy face. She continued on her way to the galley, and watched Frank Mura happily checking off the latest delivery of supplies.

"What's with Karl?" she asked. "He looks like someone just gave him a couple of planets for his own."

Frank looked up, a quick smile in his eyes. "Few days ago, while you were up at the Spin Axis, those three wranglers off that Deneb ship came and apologized—and ever since then he's been using his rec hours to go off with them to that Shver gym to try to kill each other."

Rael laughed. "Well, everyone to their own hobbies, I guess." She continued on her way through the *Solar Queen*, hugging her good news to herself as she went.

Everywhere she saw crew members busy with tasks. It had been that way in the days since the confrontation with Flindyk. On the surface, they were happy enough, and busy;

underneath, she knew, the fate of the *Ariadne* was on everyone's mind, but no one talked about it.

What could they say? The *Starvenger* papers had been surrendered back to Trade, and the *Ariadne*'s owners traced. Heirs had been found; complicated messages had been zinging back and forth across the starlanes.

Rip Shannon bounded by, tape spools in his hand. He gave her a cheery nod and she said, "The cargo masters still gone?"

Rip gave a nod. "At least Tapadakk wants to deal again."

"Tapadakk." Rael considered this. "I thought he was part of Flindyk's network?"

Rip caught himself on the up-ladder and floated in midair. "Apparently he wasn't part of Sphere Eleven, but whether he knew about it or not, Jan says no one except him will ever really know the truth. Tapadakk was certainly full of apologies for 'misunderstandings' and 'false rumors'—which is about as open as any Kanddoyd gets. The thing is, he's the best for Terran traders, so apparently we're stuck going through him."

"I'd think Jan and Dane would use moral superiority to boost our cause a little."

Rip laughed. "Oh, I think they will. Only the way Van Ryke put it was: 'Maybe if we rub his mandibles in it for a little while, he'll deal decently enough.' "

Rael laughed as well. "Did Tooe go with them?"

Rip nodded. "Everywhere Dane goes."

Rael moved aside, and Rip bounded up toward the control deck.

Rael continued on. The door to the captain's cabin was open, but he was not there. Queex saw her and squawked, and she stepped in to set his cage rocking.

Shortly afterward she handed herself through the hatchway to the control deck, and stood, watching. Jellico was there, working with Steen and Ya; Wilcox had gotten upgrades on navtapes, and Ya was monitoring the busy comlink.

You never can predict reactions, Rael thought, shaking her head slightly. The officials of Exchange had not said anything public or overt to the *Solar Queen*'s captain or crew since that day at the Movable Feast. Nothing. On the other hand, their debt had suddenly appeared canceled the day after Flindyk's arrest, and not long after, vendors had contacted them, offering ship's supplies, and when Jellico said they were cash-strapped, each vendor had insisted that they had a line of credit good enough to supply their needs for blasting off.

The officials wanted them gone, was what it came down to, Rael suspected. But the *Queen* lingered, while the red tape over *Ariadne* and *Starvenger* was slowly unraveling. Had unraveled.

It was now solved, but as yet no one knew it.

She bent her gaze to Jellico's broad back, and watched him. And after a time he became aware of her presence; he looked up, his eyes lightening when he saw her there.

"Problem?" he asked.

"Not at all," she said. "But I've news."

His brows lifted slightly. He turned to Steen, said, "Carry on."

Wilcox looked over at Rael with a little smile, then returned to his work.

Out in the hatchway, Jellico said quietly, "Yes?"

Rael smiled at him. "This news needs the appropriate setting." She watched him, saw his eyes narrow in abstraction. She was beginning to read his moods—as he was hers. "Tell you what," she said. "You're obviously busy there. Meet me at the Movable Feast in—an hour?"

"The Movable Feast?" One of his straight brows soared. "Think they'll let us in?"

"We just today received a special invitation from Gabby. I strongly suspect that business has been better than ever."

Jellico smiled, then gave a decisive nod. "An hour."

She smiled, and impulse prompted her to hold out her hand, to touch, to reaffirm what she felt but had not yet been spoken. But she stilled the impulse, sensing that it was yet too early. Míceál Jellico would have to be brought by degrees to break those barriers he had set around himself. Until then, public caresses would only embarrass him.

So she just smiled, and saw her own smile reflected in his eyes; but then he surprised her by catching hold of her hand and, with an air of gallantry, kissing it.

Then he was gone.

She made her way to the maglev for what she suspected would be the last time, reflecting on how delightful it was to be surprised by him. He would always surprise her, and they could spend a lifetime discovering one another.

As the pod sped toward the North Pole, she leaned back and watched the other passengers, and when she debarked, the business of the habitat. Everything appeared much as usual. She knew that the authorities were working in the background, that some changes would have to make their way through the elaborately sedate, polite labyrinths of Kanddoyd negotiation. But she was satisfied with what she had done. Individuals had been helped, from mere tissue repair to the possibility of a real life, for Nunku. It was Ross who had unexpectedly proved to be her biggest help in getting at least amnesty for those Spinnerites who wished to come out and seek a better life. He appeared to have shaken off the lethargy with which he'd cocooned himself—she knew, though they hadn't discussed it, that the inspiration behind his sudden energy was the realization he'd soon be going home.

Rael smiled as she entered the restaurant. Home for her had become the *Solar Queen*. Wherever it went, that was home. Its crew were now her family.

The Kanddoyd who greeted her led her up to one of the private booths, and Gabby himself soon appeared.

"I delight! The doctor, the captain? You luxuriate, exquisite foods I select meself!" He bowed and went away.

She looked out the window at the magical lighting winking along the Kanddoyd towers. When Jellico slid in next to her, she had champagne in fluted glasses.

"Crystal?" Míceál said, indicating the champagne.

"We're at point-eight grav—you can manage that," she said.

"We'll essay it," he said.

She felt the double impact of his words, and her carefully prepared speech fled.

"The *Ariadne* is ours," she said.

Jellico's hand tightened, and a drop of champagne spilled, sparkling, to his fingers.

"I asked Teague to give me my share of our inheritance early. He did, but for a wedding present, he went himself to the heirs, used my money to buy title to the ship, and I have the deed here. Now. Got it today. All we need to do is rename her, and put our names on the title."

"Wedding present?" He looked stunned.

She smiled, her heart pounding. "Is it too soon? Or do you find you can't bear after all to take the risk?"

For a long moment he was silent, and she felt the universe darken. Then he looked up and said, "This kind of talk—I don't really know how. I thought I'd cut this side of me out. You're right about risk. I never wanted to go through the grief I'd seen—" He shook his head.

"Go on," she said gently. "I think I follow."

"Why should you?" he retorted with slightly acidic humor. "I was a fool. I saw it in that instant when Flindyk threw the wine in your face. He was a cagey devil, Flindyk. He must have seen that that was the quickest way to hurt me the most. It'll always be that way—that people who want to be my enemy will seek to destroy what I love most."

"Yes," she said, gripping her hands tightly in her lap.

"But I also saw . . . well, if you had died, then I'd have all the grief anyway, and no good memories to look back on." He looked up, his emotions, for once, clear in his eyes. "Let's go and make those good memories, Rael. Soon. Now."

He held both hands out, and she brought hers up and gripped them. "As long as I live," she promised. "As long as we both shall live."

*   *   *

"**W**hat?" Ali gasped. "You mean—that's it? They've gone to Ross to marry them? And we're not invited?" He flung down the tools he'd been carrying; unfortunately the micrograv kept them from making a satisfying crash. "I'm devastated. Hear me?"

Dane sighed. Van Ryke had just given him the word—first the captain and Cofort would get the red tape out of the way on both their marriage and the new ship, and then they'd blast off for the world that came with the ship. Apparently there were still nine months left on that charter, and the cargo the *Ariadne* had found had been worth killing the crew for, so it seemed that, at last, they were heading straight for prosperity.

"Shut up," Rip said, laughing.

"They're just doing the legal stuff with Ross," Jasper said, giving them all his shy smile. "They'll do the actual vow exchange with us—after we blast off. They want to be married in space, with only the stars around, and not this place."

"Well, I can see that," Ali said. "But they might have told us."

"Telling you now," Dane said. "We've got to get our stuff together and shuttle over to the *Starv*—the *Ariadne*."

"Marriage, ship, promotion," Ali said, snapping his fingers. "What's next? I can handle it!"

"Don't tempt fate," Rip said, groaning. "Just get your kit together, and shut up."

"Wait," Dane said. "Before you go, we've got to name our ship."

The other three stared at him for a long moment.

"Name—" Jasper said.

"Our ship," Ali repeated, his brilliant eyes intense with emotions Dane couldn't name. His lips curved in a pensive smile and he said, "That's right. *Ariadne* is gone—her soul went with her old crew. And she never was the *Starvenger*. So . . . ?"

They looked at each other helplessly.

"We have to think of something," Dane said, feeling uncomfortable. "Then send a message to the captain. They'll register the name after they do the marriage legalities. So we can't take all day."

"We need a name that sounds well flying next to the *Solar Queen.*"

"Something terrestrial?" Jasper asked. He winced. *"Lunar Duke* or *Venusian Viscount* sounds kind of—"

"Idiotic," Rip said. "I think we're on the wrong starlane with the royalty. The *Queen*'s the *Queen,* and always will be, but we don't need any kings or dukes or any of that."

Dane shut his eyes, seeing an image of the heavens above Terra, remembered from his youth. And suddenly he had it. "Celestial," he said. "What did our ancestors use to guide their ships by?"

Ali sighed with satisfaction. "The *North Star.* That's it, Viking." He looked at the others, and saw Jasper nod with decided approval.

"North Star," Rip repeated, and he shoved himself toward the hatchway. "I'll send the message, then get my gear."

"Just a moment," Ali said, catching his arm. "How about the cats?" he asked, pausing.

"Tau's got them already," Dane replied. "He's gone over with them and his lab stuff."

"Tau?" Rip asked.

Dane shrugged.

Jasper said, "He had his choice, for he's senior medic. And Cofort said as long as the ships were flying together, she didn't mind duty on the *North Star.* But Tau wants to be with us—some project going on, apparently."

"I thought I heard some hinting around," Rip said. "Well, that's fine with me."

"Too bad." Ali flipped upside down and grinned. "I'll miss seeing old Viking here blush every time she appears."

"I don't," Dane said, not bothering to hide his annoyance.

"You did." Ali wiggled his brows.

"But he doesn't anymore," Rip put in, ever the peace-maker.

Ali made a graceful, careless turn and oriented right-side-up. "I told you, you just need to come with me. Get plenty of practice being around beautiful women. You'll like it, I promise."

Dane sighed. "I like them already," he said. "I like them a lot. It's when they look back at me that I suddenly grow an extra foot, and find I've got too many arms and legs."

"It's all right to look," Ali said, for once at least semi-serious. "Cofort now, she has fine taste, and she looks at me." He grinned smugly. "Everyone does. They can't help looking at such a handsome fellow. Of course that's all she does, is look. I could wait until the galaxy goes nova before she'd act on it."

"I know, I know," Dane said. "I'm learning." He wasn't going to admit to anyone, not even Rip, that he'd had a talk with Rael, and had gotten a lot of things clear just about interacting with people. Not that it would change him overnight. But at least he didn't feel quite so stupid anymore.

"Speaking of females, what about Tooe?" Rip asked, as the apprentices parted to pack their gear.

"She knows we're leaving now," Dane said.

That was all he said. He went back to his old cabin, and started packing, thinking over the events of the last few days. After all that work, it didn't really seem like much of anything was changing. Nunku still wanted to live at the Spinner, as did most of the klinti, though apparently at least they'd get ID papers, and jobs if they wanted them.

About the only concrete change that Dane could see was that Tooe had been given papers. She now was a free citizen, with no debts, ready to start her life. But though she'd worked hard and uncomplainingly, each day she'd talked less.

Would she be able to leave the klinti? Dane had been honest with her, saying he didn't know if they'd ever be back. Of course once she was out in the starlanes, if she decided not to stay with the *Queen* she could work her way back on any ship . . .

What was toughest was leaving in the first place.

Dane shook his head as he finished packing away his belongings. He looked around the bare cabin, wondering who would live there next, and how they'd feel about leaving wherever they were coming from—how they'd feel about the *Solar Queen* and her crew.

For him it had been easy. No family, no ties. This was it, his home.

In silence he joined the others, and helped push the baggage into the shuttle. Ali chattered happily, cracking jokes and singing snatches of song. Rip kept sending Dane glances of sympathy from his dark eyes, but he said nothing directly. Jasper just worked, as always keeping his thoughts to himself.

When the shuttle was ready to go, Rip made a business of checking over the com once more—and then he stopped, for a little blue figure bounded down the tube and flung herself in, clutching in her thin webbed fingers a ragged, bulging receptacle.

Dane grinned at her, and watched her drooping crest lift. No one was in sight on the dock; her good-byes had been said.

In silence the crew of the *North Star* made their way to their new ship. And not long after that, the two ships eased their way out of the great lock, and nosed out toward space.

Though there was plenty to do, Dane hovered near Tooe, watching. She stopped at the port, but her gaze was not back in the direction of the rapidly dwindling habitat.

As they built up speed for the jump to hyper, she turned and smiled out at the stars.

About the Authors

For over fifty years, ANDRE NORTON, "one of the most distinguished living SF and fantasy writers" *(Booklist)*, has been penning bestselling novels that have earned her a unique place in the hearts and minds of readers. Honored with a Life Achievement Award by the World Fantasy Convention and with the Grand Master Nebula Award by her peers in the Science Fiction Writers of America, her numerous science fiction and fantasy novels have garnered her millions of devoted readers across the globe. Works set in her fabled Witch World, as well as others, such as *The Elvenbane* (with Mercedes Lackey) and *Black Trillium* (with Marion Zimmer Bradley and Julian May), have made her "one of the most popular authors of our time" *(Publishers Weekly)*. She lives in Winter Park, Florida.

SHERWOOD SMITH is the author of over a dozen novels, including *Wren to the Rescue* and two other Wren adventures. She is also the coauthor, with Dave Trowbridge, of the Exordium series of space opera novels. Smith lives in California.

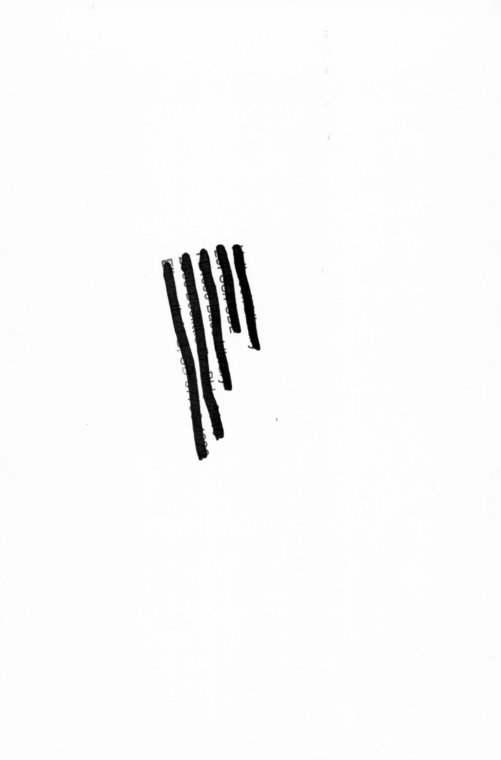